SENSUAL CONFESSIONS

NEW YORK TIMES AND USA TODAY BESTSELLING AUTHOR

BRENDA JACKSON

SENSUAL CONFESSIONS

ARABESQUE®

Recycling programs
for this product may
not exist in your area.

SENSUAL CONFESSIONS

ISBN-13: 978-0-373-83178-4

© 2010 by Brenda Streater Jackson

www.kimanipress.com

Printed in U.S.A.

To the love of my life, Gerald Jackson, Sr.

To everyone who enjoys reading about those
Madarises, this one is for you.

Dear Reader,

I never imagined when I penned my first Madaris book fifteen years ago that the series would still be going strong today.

The Madarises are special, not just because they're my first family series, but because over the years you've made them *your* family. The Madaris men have become your heroes because they represent those things you desire in a man—someone whose looks not only take your breath away, but who also makes you appreciate the fact that you're a woman. I still believe that, even with a man like Blade Madaris.

Blade, his twin brother, Slade, and their cousin Luke became special the moment they appeared on stage at the bachelor auction in *Surrender*. Of the three, I knew that Blade Madaris was a force to be reckoned with, even more so than his older cousin Clayton. There was a hint of just what type of man Blade was when it was revealed that *he* was the one who'd inherited Clayton's infamous case of condoms.

Although Blade thinks his player lifestyle is just perfect, what he doesn't count on is meeting a woman like Samari Di Meglio. A woman he can't seem to walk away from.

I hope you enjoy reading *Sensual Confessions,* the sixteenth book in the Madaris Family and Friends series.

All the best,

Brenda Jackson

THE MADARIS FAMILY

Milton Madaris, Sr. and Felicia Laverne Lee Madaris

Milton Jr. (Dora)	Lee (Pearl)	Nolan (Bessie)	Lucas (Carrie)	Robert (Diana)	Jonathan (Marilyn)	Jake (Diamond)⑧

Milton Jr. (Dora)
Milton III (Fran)

Lee (Pearl)
Lee Jr. (Alfie)

Blade and Slade (Skye)⑭, Lee, Kane, Jarod
Quantum, Jantzen

Nolan (Bessie)
Nolan Jr. (Marie)

Nolan, Corbin, Adam, Victoria, Lindsay

Lucas (Carrie)
Lucas Jr. (Sarah)

Lucas (Mac)⑮, Reese, Emerson, Chance

Robert (Diana)
Felicia (Trask)⑦

Jonathan (Marilyn)
Justin (Loren)①, Dex (Caitlin)②
Clayton (Syneda)④, Tracie (Daniel),
Kattie (Raymond), Christy (Alex)⑬

Jake (Diamond)⑧

KEY:

( ) — denotes a spouse

◯ and number — denotes title of book for that couple's story

① Tonight and Forever
② Whispered Promises
③ Cupid's Bow
④ Eternally Yours
⑤ One Special Moment
⑥ Fire and Desire
⑦ Truly Everlasting
⑧ Secret Love
⑨ True Love
⑩ Surrender
⑪ The Best Man
⑫ The Midnight Hour
⑬ Unfinished Business
⑭ Slow Burn
⑮ Taste of Passion

THE MADARIS FRIENDS

Maurice and Stella Grant

Angelique Hamilton Chenault

Kyle Garwood (Kimara)③

Trevor (Corinthians)⑥,
Regina (Mitch)⑪

Sterling Hamilton (Colby)⑤,
Nicholas Chenault (Shayla)⑨

Trent Jordache
(Brenna)⑨

Nedwyn Lansing
(Diana)⑭

Drake Warren
(Tori)⑫

Ashton Sinclair
(Netherland)⑩

KEY:

( ) — denotes a spouse

◯ and number — denotes title of book for that couple's story

① Tonight and Forever
② Whispered Promises
③ Cupid's Bow
④ Eternally Yours
⑤ One Special Moment
⑥ Fire and Desire
⑦ Truly Everlasting
⑧ Secret Love
⑨ True Love
⑩ Surrender
⑪ The Best Man
⑫ The Midnight Hour
⑬ Unfinished Business
⑭ Slow Burn

So then, my beloved brethren, let every man be swift to hear, slow to speak, slow to wrath.

—*James* 1:19

Chapter 1

"**J**ust who do you think you're fooling, Blade? You're interested in Sam. Admit it."

What was this—an interrogation? Blade Madaris thought as he ignored his cousin Luke and glanced around the restaurant before looking down at his watch. It was almost six. He had just arrived in Oklahoma City a few hours ago and Luke had picked him up from the airport.

On their way into town, Blade had persuaded Luke to make a pit stop at a restaurant downtown. He'd even suggested that Luke call his wife, Mac, and invite her to join them, conveniently extending the same invitation to the other two female partners in Mac's firm, Samari Di Meglio—better known as Sam to her friends—and Peyton Mahoney. Since Mac's marriage, the law firm that used to be known as Standfield, Di Meglio and Mahoney was now Madaris, Di Meglio and Mahoney.

"Of course I'm interested in Sam," Blade finally said,

easing back in his chair and taking a sip of water. His great-grandmother had always said that confession was good for the soul. "She's a woman, isn't she? And a good-looking one, so quite naturally I want to get to know her better."

Luke stared at him. Irritation was clearly etched in his face. "But what's the reason?"

Blade rolled his eyes. "Why? Does a man have to have a reason to want to get to know someone?"

Luke gave him a suspicious look.

Blade sat his glass down on the table. "For crying out loud, Luke," he said. "You've only been married ten months and already you've forgotten that *you* were once a skirt chaser."

"I haven't forgotten, but I consider Sam a friend."

Blade glanced at his watch again before looking at Luke. "Good for you. But to me she's a prospective conquest. Will it make you feel better if I told you she doesn't even like me?"

"Doesn't surprise me. Your reputation precedes you, even in Oklahoma. She's heard about you and detests everything you represent," Luke said bluntly.

"Whatever." Blade wasn't the least bit bothered by Luke's warning. She wouldn't be the first woman who detested him, and he figured she wouldn't be the last. Besides, women might complain about him being a player, but that had never stopped them from jumping into his bed.

Admittedly, he had picked up on the negative vibes from Samari at Luke and Mac's wedding, and had found it rather amusing—challenging in a way. It didn't bother him in the least that Sam was difficult, because the one thing he liked when it came to women was a challenge. He took it all in stride and figured her resistance would make the victory that much sweeter. He was confident that he would be getting what he wanted. And he had decided the day of Luke's wedding that he *wanted* Sam. Clarification, *he wanted Sam in his bed*. There was a difference.

Luke's phone rang. Blade watched as his cousin stood to pull his cell phone out of his jeans pocket, sliding it open as he sat back down. "Yes, sweetheart."

A few moments later Luke nodded. "All right, we're at the restaurant waiting," he said. "No problem. I love you, too."

Luke put his phone back in his pocket and glanced at Blade. "That was Mac."

"Like I thought it was anyone else," Blade said, chuckling.

"They got slightly detained but are on their way now."

He nodded and detected that Luke was just as eager to see Mac as Blade was to see Sam. "Marriage certainly agrees with you, Luke," he said after a while.

Luke grinned at him. "Hmm, maybe you ought to try it."

A scowl quickly appeared on Blade's face. "And maybe you ought to keep your opinions to yourself."

Luke couldn't help but laugh. "Not that I think you'd really care, but Mac mentioned Peyton couldn't make it. She'd made other plans."

Blade took another sip of water. It wasn't that he didn't care, especially since Peyton Mahoney was a good-looking woman in her own right, but he'd set his sights on Sam. There had been something about Samari Di Meglio that got to him, just below the gut.

"So how long will you be in town?"

Blade glanced over at his cousin. He, Luke and his brother Slade were thick as thieves—always had been, always would be. The only kicker was now Luke and

Slade were married and he was still single, and that was taking some getting used to.

"Not sure yet," he replied, glancing at his watch once again. "I'm meeting with J. W. Mosley tomorrow. Slade and I are glad we won the bid for the contract. I understand we had some pretty stiff competition."

Luke nodded. Blade's construction company, which he jointly owned with his fraternal twin, Slade, had been hired to do extensive renovations to Luke and Mac's home, as well as build the Luke Madaris Rodeo School. And now the company would also be building the new thirty-four-story Mosley Building in downtown Oklahoma City.

Over the past few years, the Madaris Construction Company had earned a reputation as one of the best firms in the country. With Blade as construction engineer and Slade as master architect, their designs were renowned worldwide.

"You're sure they're on their way?"

Luke glanced at Blade. He recognized the look on his face, since he'd seen it on several occasions over the years. It was Blade's predatory look. Luke swore silently to himself and decided it wasn't any of his business, since he'd given his cousin fair warning. Samari Di Meglio was not your typical Blade Madaris kind of woman. Sam despised players in the worst way, and Blade was definitely a player—of the card-carrying variety. Hell, he even had membership in the notorious Gentlemen's Club, and everyone in Houston knew that its members were far from being gentlemen.

"Yes, they're on their way," Luke said, taking a sip of water after deciding to mind to his own business. Blade was a grown man and Sam was a smart, intelligent woman. There was no doubt that the two would tangle, bump heads and even try to do each other in before it was over. He smiled as he leaned back in his chair. Things would definitely be interesting and all he could do was settle in for what he knew would be a wild and crazy ride.

Samari Di Meglio frowned as she glanced at the woman by her side after handing the valet attendant her car keys. "I don't know why I agreed to come here with you, Mac. You of all people know how I feel about Luke's cousin. The man is everything I detest."

Mackenzie Standfield Madaris couldn't help but smile. "Well, yeah, I know. I'm also surprised that you came."

Sam shrugged. "What can I say, it's a free meal."

Mac rolled her eyes. "Whatever."

Sam, Peyton and Mac had met in law school. The three women had become the best of friends and now they were partners in their own law firm, Madaris, Di Meglio and Mahoney. She of all people knew that the last thing Sam needed was a free meal, especially given her family—the filthy rich Di Meglios of New York.

Thanks to the proceeds from the trust fund that she had received on her twenty-third birthday, Sam had been the one to provide the financing to get their law firm off the ground, and for that Mac would be eternally grateful.

"Besides," Mac said as they entered the restaurant, "if there's any one woman who can handle Blade Madaris, it's you."

Sam appreciated Mac's vote of confidence, especially when she glanced around the restaurant and her gaze landed on the man in question at the same time he laid eyes on her. He immediately gave her one of his predatory smiles.

She could actually feel the blood rushing through her veins and felt the hard thud of her heart beating in her chest. It wasn't a good sign that a twenty-eight-year-old woman suddenly felt like a teenage girl swooning over one of those "I-heart-you" smiles from the cutest boy in school.

Luke and Blade saw them as they entered and stood up to greet the two women, stretching their muscular bodies to their full height. Sam's gaze immediately went to Blade's broad shoulders, and with his jacket off she could actually see the muscles rippling under his starched white dress shirt. He was wearing a pair of jeans that hugged his firm muscular thighs. She'd seen him only a few times and the one thing that stood out, besides the fact that he was truly a handsome man, was that he was a sharp dresser, whether it was business or casual attire. He was Mr. *GQ* in living color, and he had an air of machismo about him that women could sense and few could resist.

He stood tall—almost six foot four—with a body that had her insides quivering in appreciation. She hated being reminded of how long it had been since she'd been intimate with a man. She was used to flirting with men who had the word *player* stamped on their foreheads, and setting them up for heartbreak. She enjoyed showing them that two could play their games. Thanks to the hurt and humiliation she'd suffered at the hands of Guy Carrington a few years back, on what should have been her wedding day, she got great pleasure from pretending to be the needy, airhead, spoiled little rich girl. She enjoyed getting to them before they got to her, but not in the same way, of course. She figured it was their just deserts, and the least she could do to retaliate for their thoughtless behavior toward women.

Mac touched Sam's arm, regaining her attention. "Wait a minute. You didn't bring it up so I will."

Sam lifted an eyebrow. "What?"

"The vase of flowers you got today."

She shrugged. "What of it? I have a secret admirer who evidently hasn't gotten the message that I'm not interested."

"Or one of those players who didn't appreciate your turning the tables on them, perhaps?"

Sam looked at Mac as she planted her hands on her hips. "Trust me, if that was the case I wouldn't be getting flowers."

"Still, I think you should consider investigating just to be on the safe side. You could have a stalker."

Sam shook her head. Of course Mac would think that way. "I really don't think it's *that* serious. Besides, I have an idea who they might be from."

She glanced back at Blade and her gaze went directly to his face. The eyes staring back at her were dark, piercing and determined. They were filled with a hunger like he wanted to eat her alive. She could just imagine what was going through his mind. He wouldn't hesitate to seduce her if given the chance. She tilted her head, knowing he would never get the opportunity.

Okay, she would admit there was a sexy air about him, and there was no doubt in her mind that he proudly lived up to his womanizing reputation. A part of her knew she probably should not have come, since tonight she wasn't at the top of her game. But because she *was* here, she would just have to deal with it and handle the notorious Blade Madaris in her own way.

And notorious he definitely was, with a face too gorgeous to be real. He possessed a ruggedly handsome square jawline, high cheekbones and a straight nose. And then there were his lips, the most sensuous looking pair she'd ever seen. They were curved in a smile that was trying really hard to seduce her, get on her good side and break down her defenses.

She found his efforts annoying and was determined not to let him get past her guard. Some men just didn't know when to give up. Her mind went back to the flowers she'd left sitting on her desk, and felt the same held true for whoever had sent them. For the past three weeks she'd received a bouquet of flowers. They were beautiful, and she could tell by the blossoms in each arrangement that they had to have been expensive. Although she wasn't one hundred percent certain, she believed they had come from Blade.

If he was the culprit, and assumed liked a lot of players did that a quick way into a woman's panties was with sweet-smelling roses, he would be sorely disappointed. Maybe there were some women who were that naive, but their name wasn't Samari Di Meglio.

Mac nudged her shoulder, interrupting Sam's thoughts. "Our guys are waiting."

Sam frowned, feeling a migraine coming on. "One of the guys is definitely yours, but the other is *sooo* not mine. I wouldn't claim him if my life depended on it."

As they began walking toward the two men, Sam wanted to believe what she'd just said.

Blade glanced at the two women who were making their way toward him and Luke. Both were stunningly beautiful. One was already taken by Luke. The other… well. He studied all five foot eight of her. He looked her up and down, top to bottom, taking note of her blue business suit with its short skirt that showcased a pair of lush brown thighs and long, sexy legs. They were legs that went on forever, and one of these days he intended to see just where they stopped. He could just imagine the body hidden under her suit—a body he was convinced needed a master touch. *His.*

He smiled at the thought before his eyes moved up to her face. She was a mix of Italian and African-American. She had a pair of beautiful dark exotic eyes, a cute nose and delicious looking lips. Her caramel-colored skin looked soft and smooth, and the mass of black hair that flowed around her shoulders gave her a sexy look. Samari Di Meglio was the kind of woman who easily drew men to her, made them drool mercilessly and compelled them to include her in any wicked fantasies they had. But he also knew that she was a woman with no intention of ever being claimed by any man—not now or forever.

That was fine with him, since the word *forever* wasn't in his vocabulary, anyway. He wasn't interested in any woman beyond the first two orgasms, maybe three on a hot night. To go beyond that was asking for trouble, especially if she had a tendency to become possessive, or assumed that most men's brains were controlled by what happened below the belt, and that if you kept a certain part of their anatomy satisfied, then that's all it took. But that was a false assumption where Blade was concerned.

That might be true for some men, but he had yet to encounter a woman who could make him forget what day it was, whose bed he was in or whose legs he was between. And when the time came, he had no qualms about pulling back, pulling out and getting the hell out, if necessary.

"Hello, Blade."

"Hi, Mac."

He kissed her on the cheek and then watched as her face broke into an incredible smile when she looked at her husband. Luke leaned over and kissed Mac's lips as she slid into his open arms, almost instinctively. The gesture was as natural as anything Blade had seen in a long time. He had known—from that first night more than seven

years ago when Luke and Mac had met at a charity
bachelor auction in Houston—that the two had the hots
for each other. And he was still having a hard time getting
used to the public displays of affection between them, especially since Luke had always been aloof where women
were concerned. Marriage had certainly made him a different man.

Blade shifted his gaze from the loving couple to the
woman standing in front of him—who was so damn
delicious looking he could eat her for dessert. And one
day he intended to do just that. As usual, whenever they
were around each other, the sexual tension was so thick
you could cut it with a knife.

"Hello, Sam."

"Blade."

She held her hand out and he took it, liking the soft,
warm feel of it. She reclaimed her hand as he pulled out
her chair. "Glad you could make it."

She smiled politely. "I'm sure you are."

He sighed inwardly. He had a feeling that all the lines
he had planned to use on her tonight would be wasted. The
woman was what most would call a lost cause, but he
didn't intend to give up. All it took was a whiff of her
perfume to know the battle wouldn't be easy, but the
victory would be well worth it. Besides, she hadn't yet
tangled with the likes of Blade Madaris—on a good day
or an even better night.

He glanced over at Luke and Mac. The couple had
finally sat down. "How are you, Mac?" he asked.

She smiled at him. "I'm fine. Luke mentioned that
your company was awarded the contract for the Mosley
Building. Congratulations."

"Thanks."

"How long do you plan on being in town?" she asked.

"Not sure. That depends."

"On what?" Sam asked.

She watched Blade shift his gaze from Mac to her with a smile that would have made her drool if she was the drooling type, which she wasn't. But she would give it to him for being the kind of man who could make her feel hot all over, whatever the temperature. And then there were his eyelashes, which were just as deadly as his lips. His lashes were long and thick—lashes most women would envy.

"As chief engineer of Madaris Construction Company, I need to make sure the groundwork is laid before my crew can start work. There are surveys I need to complete, research that needs to be done, soil samples to be analyzed, as well as planning the construction schedule from start to finish. I also need to work with the Mosley people to keep the public informed as to what's going on."

He took a sip of water. "The design of the Mosley Building will be unique, and it's my job to make sure the materials we use and the work we do meet our highest standards. So there's no telling how long I'll be here— maybe four to six months."

Sam nodded. Regardless of what he'd just said, she knew there was more to him hanging around Oklahoma City than he let on. The look in his eyes said as much. The man just refused to give up. She would hate to make him another casualty, like every other player who thought she was fair and easy game. Evidently, he felt pretty damn sure of himself.

Any other time she would have jumped at the opportunity to prove him wrong, but with the phone call she'd received from her parents before leaving the office, she didn't have the time or the inclination. Although she was pretty good when it came to multitasking, she didn't want to take on both Blade and her parents at the same time.

Her mom and dad, who had been responsible for choosing Guy as their future son-in-law, were at it again. For some reason they couldn't leave well enough alone. At first, when they had called last week, they'd insisted that she fly home to New York to meet the man they thought was the perfect match for her.

When she had refused, they had tried playing on her sympathy by claiming that they would be too old to enjoy grandchildren when she and her brother, DeAngelo, finally settled down and produced offspring.

"Peyton sends her regrets, but she wasn't able to make it, Blade," Mac said, diverting his attention.

Sam glanced at him to see if any disappointment registered on his face. He smiled. "Luke told me and I'm disappointed," he said evenly.

Was he really? Hmm. As if she'd spoken out loud, Blade shifted his gaze from Mac to her and once again gave Sam that predatory smile. She was relieved when the waitress appeared and placed glasses of water in front of her and Mac, and gave everyone menus. She had dined at this restaurant before, so it didn't take long to decide what to order.

Sam closed her menu and glanced up to find Blade staring at her. She was about to ask if there was anything wrong, but decided not to. Instead she stared back at him. She smiled to herself. If he thought he could outstare her, he was *so* wrong. This was one of the games she and her brother would play as children, when they didn't have anything better to do. Not only did she play it well, oftentimes she beat her older brother. She could hold her own with the best of them and could stare down anyone without blinking.

It didn't take long for her to see that was exactly what Blade was trying to do. Evidently he'd played a similar game as a child and could definitely hold his own. But she had to admit—even though it bothered her to do so—that staring at him was affecting her in ways that the game she'd played with DeAngelo never did.

She felt a stirring sensation emanating from Blade's dark eyes. They seemed to be staring right through her, reading her thoughts.

"Blade, I understand Jake will be hosting a huge party in a few weeks to celebrate Sheikh Valdemon's marriage," Mac said.

It was only then that he looked away from Sam, to answer her. "Yes, he is. And you know nobody throws a party like Uncle Jake and Diamond. They would have given the party sooner, but it's been hard for the newlyweds to visit the States because of commitments between the two countries."

"I can't wait to meet the woman the sheikh chose as his bride," Mac said excitedly.

Blade shrugged. "Everybody who attended the wedding celebration said she's a beauty. Still, I thought Rasheed would remain a bachelor forever. But I guess he had to marry sooner or later to produce an heir."

Sam remembered the sheikh. What woman who'd attended Luke and Mac's wedding hadn't? She had certainly checked him out herself. "Who did he marry?" she asked.

"A young woman from his country," Blade said. "One chosen for him by his family. If I remember correctly, she's the reason he had to unexpectedly leave Luke and Mac's wedding. Rasheed wasn't happy about that. But according to Uncle Jake, it ended up being a love match anyway, and I'm glad. I would have hated for him to have gotten tied down for the rest of his life, married to a woman he didn't love," Blade concluded.

Sam took a sip of water and looked over the rim of her glass at him. "So when you marry, it will be for love, Blade?"

She knew by the look in his eyes that he didn't appreciate her question, and from the silence at the table it was evident that, like her, Mac and Luke were waiting for him to answer. Sam wasn't exactly sure what had possessed her to ask such a question when she already had a pretty good idea what his response would be. But she had asked, and there was no doubt in her mind that he would make it crystal clear for her, so that there would never, ever be any misunderstanding. He enjoyed being a womanizer, and he proudly played the part.

He took another sip of water before flashing a smile that revealed a pair of dimples she hadn't noticed until now. His eyes locked on her face. "I don't ever plan to marry, Sam—for love or any other reason. I enjoy my life just the way it is. I could never be a one-woman man. What's the point?"

"Yes, I agree with you one hundred percent. What's the point? I don't plan to marry, either. Like you, I like my life just the way it is, and I could never belong to one man exclusively."

She wasn't quite sure what he had expected her to say, but from the look on his face she could tell that hadn't been it. He evidently thought men were the only ones who could play the field.

Sam was spared from saying anything else when the waitress returned to take their orders. But that didn't stop her from glancing across the table at Mac and seeing the sly smile on her friend's lips. Luke seemed inordinately preoccupied with his silverware.

It was obvious she had stunned Blade, so everyone was giving him a chance to recover. From the way he was staring across the table at her, he had to be wondering why—since they had the same outlook on life when it came to commitment—she had refused to give him the time of day.

Sam looked away as she ran a finger around the rim of her glass, then seductively touched the tip with her tongue, knowing Blade's eyes followed her every movement. She tried to ignore the shudder that passed through her each time their eyes connected. When the waitress delivered their food, and she began eating, she tried to overlook the intense sexual chemistry between them even as they shared the table with others. She wasn't sure whether Mac and Luke were aware of what was taking place between them or not, but both she and Blade knew it. Dinner was as enjoyable as it could have been under the circumstances, and at the end of the meal she thanked everyone for inviting her, and stood up to leave.

"Where are you rushing off to?" Blade asked, quickly rising to his feet.

The tone of his voice, to her way of thinking, sounded a lot throatier than it should have. It sent shivers up and down her body.

She met his gaze. "I'm going home. I drove Mac over. But since Luke's SUV is here, I'm sure all three of you will be riding back together and—"

"No," Blade said smoothly. "I'm staying at a hotel in town."

That surprised her. "You are?"

His smile widened. "Yes. I didn't want to impose on the newlyweds. Would it be a bother to drop me off at the hotel?"

"Drop you off?" she asked, as if she hadn't heard him right. She inhaled deeply, silently telling herself to get a grip. Handle her business. So what if she had to drop him

off at some hotel? She could do that. Put him off at the
curb and keep going.

"Yes, at the hotel."

Before she could answer, Luke spoke up, giving her an
out. "No need to bother Sam. Mac and I can drop you off
at the hotel, Blade. Besides, your luggage is in my truck."

She cast Luke an appreciative smile. "Then it's all
settled. Luke and Mac will make sure you get to the
hotel," she said, looking back at Blade. "It was good
seeing you again, and thanks for dinner."

She was about to turn for a quick getaway when he
said, "I'll walk you to your car."

Sam forced herself not to tell him she preferred if he
didn't. She knew he hadn't intended to let her go that
easily, not until he found out what he wanted to know.
"Fine." She glanced at Luke and Mac. "It's always good
seeing you, Luke, and I'll see you in the morning, Mac."

"Yes, bright and early," she responded. "We have to go
over our notes for the Penton's case."

Sam nodded and gave her a thumbs-up before turning
to leave, with Blade by her side.

He didn't say anything until they had walked out of the
restaurant and were waiting as the valet attendant went
to get her car. Then Blade faced her and said, "I think you
owe me an explanation."

"About what?" she asked, deciding to play innocent as
she tilted her head back. He held her gaze with an intense
look in his eyes.

"If you don't have any problems with casual dating,
then why have you been giving me the cold shoulder
every time I approach you?"

Before she could answer, the valet brought her car
around. "The reason is rather simple," she said, opening
the door and tossing her purse on the passenger seat.

"Is it?" Blade asked, watching as she slid into the driver's side of her sporty red Mercedes two-seater.

"Yes," she replied, buckling her seat belt and rolling her window down.

He gazed at her. "And what reason is that?"

She turned the radio to a station that played soft music before looking back up at him, staring straight into his eyes and stating what she knew was the biggest lie of her life. "You, Blade Madaris, don't interest me. Good night."

And before he could utter another word, she revved the engine and drove away.

Chapter 2

Blade tossed the hotel key on a table after settling into his suite. He couldn't help the smile that touched his lips as he recalled Sam's parting words. He didn't for one minute believe she had been serious.

Of course, what she'd said had sounded pretty damn convincing, like saying it would be the end of it. If those words had been spoken by any other woman, it would have been. He didn't have time to waste on anyone who refused his advances. But Blade knew for a fact that he *did* interest Sam, just as she interested him. It had been obvious tonight, although she probably wanted to deny the truth. But he wouldn't deny it. He didn't intend to give up on her so easily, and evidently, she was counting on that fact.

He was a man who knew women inside and out. He was thirty-four and knew the female gender a lot better than men with twice his experience. And for him to make that claim said a whole hell of a lot.

From the time they were teenagers, it was clear that he and his twin brother, Slade, had a different take on women. Slade had been easygoing and had put his career first. Blade, on the other hand, had been able to juggle both. His sexual exploits rivaled those of his cousin Clayton, who ten years earlier had had the same reputation.

At one time, the thought that Blade was following in Clayton's footsteps had been cause for major concern in his family. They figured once Clayton had settled down and was married, that would be the end of the playboys in the Madaris family. He chuckled as he removed his jacket, thinking about how he had proven them wrong. He probably had more notches on his bedpost than his cousin Clayton ever thought of.

Times were different now. Things had changed. He probably didn't have to work as hard to get a woman in bed as Clayton had. Nowadays, women were liberated, freethinkers. The ones he dated didn't mind the fact that they weren't the only one. They enjoyed a challenge and preferred getting physical in the bedroom more than anything else. The sky was the limit behind closed doors and he'd had no complaints. He dated women whose only concern was *not* having to "fake it," and who didn't give a damn that come morning, when he walked out the door, chances were he wouldn't be back. They weren't into long-term relationships any more than he was. He dated women who not only knew the score, but played the game as much as he did.

He had accepted early on in life that marriage wasn't for everyone, and he didn't lose sleep over the fact that he wasn't settling down to the kind of marriage his parents had. More than anything, the two words that scared him to death were *settling down*. There was still too much fun out there to be had, too many women out there to sleep with. Marriage demanded faithfulness and he was convinced there was not a single woman capable of holding his interest forever.

He had tried to explain his position to his family time and time again. But that hadn't stopped them, even Clayton, from worrying about the number of women coming and going in and out of his life—namely, his bedroom. His great-grandmother thought he had *issues*. But as far as he was concerned, he just had a healthy Madaris sexual appetite.

He would never forget the day Clayton had given him a huge case of condoms and told him that at the rate he was going, he would definitely need them. Clayton had been right. Blade had gone through that case and was working on several more.

Some women he met definitely had marriage on their minds. He quickly let them know, up front, he wasn't going there. He never intended to marry. It was okay for some, like his brother Slade and cousin Luke, but not for him. He enjoyed life too much. He enjoyed having fun in the bedroom. And as they say, variety is the spice of life— at least when it came to his *sex* life. What was a sexual taboo for some was a welcome change for him.

He had no intentions of ever getting stuck with a wife who would eventually turn their bedroom into nothing more than a place to sleep. He worked hard and enjoyed playing harder. The thought of being stuck in a marriage that was limited to predictable sex—"PS," as he referred to it—was enough to make him break out in hives.

And he didn't want to have to answer to any woman. He wanted to come and go as he pleased. He was always getting calls from different women, but he answered them when he got good and ready, and not before. He didn't mind dropping one if he had to, because she could quickly be replaced. He would never trade in his long list of numbers in his little black book for a long, drawn-out, till-death-do-us-part marriage. What was the point?

It didn't bother him that he had acquired quite a reputation, one that rivaled that of Clayton, who had been his idol growing up. As best he could remember, he'd never seen Clayton with the same woman twice. But now, even Clayton was happily married and a proud father.

Blade shook his head. Imagine that. He'd be the first to admit that Clayton had hit gold with his wife, Syneda. In fact that's how he always thought of her—as Clayton's golden woman—with her green eyes and mass of golden-bronze hair. She was fun to be with, witty and beautiful, and it seemed as if she was handling her man. It was easy to see why Clayton only had eyes for his wife. He adored her. But Blade knew for a womanizer like Clayton to find a woman like Syneda was indeed a rarity.

Blade was a man who loved women, but he loved his bachelor lifestyle even more, which was why practicing safe sex was critical in his book. He was selective with the women he slept with. In certain situations, he even asked his bed partner to produce medical verification attesting to her sexual health, and he did likewise. Nothing personal, just covering all the bases.

His thoughts shifted to Samari Di Meglio. There was something about her that stimulated him sexually just thinking about her. Sure, she could claim all she wanted that she wasn't interested in him, but he knew for a fact that she was. He recognized the look whenever their eyes met, and he felt the heat when he'd touched the palm of her hand. He had also picked up on the sexual vibes that were just as obvious as if she'd opened her mouth and said it aloud, letting him know she wanted him as much as he wanted her.

Maybe she was the kind of woman who liked to be pursued by men, and with her beauty he could easily imagine that happening. He could see a man wanting her so bad that he'd do just about anything to have her, knowing that one night in bed with her would be well worth it.

Whether she knew it or not, she had done the unthinkable to a Madaris—at least this particular Madaris. She had issued a challenge that struck a nerve with him, and he intended to make her eat her words. And he would take great pleasure in doing so.

He headed toward the bathroom to take a shower.

Sam's town house was in a secure gated community called Windsor Park, situated on a beautiful lake with mountains in the background. It was considered one of the safest areas in the city.

A few months after she'd come to Oklahoma, Sam's parents had insisted that she move to Windsor Park. At the time, a man her father had prosecuted more than twenty years ago had escaped from prison and was determined to get back at him.

Since threats had been made against the entire Di Meglio family, her parents decided not to take any chances, especially after there had been several attempts to run her brother off the road. The man was eventually caught. But before he could be apprehended, he was killed in a shoot-out with the police.

Sam's home was much too large for one person. In her opinion, it was definitely more space than she needed. There were two bedrooms on the ground floor, a bathroom, a living room, dining room and spacious kitchen. On the upper floor were two more bedrooms—one that she used as an office—an entertainment room and a huge bathroom that included a sauna and a Jacuzzi. There was a screened-in balcony with a hot tub off the master bedroom.

At first, she had intended to move out of the town house into a smaller place once the threat had passed. But by then she had fallen in love with her home. She loved the close proximity to the office and enjoyed all the amenities the exclusive gated community provided, especially the scenic walking trail and recreational park. On the weekends she would spend hours relaxing or sitting on a blanket by the lake and reading.

Sam pulled into her private garage and within minutes was entering her house. The moment the door closed behind her, she kicked off her shoes. It was only then, in the comfort of her home, that she allowed her mind to drift back to Blade Madaris.

She wondered if he would take her words at face value. Any man with an ounce of pride would. For a woman to come right out and say that she wasn't interested in him was bold, not to mention ego-crushing.

She had been looking in his eyes when she'd said it, but his reaction was unreadable. But then, she hadn't hung around long enough after that to really find out. She had driven off like the devil himself was on her tail.

She put her purse and briefcase on the table as she made her way into the kitchen, thinking she'd have a cup of tea before getting ready for bed.

She, Mac and Peyton had decided to take on Clarissa Penton's sexual-harassment case, but the three of them had agreed that it sounded a lot like Clarissa was trying to get even with her boss for refusing to return her advances.

After turning on the stove to heat the water for her tea, Sam glanced out the window at the lake. She had intended to pull her notes together and go over what they knew about the case so far. As Mac had reminded her, they would be meeting to discuss the case in the morning. But any plans to review those notes had been made before tonight's dinner. And being in the presence of Blade Madaris for an extended period of time had been unnerving. Although she had tried downplaying the chemistry and mutual attraction between them, it had been there, and blatantly so. But that didn't mean she would act on it, even though her body was daring her to do so.

It wasn't because she thought he was too much to handle. To her way of thinking, no man was once he met the right woman. She'd heard a lot of stories about Blade and figured someone needed to knock him off his high horse. But it wouldn't be her. Not this time. She had enough to deal with. There was her share of the caseload that had been divvied up among the three of them, and her parents were still trying to run her life even from New York.

Antonio and Kayla Di Meglio still hadn't learned their lesson with Guy, she thought, settling down at the kitchen table with her cup of tea. Guy had joined her parents' law firm and, according to her father, had a bright future. He was highly intelligent, articulate, a smooth dresser, a sharp lawyer, and he had an interest in politics, which had once been her father's dream. Guy had even told her parents he had Italian ancestors somewhere in his family. That made him a shoo-in.

Yielding to her parent's wishes—and against her better judgment—Sam had begun dating Guy. To her surprise she'd really liked him, although she wouldn't go so far as to admit that she fell in love with him. They dated for almost a year before he popped the question. Because she thought she'd gotten to know him, and believed he was the one man she could live the rest of her life with, she had said yes.

Her parents had turned her wedding into the social event of the year, inviting more than five hundred guests. She'd had bridal showers galore and her wedding dress had been designed by Vera Wang. Her parents had assumed, as she had, that she and Guy would share a long and prosperous marriage, and the storybook wedding would be one they would all remember.

Sam shook her head as she finished her tea and walked over to the sink to rinse out her cup before placing it in the dishwasher. Yes, her wedding day had been one she and Guy would remember, all right, along with her parents and all five hundred invited guests, but for all the wrong reasons.

She had walked down the aisle to take her place by Guy's side when a commotion in the back of the church got everyone's attention. Two women with screaming babies came forward to announce that Guy was their babies' daddy. One even claimed she was pregnant with another child of his. Talk about drama. It took the reverend and the ushers a full hour to get things under control. Later, in Reverend Caldwell's study, Guy had confessed that the two women's claims were true. However, he felt the situation had nothing to do with Sam, and they should go on with the wedding anyway. He'd certainly been a fool to think that. She'd told him so, and none too nicely.

Sam walked out of the kitchen and went upstairs to her bedroom, remembering how she'd gone on her honeymoon without Guy. When she'd returned two weeks later, she had gotten a call from Mac, asking if she wanted to become a partner with Peyton and her, realizing their law-school dream of forming their own legal practice.

Mac had been living in Louisiana, and her boyfriend had proved to be no better than Guy when he up and married someone else. Peyton, who'd grown up on Chicago's South Side, had been working as a community activist and lawyer, wasn't involved with anyone and was ready for a change. Mac, who was a black Cherokee, was ready to move back home to Oklahoma. Considering everything, the timing was perfect.

Over her parents' objections, Sam left New York and headed for Oklahoma. But distance had not stopped her parents from trying to interfere in her personal life or wanting to play matchmaker on occasion. In a way, she understood her parents' desire to have grandchildren. Their friends—the social elite of Manhattan and the Hamptons—were all bursting with pride about their grandkids. At thirty-two, DeAngelo, who was still very much a player, had no intention of settling down and getting married, so her parents had focused their attention on her.

As she stripped off her clothes to take her shower, she couldn't help but think again of Blade Madaris. Maybe now the flower deliveries would stop coming to the office, since she had a strong suspicion he was behind them. During dinner he had mentioned to Luke that one of their aunts had opened up a florist shop on the ground floor of the Madaris Building. Had he just been bringing Luke up-to-date on what was going on in their family, or was it meant to let Sam know he was her secret admirer? Thanks to Angelo, which is what friends and family called her brother, she knew firsthand how players operated. Send a woman flowers to break down her defenses, her brother would say. Who could resist a beautiful, sweet-smelling, romantic bouquet?

Samari Di Meglio, for one.

She knew from the conversation at dinner that Blade would be in town for only a day or so, not long enough for them to run into each other again. Since he was Luke's cousin, and a close friend at that, and she was one of Mac's best friends, chances were their paths would cross again, but hopefully none too soon. Blade was a player who had little regard for the women whose hearts he broke. He was the type of man she wanted no part of, the kind she detested. And after what she'd said to him tonight, she was certain he would stay as far away from her as he could.

Blade chided himself, silently scolding himself for being a fool for getting up at the crack of dawn and hurriedly eating breakfast just to chase behind a woman. It was certainly not the way he usually operated.

He appreciated the car rental company for delivering the vehicle to him and having it ready for him when he walked out of the hotel that morning. A man with a plan, he slid behind the wheel, and now he stood watching from the office window the object of his curiosity as she parked her car. She had no idea he was there awaiting her, and he couldn't wait to see her face when she did. He liked having the element of surprise on his side.

"I'm not sure it was a good idea to let you in, Blade."

He glanced over his shoulder and met Mac's gaze and couldn't help but smile. Dressed in a blue pantsuit, she looked sleepy but in a beautiful sort of way. It was obvious she wasn't used to getting to the office this early, but had let it slip that they would be here early since she had to be in court by ten.

"Why do you feel that way?" he asked.

She rolled her eyes. "I think it's obvious. Sam doesn't like you."

He knew that was probably putting it mildly. "I intend to change her mind about that," he said.

"Personally, I don't think you can. You didn't make such a good impression on her at my wedding or my birthday party. That said, I'm going into my office. I've seen Sam's hot-blooded Italian temper in action and I don't want to be around when she walks through that door and finds you here."

He watched as Mac hurried into her office and closed the door, and then he glanced out the window in time to see Sam get out of her car. He felt his heart flutter in his chest as she swung her legs around to get out. She was wearing a business suit, with one of those short skirts again, the kind that showed off just what a nice pair of legs she had.

She crossed the parking lot carrying a deli bag in one hand and a cup of coffee in the other. But his eyes weren't really focused on what she was carrying. They were focused on her and just how good she looked this morning.

Why am I so drawn to her? He couldn't help but ask himself that. He couldn't blame his fixation on her beauty, since he'd been attracted to beautiful women before. The fact that she presented a challenge was part of it, he was sure. For some reason, he wanted to best her at her own game. He had to represent the players out there.

As he continued to watch her, he saw her smile at the security guard standing by the entrance. Blade frowned, remembering how the guy, who looked about twenty-four or twenty-five, had given him the third degree until he showed him proof that he was related to Mac. He knew the guard was just doing his job, but Blade thought he'd been more of a stickler than he needed to be.

He watched as the same man who'd given him grief just an hour or so earlier gush like a besotted fool when Sam greeted him with a smile. Sure, Blade would be the first to admit she had that effect on men. But still he didn't like the way the man was looking at her, mainly because he recognized the look even if Sam didn't.

He tried to ignore the mounting irritation he felt, and refused to consider, even for a moment, that he was jealous. Being jealous of a woman didn't fit who he was. Admittedly, he was more than slightly annoyed that she never smiled at him that way, but he intended to change that, as well. He was a smart enough man to know that getting a smile out of her would take time.

He continued to study the two and rolled his eyes. Now they were standing and chatting like old friends. He glanced at his watch, and when he looked out the window again he tried to ignore Sam and the security guard by looking up at the sky. It was the second week in April and the temperature that morning had been cool, but the weather forecast said warm air was moving their way. The sky was a beautiful blue and he couldn't help wondering how the weather was back home in Houston. When he glanced back at Sam, he realized she was about to enter the building. The clock on the wall said seven-thirty as he quickly moved toward the door.

She opened the door, nearly gasped in surprise when she saw him standing there. Before she could open her mouth to say a single word, he smiled at her, leaned in the doorway and said, "So tell me, Sam. Just what kind of man does interest you?"

Sam stared up at Blade. It had been a long time since any man had rendered her speechless. What was Blade Madaris doing in her office at this time of the morning? She quickly answered her own question when she thought about the question he'd just asked. He was a man whose advances were probably never rebuffed. He was used to

women thinking he was the greatest thing since
Grandma's apple pie. For him to show any interest in a
woman was a privilege, an honor, or so he thought.

She'd heard that back in Houston he had his choice of
single women at his beck and call. Considering that, it was
no wonder he was so conceited. The mere thought that she
wasn't like all those other women, and that she'd had the
nerve to come right out and tell him he didn't interest her,
probably had him in a tizzy to find out why, or better yet,
to prove her wrong.

Instead of answering, she moved passed him and
headed toward her office, since she needed time to regain
her composure. "Good morning, Blade. You're the last
person I expected to see today."

"I'm sure I was," he said, walking in step beside her.

She wasn't sure what cologne he was wearing but he certainly smelled good. How could his scent be more seductive than a breakfast sandwich and coffee from Walter's
Café?

"I guess you figured what you said last night would
have kept me from coming back," he added, as he
followed her into her office and closed the door behind
them.

She had figured that. "I was being honest with you,
which I felt was best."

"I appreciate it but I don't believe you."

Sam placed the bag and coffee on her desk, and by the
time she turned to face Blade a frown had settled on her
face. "Excuse me?"

He smiled. "I said I don't believe you."

She crossed her arms over her chest and leaned back
against her desk. "Are you so conceited that you think
every woman alive should want you?"

His smile widened. "For starters, we're not talking

about every woman, we're talking about you. And yes, I think you want me."

She gave him a chilly look as the muscles in her neck actually knotted. "Please explain how you figure that."

He shrugged. "You've been sending sexual vibes my way."

Her brow wrinkled at the center of her forehead. "What?"

"I said you've been sending sexual vibes my way. It started at the wedding. I have this uncanny ability to detect when a woman and I connect in the most sensual way. I have a built-in radar that lets me know she's attracted to me. When that happens, it's up to me to let her know whether or not *I'm* interested. If a woman picks up on the 'I'm interested' signal, that's cool. If she doesn't and if it's someone I really want to hook up with, then I take things a step further. I picked up on the fact that you're attracted to me. However, when I responded, so to speak—on two occasions, I might add—for whatever reason, you retreated."

Sam kept her jaw clenched tight. He was right. She had been interested in him, but not for the reasons he thought. She knew immediately when she saw him at the wedding and observed how he worked the room at Mac and Luke's reception that he was a player.

The only reason she *had* singled him out was the same reason she targeted most men like him, and that was to teach him a lesson. By the time he noticed her, she had decided not to pursue her plan, since Luke and Mac's marriage officially made him a relative of her best friend. She figured the best thing to do was to spare him.

Then last month, when she'd seen him again at the birthday party Luke had given for Mac, she'd known he was once again on the prowl. More than once he had tried hitting on her and she'd ignored him. By the time the party had ended, she'd pretty much decided that if she ever saw him again she would finally take him down a peg. Now would be a perfect time if she didn't have her parents to deal with.

A week after the party the flowers had begun arriving, a beautiful bouquet each week, but without a card. The florist explained the flowers had been ordered over the Internet so she had no idea who'd sent them. It could have been anyone. Although Sam had never mentioned it to Mac, a part of her had believed they were from Blade, since he had been the last man to come on to her and he had the money to do something that extravagant. It was obvious that the weekly floral arrangements she'd received weren't cheap.

"I can see I've left you speechless."

Her response would have been a snort, but she suppressed the instinct. Her first inclination was to give him the reading of his life, something Angelo said she was good at when it came to men who were womanizers. He and Sam's three male cousins had been the recipients of such a dressing-down.

She lifted her head, locked onto his gaze. "Read my lips, Blade. There weren't any vibes. Anything you thought you sensed was a figment of your imagination. Contrary to what you believe, not every woman is interested in you. If you knew anything about me, the one thing you would know is that men like you turn me off. I can chew them up and spit them out."

"Prove it. Prove that I can't break through the defenses you have set up around yourself." His voice was deep, controlled and sexy. The expression on his face was intense and just as sexy as his voice. She wanted to roll her eyes. But for the moment, she couldn't move her gaze from his.

Defenses?

"Besides," he continued, interrupting her thoughts as a cocky grin spread across his face. "I sort of like the thought of you chewing me up. You can even go ahead and bite me a few times and I won't complain."

He took a step forward, standing in front of her. "But what I will do, Sam, is retaliate in a way that will have you moaning for days and groaning for nights."

A shudder passed through Sam's body at his threat. Maybe it was the fact that she hadn't gotten a good night's sleep and was still feeling tired. Or it could have been that Blade was standing too close to her and his scent, the sound of his voice and the look in his eyes were all getting to her. Or it could have been the fact that it had been more than four years since she'd been intimate with a man. And the last time had been so quick she would've missed it if she had blinked. Not only had it been rushed, it had been thoroughly unsatisfying.

She stared at him. "You're sure of yourself, aren't you?"

A soft smile touched his determined lips. "Yes."

She shook her head. When they had been doling out arrogance, he had been first in line, she was sure. There was nothing wrong with being confident, but this man was as conceited as they came. "Sorry to disappoint you, but you're wrong."

"Then prove it."

Famous last words, she thought. But he was beginning to annoy her. "I don't have to prove anything. I told you how I feel. It would be so much easier on the both of us if you respected that."

"And I will once you answer my question. Just what type of man does interest you, since I don't? Based on what you said last night, you have no problem with a man who's not into long-term relationships, so just what turns you on, Sam Di Meglio?"

She glared at him. "A man who respects my wishes, for one."

He took a step closer to her and put both hands on her desk, effectively pinning her in between. He smiled faintly. He smelled heavenly. And her heart was beating like crazy in her chest.

His mouth was inches from hers. "And I will respect your wishes," he said in a silky voice that sent all kinds of erotic sensations through her body. "But first, since you won't answer my question, let me give you my opinion and tell you what I think."

She breathed slowly and deeply, inhaling his scent through her nostrils. "You really don't need to bother."

His smile widened a bit as he leaned closer to her. "Humor me."

His breath was hot on her lips and she fought back the urge to do more than just humor him, to do something crazy like stick her tongue out and lick his lips from corner to corner. So she did something probably even worse; she concentrated on those lips. They were beautiful, firm and full, curved and clearly defined and shaped in a perfect bow.

She would be the first to admit she was one of those women who were drawn to a man's lips. Even though he'd ended up being a deceitful ass, Guy's lips hadn't been all bad. But no one's lips could compare to the ones she was staring at now, the ones sending shivers through her body, making her feel hot all over, so much so that she wanted to remove her jacket, take off her blouse, slip out of her skirt, take off her bra and panties and…

She blinked. What in the world was happening to her? What could she be thinking? What was *he* thinking? She opened her mouth to ask Blade that very thing, when, too late, she realized he'd been waiting for her to do just that.

Before she could draw in her next breath his mouth captured hers and began eating away at it like she was his breakfast and he intended to devour her right up until lunch. The moment his tongue touched hers, stroked it in such a way that blatantly reminded her how long it had been since she'd engaged in foreplay with a man, he conjured up all those deep-seated, wild fantasies no other soul knew about, not even Mac and Peyton.

Any thoughts of what Mac and Peyton didn't know fled Sam's mind when Blade deepened the kiss. She knew she had to do something before he went any further or before she succumbed any more to his passion. If that happened, considering the last time she'd been intimate with someone, he could drag her to the floor and she wouldn't put up much of a fuss. In fact she might be the one dragging him first.

She had no idea just how long they'd been kissing or how long they would have continued had the intercom on her desk not buzzed, and if their secretary, Priscilla Gaines, hadn't chosen that moment to say, "Ms. Madaris wanted me to remind you of the meeting this morning, Ms. Di Meglio."

Sam drew in a deep breath as Blade reluctantly let go of her lips. "Bad timing, wouldn't you say?" he whispered, straightening his physique and taking a step backward.

She exhaled, still wondering what the hell had happened. She shook her head, sending a mass of curly locks flying around her shoulders as if that would help screw her head back on, not only right but tight. She knew at that moment that this man was dangerous to any woman. He was smooth and lethal all rolled into one. She

wondered how many hearts he'd already broken and how
many more he would be breaking. Maybe not intentionally, but with total disregard for the fact that although he
might not fall in love with a woman, some would ulti-
mately fall in love with him and painfully watch as he
swaggered out of their life without even a backward
glance.

"I'd better leave and let you get back to work now," he
said, smiling as if coming to her office and kissing her
senseless first thing in the morning was an everyday oc-
currence. "I'll be returning to Houston later today, but I
plan to come back to Oklahoma City in about three
weeks."

She frowned. "Why?"

His smile widened. "The Mosley Building, or have
you forgotten?"

She had forgotten, sort of. "Why do you need to come
back? I thought your construction crew would be taking
over now that things have been finalized."

He chuckled as he smooth out his jacket. "Not yet. As
chief engineer, I'm hands-on from start to finish. That
means you'll be seeing a lot of me for at least the next six
months or more."

Her entire body stiffened when she remembered his
spiel at dinner last night. For Pete's sake, she didn't want
to see any more of him. Less of him would serve her nicely.
She had let her guard down with him today, and judging
from the smirk on his face, he evidently assumed he'd
gotten the upper hand. "I don't want to see more of you,
Blade."

The smile that appeared on his face at that moment
would have been priceless to any other woman. "You need
to stop doing that, you know," he said as he headed toward
the door.

She crossed her arms over her chest again. "Doing what?"

He glanced back over his shoulder and paused long enough to reply, "Saying one thing when you mean another."

She glared at him. "I mean what I say, Blade. You just can't seem to get the message."

He put his hand on the doorknob and angled his head to the side to look at her, a pose she found unnerving. "No, Sam. I read you loud and clear, and if you do mean what you say then you need to stop sending mixed signals. I'll see you in three weeks."

He opened the door and was gone.

Chapter 3

"So there you have it," Peyton Mahoney said, as she threw her pencil in the middle of the conference table. "According to the photo lab, those pictures were doctored."

A disgusted look appeared on Mac's face. "So Clarissa Penton lied to us. Those are not pictures of her and Sidney Gresham in bed together."

"Nope. So what do we do now?" Peyton asked.

"There's only one thing left to do," Mac replied, as she rubbed the back of her neck. "Get her on the phone and ask her to meet with us. We'll let her know what we've found out and advise her to get someone else to represent her. We should also suggest that she drop the charges, and let her know what can happen if she doesn't."

Mac glanced over at Sam. "What do you think?"

Sam had been staring into space, but now looked across the table at her two friends. "The way I feel right now, I want to call her in and kick her you-know-what for wasting our time."

Mac couldn't stop the smile that spread across her face. She saw that Peyton was doing a better job than she was at holding back. Both of them were well aware that Sam was in a lousy mood and had been since Blade left. They were also aware that Sam and Blade had spent almost twenty minutes together in her office before he'd finally departed, and that was only after Priscilla had reminded Sam of their meeting. They had both noticed that although Sam had reapplied her lipstick, her lips were kiss-swollen nonetheless.

"I think," Mac said, "that we go with option one—call her in and let her know we won't be representing her in her sexual harassment case against Sidney Gresham." She glanced at Sam again. "You might want to take a chill pill before she arrives, Di Meglio."

Muttering something under her breath, Sam stood and walked over to the coffeepot to pour a cup. "I don't need a chill pill. What I need is my head examined."

"Um, Blade Madaris was that bad, Sam?" Peyton asked, grinning.

She turned around and stared at her friends for a long, steady moment before rolling her eyes to the ceiling. "No, he was that good," she said in a disgusted tone. "Damn it."

From the stares and arched eyebrows, she immediately knew what Mac and Peyton assumed. "For crying out loud, stop staring at me like I don't have any panties on. We didn't go *that* far. Jeez. He was only in my office for twenty minutes. It was only a kiss."

Peyton stood as she gathered her folders. "Hey, a woman and her man can do a lot in twenty minutes. And please don't ask me how I know."

Since Peyton was the argumentative type and no one was in the mood for a debate this early in the morning, they didn't say anything as she left the room. As soon as the door closed behind her Sam felt Mac's eyes shift to her.

"Sam, if Blade is making a nuisance of himself and is harassing you, I can have Luke talk to him."

Sam waved off her words as she returned to her seat. "It's not that serious, Mac. He's not harassing me. There's a difference between a man openly pursuing a woman and when he's harassing her."

"And usually the difference is the attitude of the woman," Mac pointed out. "Do you or don't you want to be involved with Blade?"

"No, I don't and I've told him that. But of course he thinks he can change my mind. I think he sees me as some kind of conquest. I'm the one woman not falling at his feet, not eagerly crawling between his sheets. He wouldn't be a true-blue player if he didn't get the woman who rejects his advances, namely me."

She leaned back in her chair, stared into her coffee and then added, "He thinks I'm being defensive, whatever that means. And I didn't help matters this morning by letting him kiss me."

"Mmm, sounds interesting."

Sam looked at her friend. "Damn it, Mac, it was better than interesting. I've never been kissed like that before. The man makes using his lips and tongue some sort of art form."

Mac chuckled as she stood up. "Must be a Madaris trait. And I hope you know that unless you put your foot down and give him a reason not to, Blade will be back, and he won't give up until he gets what he wants." She shook her head. "Neither of you are acting rational. I've

known Blade for more than seven years, and I've never
known him to pursue a woman the way he's chasing you
for any reason, conquest or otherwise. I've known you
even longer, and I've never known you to let a bona fide
player get under your skin."

Sam didn't say anything for a moment and then said,
"He claims I'm sending mixed signals."

"Are you?"

She paused, then admitted, "Possibly. You and Peyton
of all people know how I handle players."

"Yes. Which has me wondering why you're handling
him differently?"

"He's Luke cousin. Besides, my parents are beginning
to act crazy again by playing matchmaker. There's this
new guy who's working at the law firm. My folks are all
but shoving him down my throat. My mother sent me
pictures of him over the Internet, but I've refused to open
the file."

Mac shook her head. "Will your parents ever learn?"

"Apparently not. I see now that I made a mistake after
law school when I let them talk me into coming home
and working in the family firm. Those years I spent at
Di Meglios were the worst. My parents were determined
that I not have a life, at least not one they couldn't
control."

Sam couldn't help but remember those years. Her
parents were highly respected attorneys who'd earned a
name for themselves in New York circles. The firm
included her mother and father, her father's two brothers,
Federico and Leandro, and their sons, Maddox and
Damon, as well as her brother. They were all Di Meglios
and they made their name representing the rich and
famous.

Besides her mother, Sam had been the only Di Meglio

woman in the family practice. All her female cousins had
been smart enough to choose some other profession, since
they'd known they would have been expected to work at
the family-run law firm.

She cringed each time she remembered her parents'
angry words when she'd told them of her decision to move
to Oklahoma and form a law practice with Mac and Peyton.
She knew they were still holding out, hoping that eventually she would come to her senses and return home to Manhattan to the plush, prestigious office overlooking the
Hudson River, which was still empty and waiting for her.
Angelo was the only one who knew for certain that she
wouldn't be coming back, and she had left with his bless-
ings.

"You're a big girl and I know you can take care of
yourself," Mac said, interrupting her thoughts. "And as far
as Luke is concerned, he knows that Blade is capable of
handling himself, as well. Just so you know, Luke and I
talked about it last night, when Blade walked you to your
car. We've made a decision to stay out of it. Whatever
happens is between you and Blade. Like I said, you're a big
girl."

Sam didn't say anything for a moment and then,
smiling, she stated, "Well, the first thing this big girl
needs to do is clear her calendar for a week and fly to New
York to pay her parents a visit. I need to settle a few
things and get them to understand my life is my life, and
I won't have them interfering. And as for Blade, if he con-
tinues to be a nuisance, I will settle a few things with him,
as well."

Later that evening Blade entered his condo. In a way
he was glad to be back home in Houston. His meeting
with J. W. Mosley had gone well and the man was looking

forward to working with Madaris Construction Company. The building would be a magnificent addition to downtown Oklahoma City's skyline.

Blade had slept through most of the flight. But right now, he was wide-awake and Sam Di Meglio was on his mind. He was convinced that the only reason he was still thinking about her was because he hadn't met anyone quite like her. Besides her beauty, he knew there was a passion in her just waiting to be unleashed. He saw it in her walk, was moved by it whenever their eyes met, and had felt it in their kiss that morning. He was definitely looking forward to returning to Oklahoma City, and would make it his business to see her again.

He had talked to Luke on his cell phone on the way to the airport. His cousin had given him fair warning and tried to convince him Sam wasn't a woman a man wanted to toy with. Blade didn't want to toy with her. He wanted to spend an entire night in bed with her. He wanted to get her out of his system. He was convinced the kiss they'd shared that morning had definitely been the reason she was still on his mind.

He had put his overnight tote and garment bag on the bed when his cell phone rang. He quickly pulled it out of his pants pocket. "This is Blade."

"I know who you are."

He couldn't help but chuckle upon hearing his great-grandmother's matter-of-fact voice. "Yes, ma'am, Mama Laverne, I'm sure you do. And how are you doing today?"

"As well as can be expected. And how was your trip to Oklahoma?"

Blade lifted a brow. "How did you know I went to Oklahoma?"

"Slade told me when I called to check on Skye. She's been a little under the weather."

"Oh," Blade said, leaving his bedroom and heading for the kitchen to get a beer out of the refrigerator. He hadn't known his sister-in-law was sick. "How is she doing?"

"She's doing fine for someone who's having a baby."

Blade blinked. "Excuse me? Skye's pregnant?"

"I dreamed about fish last night, so you know what that means."

He nodded as put his great-grandmother on speaker-phone, placing his cell phone on the table while he un-screwed the beer cap. Yes, he most certainly knew what that meant. Everybody in the entire Madaris family did. If Skye wasn't pregnant, someone else was. It seemed whenever his grandmother dreamed of fish someone ended up pregnant.

"Yes, I know," he said, before tipping the beer bottle to his mouth to take a huge swallow.

"I'm guessing it's Skye, which would be my first great-great-grand. So I'm tickled pink at the thought of that. But who knows. It might not be Skye. It just as well could be one of your girlfriends."

Blade nearly choked on the beer he'd been drinking.

"Blade? You okay?"

He coughed to keep from choking. "Yes, I'm fine. You don't have to worry about it being one of my girlfriends. I don't do babies."

"But you *do* women and all it takes to make a baby is a man and a woman who—"

"Excuse me, Mama Laverne, but I think I hear someone at the door," he said, quickly deciding the last thing he needed was to hear his great-grandmother's version of how babies were made. "I need to go answer it."

"Oh, okay. Will you be at church Sunday?"

He rolled his eyes. He hadn't planned to go. "Why? Is there something happening there this Sunday?"

"Something happens at church every Sunday, Blade."

He rolled his eyes again. "Yes, ma'am. I'll see if I can make it."

"Elsie Fowler's niece is back in town and she'll be there."

Blade shook his head. Now he knew for certain that he wouldn't make it. Elsie Fowler's niece, Sharon what's-her-name, was not his type. She was the clingy kind who hadn't been all that great in bed. "Okay, Mama Laverne, I'll talk to you later."

He hung up, glad to end the call. His great-grandmother meant well, but they had different opinions about things, namely his marital status and his social life. The old gal was a die-hard matchmaker. And from what he'd heard, she used to be good at it back in the day. Five of her seven daughters-in-laws had been handpicked. And now she was trying to step back into that role. All of her great-grandchildren were well aware that she was trying to marry them off. Blade even suspected she had something to do with Luke and Mac getting together. It was a good thing she didn't know of his interest in Sam or she would have taken it the wrong way. The only thing he was interested in was getting her in his bed, nothing more.

After emptying his beer bottle and putting it in the recycling bin, he made his way to the living room. It was a Thursday night and in his corner of the world, the weekend didn't start on Friday. It started tonight. He picked up the phone to call his friends Wyatt Bannister and Tanner Jamison to see if they were interested in heading over to Sisters, a restaurant where they knew single women liked to hang out. He was back on familiar turf and he felt good about it.

Chapter 4

"Welcome back, Sam. How did things go with your parents?" Mac asked as soon as Sam walked into the conference room.

She made a face as she sat down in one of the chairs at the large oval table.

"Mmm, that bad?" Peyton inquired as a grin spread across her lips.

"Worse. They weren't expecting me, so I figured I would have the element of surprise on my side, but that wasn't the case. Even with such short notice they were able to make sure Cash Larkin made an appearance."

"Cash Larkin?" Peyton asked as she spread cream cheese on her bagel. "Who's Cash Larkin?"

"He's a new attorney at the firm. He's been there for about six months or so. My parents think he has a promising career and is just the man to marry their daughter. Sound familiar?"

"Will they ever learn?" Peyton asked, smiling.

"Apparently not."

Mac shook her head and then asked, "Did you accomplish what you set out to do?"

"With my parents, maybe. But I'm not sure about Cash. I don't know what my parents said to him, but I think he assumed that a serious relationship with me was a done deal. I hate to burst his bubble because he is a cutie."

"If he's a cutie then why burst his bubble?" Peyton asked with a serious expression on her face. "You shouldn't assume he'll be like Guy. Who knows? He just might be the one."

Sam didn't reply, since Peyton was only echoing what her parents had said. She couldn't go through life blaming every man for what Guy had done to her. All men weren't like him.

"It doesn't matter if he's nothing like Guy," she finally said. "I'm not interested in Cash. Besides, there wasn't any chemistry between us. No heat."

Peyton raised an eyebrow. "None?"

"Not enough to make me pause. Like I said, he's good-looking. He has a good body, nice teeth, but that's about it," she said. What she wouldn't say was that compared to Blade Madaris he lacked just about everything. He didn't have that swagger, that intense look in his eyes, and when she shook Cash's hand, all she felt was a warm, clammy palm—not a spark of hot desire.

"How does he kiss?" Mac asked.

Sam shrugged. "Don't know. We didn't get that far." And it wasn't for lack of trying on his part, she thought, remembering the couple of times he tried to get her alone. She just wasn't feeling him. Maybe it had been the wrong thing to do, but she had compared Cash to Blade. There had been more than just chemistry between her and Blade, even when she hadn't wanted to admit it. Even when she had denied it to herself and to him.

The moment he'd showed up at Mac's rehearsal dinner, Sam knew he would be trouble. She had watched him out of the corner of her eye as he smoothly checked out the women, mostly single female friends of Mac. And she knew the moment his gaze landed on her. Later that night, when everyone left the church for the rehearsal dinner, he'd approached her to make small talk. But she'd stopped him cold with an icy look before he could even get in a word.

"Well, I hate to change the subject, but I have some good news to share with everyone," Mac said.

Sam sat up straight and looked over at her expectantly. "What's your good news?"

Mac was beaming brightly. "Well, it's not really *my* good news personally, but good news about people I care about. First, Ashton called yesterday to say that Nettie is expecting."

"Wow!" Peyton said, clapping her hands. "That's wonderful!"

"He didn't predict triplets again?" Sam asked, smiling. Everyone knew the story of how Mac's cousin had said Nettie would be having triplets—three sons—even after the doctor had convinced Nettie she would never have children.

"No, he says it's just one baby this time. A daughter," Mac said, chuckling. "And," she continued, "Luke talked to Slade last night. He and Skye are expecting."

"I think we really do have a reason to go over to Twains after work to celebrate," Sam said. She had met Skye at one of Mac's bridal showers and had immediately liked her. She was down-to-earth and friendly.

"I agree," Peyton interjected.

Mac chuckled. "Count me in."

Sam nodded. She was happy for Nettie and Skye. They had fallen in love and married good men. Sam had met Ashton while she and Mac were roommates in law school. Sam had had a crush on him for a while. It was a man-in-uniform thing. As far as Slade was concerned, although he was Blade's twin brother, the two looked and acted nothing alike. Slade was handsome in his own right, but his disposition was entirely different from Blade's. They were like night and day. It was easy to see that Blade was a man who enjoyed women, and it was just as obvious that Slade was a man who could be loyal to only one woman. It was there in his eyes whenever he looked at his wife. Blade wouldn't know how to look at a woman like that. He wouldn't know the first thing about making a woman feel like she was the only one, mainly because with him she wouldn't be.

"Okay, it's time to get down to business," Mac said.

Sam put her case files on the table. Mac was right. It was time to get down to business and that meant eliminating any thoughts of Blade Madaris.

Blade drove the rental car to the rodeo construction site. After he parked the car, he turned his attention to the men from Madaris Construction who were hard at work on what would be Luke's rodeo school.

Weather permitting, the project would be completed on time, and Luke's school would be finished by the end of the month. Mac was hoping to host a grand opening the first of June, which meant landscape work had to be finished by then, as well. The timing was good, since some of the same men on Luke's project would be working on the Mosley Building.

Blade got out of the car and pushed his Stetson back

off of his forehead with his thumb. He hadn't had time to drop by and check on the progress at the site when he'd been in Oklahoma City a couple of weeks ago. In fact, he hadn't been to the construction site since the foundation had been poured.

The building was huge and consisted of two floors, which would give Luke all the space he needed to teach others what he had been taught. From what Blade had heard, there was already a waiting list of eager rodeo students.

"You're back?"

Blade turned and saw Luke coming out of the barn. He couldn't help but chuckle and say, "Hey, you could act like you're glad to see me."

"Whatever," Luke said, giving him a bear hug. "Like I don't know the real reason you returned."

Blade looked away and observed one of the men installing a window on the second floor. His cousin was the last person he would have told that he hadn't been himself lately. He'd done what he always did when he'd returned to Houston and had gone out with Wyatt and Tanner to their usual spots. But he hadn't had a burning desire to sleep with any of the women he saw there. He actually thought he was coming down with something until he'd figured out just what was wrong with him. The kiss he'd shared with Sam had done him in. He'd never kissed a woman that way without the two of them ending up in bed. That meant that he and Sam had unfinished business. In order for him to move on, he needed to get her out of his system.

"Any news from the home front?" Luke asked, prompting Blade to turn around and look at him.

Blade couldn't help but smile. "I'm sure you've heard about Ashton and Slade."

Luke nodded.

"And I don't know if you've heard about it yet, but Reese got a promotion," Blade added.

"No, I hadn't heard," said Luke. "A promotion to what?"

"He's foreman of Madaris Explorations."

Luke frowned. "But that's Trevor's job."

Blade chuckled. "Not anymore." Trevor was a family friend and had worked as their cousin Dex's foreman for years.

"Trevor is opening a facility to train ex-military men. It's for those interested in tactical military operations."

"Sounds deep."

Blade laughed as he shoved his hands into his pockets. "Knowing Trevor, it will be. And I understand Drake Warren might be working with him at some point. And if Ashton ever decides to retire from the military, he'll be joining them, as well."

Luke leaned back against the post. Blade could feel his cousin studying him. He looked at him. "What's wrong?"

"You tell me. Why are you back?"

Blade took a breath and looked away momentarily to where three of his men were working on the roof of the building, installing shingles. There was no way he was going to confess to Luke the real reason he was back in town, especially since Sam was Mac's best friend. Since getting married, Luke had become a damn knight in shining armor.

He glanced back at his cousin. "I told you I would be coming back."

"You said in three weeks, not two."

Blade leaned against the post that was supporting Luke's weight. "There are more permits I need to file at the courthouse for the Mosley Building," he said. He didn't like having to explain his reasons for anything he did to anyone, not even Luke.

"That's it?"

Blade met Luke's gaze directly. "Is there supposed to be more?"

"You tell me."

Blade knew he couldn't very well do that. The less Luke knew of his plans for Sam the better. Besides, there were certain things he couldn't explain to Luke because he didn't understand them himself. Like why the women back in Houston had suddenly become uninteresting to him. While he had been home, he had begun to take a closer look at the women he'd been dating and had found them lacking, except in the bedroom. But now even that wasn't enough to hold his interest.

"There's nothing to tell. When is Mac coming home?" he asked, changing the subject.

The look Luke gave him let Blade know his cousin knew exactly what he was doing and that he wasn't taking the bait.

"Usually she's home by now, but she called a few minutes ago to say that she, Peyton and Sam are going for drinks after work to celebrate."

"To celebrate what?"

"Ashton and Skye's news. They'll be going somewhere to eat afterward, so if you haven't eaten yet you might as well join me for dinner. And if you don't have a place to stay while you're in town, you know you're welcome to stay here."

"Thanks, but I'll be at the hotel. It's located downtown near the courthouse where I need to transact business. There are a number of permits I need to get pulled."

Although Luke wasn't saying anything, Blade was aware that his cousin knew enough about the construction business to know that he didn't have to come to Oklahoma City himself to pull any permits. Blade had people working for him who could have performed those tasks.

He glanced over at Luke. "So what's for dinner?"

"A casserole."

Blade smiled. At Morehouse that had been Luke's specialty. He, Luke and Slade had shared an apartment not far from campus, and the one thing they could look forward to was Luke's casseroles.

"You didn't say how long you plan on being in town, Blade."

No, he hadn't, Blade thought. "Not sure yet," he answered. And then he added. "I'll know by the middle of the week."

Hopefully by then I'll have a plan, he thought. There was no way he could tell Luke that he would remain in town for as long as it took to get Sam into his bed.

The man glanced around thinking this particular restaurant seemed as good a place as any for them to meet. He glanced over at the woman who was already there waiting for him.

She looked a little different today and he immediately knew what it was. She was wearing makeup. No doubt to impress him, since she fancied herself in love with him. And she probably thought he had fallen in love with her, as well. He shrugged. What she thought wasn't his concern. But if believing such would assure that she continued to provide him with the information he needed, then so be it.

He sat in the chair across from her. "You look pretty today."

"Thanks." She smiled. His compliment had pleased

her, so he would make sure to shower her with more in the future. After a few minutes of small talk, in which he told her again how nice she looked, he said, "The flowers are still being delivered." It was a statement and not a question.

"Each week, and they are beautiful, too. She likes them and doesn't suspect a thing."

He nodded, glad to hear it.

"She thinks she has a secret admirer."

He couldn't help but smile at the thought of that, and thanks to Samari Di Meglio he'd had very little to smile about over the past few years. He wasn't a secret admirer—far from it. But if she wanted to think that she could certainly do so. When she discovered the truth it would be too late to do anything about it.

"How long will you continue to send the flowers to her?"

The annoyingly soft voice had interrupted his thoughts. Now she was asking a question that really wasn't any of her business. His jaw tightened. His gaze narrowed. "For as long as I want," he said in a chillingly cold tone.

He saw the look in her eyes, the flash of fear. He breathed in deeply, knowing that he had to get his feelings under control. The last thing he needed was to make her wary of giving him the information he needed.

He reached out and touched her hand, held it in his for a while. "I didn't mean to scare you. But I've told you why I need to make her remember what she's done, and why she has to pay for doing it."

The woman nodded. Of course, he hadn't told her everything. He'd told her just enough to get her sympathy to do what he needed her to do. She assumed the most he would do was scare and harass Samari Di Meglio for a while, and not do anything really serious to harm her. He smiled to himself at the thought of that. Little did the woman sitting across from him know, but he had a much bigger and more sinister plan. It was one he had worked on for years. Now the time had come and no one, and he meant no one, would stand in his way.

Chapter 5

Sam glanced up when she heard the buzzing sound from Security. She reached over and pressed the button on her intercom. "Yes, Rita?"

"There's someone here to see you."

Sam arched an eyebrow. The office had closed hours ago. After work, she, Mac and Peyton had gone to Twains, the bar and grill on the corner, to have a drink to celebrate Ashton's and Skye's news. They'd also ordered dinner. Afterward, Mac and Peyton had left for home, but since she had been out the past week, Sam had decided to return to the office to catch up on paperwork.

Their building was in a very busy section of town with a popular restaurant a few doors down. But that hadn't stopped someone from ransacking Mac's office last year. That incident had prompted them to hire a twenty-four hour security service, since at any time of day, any one of them might be working late at the office. Rita Wilder, one of their three security guards, worked twelve-hour shifts three days a week—from nine in the morning to nine at night. On occasion, however, she made extra money working overtime by staying late. Frank Denson worked the same number of days from nine at night to nine in the morning. And Marlon Fisher covered everything else. Sam was confident they had a top-notch security team, although Rita sometimes got lost in her romance novels.

"Who is it, Rita?" she asked. She couldn't imagine anyone dropping by the office this late. If anyone glanced in the window, however, they would see the lights were still on in her office and her car was still parked outside.

"He says his name is Blade Madaris."

The air in the room seemed to suddenly evaporate, and she could hear the pounding of her heart in her chest. What was Blade doing here? When had he returned to Oklahoma City? The last time she'd seen him, his parting words had been that he would see her in three weeks, and it hadn't been three weeks yet.

"Ms. Di Meglio?"

She could tell from the sound of Rita's voice that she was probably annoyed that someone had interrupted her novel. "Yes, Rita?"

"Well, do you want me to send him up or not?"

Sam's first impulse was to say no, to tell Rita to advise him to come back during regular business hours. A smile touched Sam's lips at how that sort of message would be received. It definitely wouldn't go over well.

She wouldn't put it past him to sit in the parking lot and wait until she finally left the building, since he knew she wouldn't be working all night. Against her better judgment, she inhaled a deep breath and said, "Yes, Rita. Let him in."

Realizing the impact of her words made her blood surge through her veins. There was a tightness that wedged in her chest. Suddenly, her tongue remembered the taste of him and she forced herself to swallow hard, to fight back the tingling sensation that was sweeping through her body.

Her ears perked up. She could hear the sound of his footsteps as he walked down the hall toward her office. They were paced with practiced precision. The sound of his feet making contact with the floor was hypnotic. She could just imagine the swagger in his every step.

Sam turned to her computer to save the document she'd been working on, and began wondering why Blade was here in her office. Deep down she knew the reason. She had explained it all to Mac a week ago. He saw her as the one who got away. The one he wasn't finished with yet. The one who refused to let him get to first base. And for a man who was used to hitting home runs, a strikeout was unacceptable.

Usually she would enjoy flirting with a man, especially one who was a player and who she intended to set up for a fall, but not tonight. Blade had a way of unnerving her, and she knew she had to be on her guard around him.

She pushed her chair back and stood, deciding she needed to be on her feet when he entered her office. He was a lot taller than she was, and she still had to look up at him, but not as far.

She came around her desk and leaned her bottom against it. Too late, she realized this was the exact position he'd left her in the last time he'd seen her two weeks ago. The very same day he had kissed her senseless.

Before she could change positions or move to another spot in the room, she heard him take the final step down the hall, and when she looked toward her door, he was there. Her eyes locked on his face, but her breath took in all of him. His manly scent was forcing her to exert a degree of self-control she hadn't had to exercise in a long time.

She allowed her gaze, just for a moment, to take in his entire body. He wore a pair of dark tailored trousers, an expensive looking dress shirt, a designer sports coat and Italian loafers. As usual, he looked far too sexy for his own good and for hers. He had a body built for whatever he wanted to use it for, and she had more than an idea just what that was.

She inhaled deeply, remembering two could play his game, and at that moment she decided that yes, she would play. And win. She had given him fair warning and he hadn't heeded it. Instead, the last time they were together he had taken her mouth and done delicious things to it, things she was still losing sleep over. His kiss had been greedy. He'd made it wet. He had flavored it with desire and seduction and then delivered it with a tongue that should be outlawed. But she couldn't think about any of those things now. This was war.

"Blade, what are you doing here?"

He leaned in the doorway, showcasing impressive muscles, a sleek build and a flabless, taut body that most men would give just about anything to have.

"I came to see you."

His deep, sexy voice was as potent as anything she'd ever heard, and it sent a yearning, a kind she'd never felt before, through her. Deciding that standing on her feet wasn't such a good idea, after all, she forced her legs to move as she went back to sit behind her desk.

"Why? And how did you know where I was?" she asked, forcing herself to breathe, and at the same time concentrate on the question she'd just asked.

He took his time answering and continued to look at her. The heat of his gaze was like a soothing caress. "I needed to see you again," he finally said. "And I knew you were here from Mac. I was at her place when she came home. And when I asked about you, she mentioned you were working late tonight."

Sam frowned. "She would not have told you that had she known you were going to disturb me."

He shrugged easily. "Probably not. It wasn't my intention to disturb you, but my hotel happens to be right up the street."

How convenient, Sam thought, and then let her mind wander, thinking about all those things they could do in his hotel room. All those things they could do right here. Thank God Rita was up front, although the security guard was probably sitting at her desk, consumed by her novel. But if she heard a lot of unusual noises she would come and investigate. And what Rita would see with her own eyes would put those romance novels to shame.

Sam felt her knees get weak and was glad she was sitting down. Now was not the time to think of all the things Blade could do to her or all the things she could do to him. Nor should she dwell on all those things they could do to each other. The man standing across the room looking so delicious she could eat him alive was a bona fide player. He needed to be taught a lesson, regardless of the sexual chemistry between them. He was too arrogant, too sure of himself to suit her. And when she finished with him he would regret the day he'd ever broken any woman's heart.

But she knew Blade was not a fool. If she appeared too eager, then he would know she was up to something. So she would take her time, play the part of the reluctant but horny woman, and let him work hard for her. Eventually, he would assume that he was getting close to breaking down her resolve. She, of course, would let him think that. She would tease him mercilessly, even give him a little sample of what he thought he would be getting. She would enjoy building him up, just to break him down. She would be the one to teach him the lesson he sorely deserved to learn.

Blade Madaris had finally met his match.

Blade wondered what Sam was thinking, since he knew for certain that something was going on in that pretty little head of hers.

As far as he was concerned, a one-night stand—as long as it was an all-nighter—was just what he needed to get her out of his system. He was convinced that she was feeling the same sexual tension that was gripping him all the way to his toes. She was trying to be cool, calm and collected. Other women had tried that same tactic, fearful of letting him know the depths of their desire. He hoped that wouldn't be the case with Sam, because he wanted to know. He needed to know.

It was killing him to find out.

"Come to my hotel room with me," he said, deciding not to beat around the bush. He had made a pit stop for one reason and one reason only. He knew it and she knew it, as well. They were adults. There was no reason to be coy or deny what just wouldn't go away.

Her chuckle was like a kick in his groin. "Don't hold your breath, cowboy."

He winced, disappointed. She was still denying those needs, still being coy. This wasn't going to be as easy as he had hoped.

"May I ask you something, Blade?"

Can we go ahead and get naked? was the question

he hoped she would ask. "Yes, you can ask me any-thing," he replied.

She placed her hands on the desk and held his gaze. "What part of what I said the other night at the restaurant didn't you understand? I thought I was very clear when I said you don't interest me."

A smile touched his lips. "And I thought I was just as clear, Sam, when I said that you were sending mixed signals."

She narrowed her eyes. "If that's the case then I need to immediately make a correction."

He slowly crossed the room toward her desk. "Don't bother."

When he got to her desk he walked around it and sat on the edge, facing her. He could tell by the look in her eyes that she was surprised by his boldness.

"Why are you playing hard to get, Sam, when you know you want me? One night is all I'm asking for, and I'll have you climaxing in your sleep for the rest of the week. The memories will be just that strong and power-ful."

She arched an eyebrow. "You're pretty sure of yourself, aren't you?"

"Yes, especially since I haven't had any complaints, just requests for repeat performances."

He saw the smile that touched the corners of her lips. He was not in the mood to humor her. He wanted to make love to her. Get her naked and get inside of her and stay there until he'd gotten his fill. Was one night too much to ask for?

He held her gaze and felt the air surrounding them thicken with the same intensity of his erection, and was glad that he was sitting down. But he knew she was very aware of his aroused state.

"Have you ever considered the fact that I might be a different breed of woman than what you are used to?"

Yes, he had considered it, and he believed that was one of the reasons he was so hot for her. "That thought has crossed my mind once or twice," he replied smoothly.

"And that doesn't bother you?"

He thought her question was odd. "No. Why would it bother me? I'm a flexible guy. I can roll with the flow."

"Even if it takes you on some very wild fantasies?"

He lifted his brow at the same time he felt his erection twitch in his trousers. Whether she knew it or not, she was trespassing onto his turf. Could it possibly be that they were of like minds? Did they have the same kind of wild, wicked and naughty fantasies?

He couldn't help wondering just what she had on her mind. He would draw the line at a ménage à trois, since he didn't like sharing. But if she wanted to blindfold him and tie him to the bed and have her way with him, then bring it on—the ropes and the blindfold. "How risqué are we talking?" he asked, now that his curiosity, among other things, was piqued.

"Not sure. Forget I asked."

The hell he would. He doubted that he could.

"It's late and I've stayed here longer than I should have," she said, pushing her chair back to get up. He watched the movement of her hips and got turned on even more. She liked wearing those short business suits and he liked seeing her in them. She had the legs to wear them.

"And before you ask again, the answer is still no. I won't go to your hotel with you, Blade. I'm going home. Alone."

His gaze moved from her legs back to her face. "Are you sure you want to do that?"

"Tonight I do. Tomorrow, maybe not."

A tightness formed in his stomach. His heart began pounding. She had just given him hope and he caught it like it was a lifeline, something he'd never done before. "Have dinner with me tomorrow," he said, standing up.

"Why?"

"So I can convince you that I do interest you."

She held his gaze for a long moment, as if tossing his offer around in her head, and then she said, "All right. But you won't get too many opportunities to convince me of anything."

He hadn't thought that he would, which meant that he needed to use every minute of his time wisely. He stood back to gave her room to clear off her desk and to log off her computer. She was about to put the strap of her purse over her shoulder when he reached out and gently pulled her to him.

He figured he had been in her office less than thirty minutes, but it had to have been the most intense half hour he'd ever shared with a woman outside of the bedroom.

She didn't resist when he wrapped his arms around her waist, pulled her even closer and stood in such a way that she felt his arousal. Every inch of it, and it felt so damn good cradled in the juncture of her thighs. "Let me give you something to think about until I see you tomorrow."

And then he lowered his mouth to hers.

Sam saw his mouth coming and was ready for it. They had talked long enough and she needed this to take the heat off. The moment their mouths touched she could feel her heart slam against her chest, automatically causing an ache between her thighs. The way his erection was pressing against her wasn't helping matters. But she could handle it.

Or she would die trying.

Moments later she thought she would be dying anyway, if he continued to kiss her the way he did. His tongue was greedier tonight than it had been the last time. There were no parts of her mouth that hadn't been licked, sucked and teased. He was thorough and by the time he was finished she was moaning deep in her throat. But then she'd heard his groans, those husky sounds he'd made, letting her know his enjoyment was just as pleasurable as hers.

Once again it was the intercom that had them reluctantly pulling their mouths apart. "Ms. Di Meglio, it's eight o'clock, and you wanted me to let you know so that you wouldn't stay here too late," Rita said.

Sam licked her lips, sealing in Blade's taste. She was surprised Rita had remembered. Usually she was so absorbed in her novel that she forgot everything. Sam leaned over and pressed the button on her desk. "Thanks, Rita, I'm getting ready to leave now."

Thankfully, Blade stood back to let her lock her desk drawers, and then he moved in step with her when she headed out the door. She bade Rita a good-night when they passed through Security. She and Blade didn't say anything until they were walking out the door to the parking lot.

"She's a lot nicer than that security guard that was here the morning I stopped by," Blade said.

Sam looked over at him. "That was Frank Denson. He takes his job seriously."

Blade snorted. "Yeah, I can tell." He decided not to mention that as far as he was concerned, the man took her seriously, as well. He had watched how Denson had hung on to her every word. Had the man been a dog he would have been panting and wagging his tail. A low growl rumbled in Blade's chest at the memory.

When they reached her car he waited until she opened
the door and slid inside, appreciating the glimpse of her
thigh. "And you're sure I can't persuade you to come to
my hotel room tonight?"

Sam couldn't help but grin. Blade was persistent if
nothing else. "I'm positive. I agreed to have dinner with
you tomorrow night, that's a start."

He smiled down at her. "I prefer thinking about the
finish. It will be a lot hotter and steamier."

"We'll see."

"No, Samari Di Meglio, get ready to feel. And
because I was taught to make sure ladies get home safely,
I'll follow you."

She nodded. There was no reason to tell him that he
would only be allowed to go so far, because she lived in
a gated community. He would find out soon enough, especially if he assumed she would be inviting him inside
for a nightcap. It wouldn't be happening.

"Good night, Blade.

"Good night, and I'll pick you up here tomorrow at
five."

"All right." And without giving him time to say
anything else, barely giving him time to get into his own
car and start the engine, she pulled off.

Chapter 6

Scowling, Blade sat outside the gate while Sam drove through it. She had conveniently avoided mentioning that she lived in a gated community—a very upscale one at that. The engineer in him couldn't help but admire the design and structure of the complex—at least what he could see from the outside.

Windsor Park.

He knew the price of the townhomes in this development weren't cheap. And judging from the fortress surrounding it, the complex looked as secure as Fort Knox. Was there a reason she had decided to live someplace that provided her such high-level security and protection?

As he drove away, he tried to remember just what he knew about Sam. Since meeting her he had asked Mac a number of questions. Some she had answered and others she had not. Luke had been just as tight-lipped as his wife, and the only thing he had said, other than a warning that Sam wasn't the kind of woman he should go after, was that her family had money.

That was all well and good, since Blade wasn't exactly broke himself. Thanks to the Madaris Construction Company, and his uncle Jake Madaris—not only a highly successful businessman, but one hell of a financial adviser, who had made some wise investments on Blade's behalf—if he never worked another day in his life, he could still live a very wealthy lifestyle.

Minutes later, when he entered his hotel room, an idea took shape in his head. He would be meeting with some of Mosley's employees tomorrow to start the ball rolling, so everything would be in place to break ground in a few months. But that didn't mean he couldn't remain in Oklahoma City a little while longer than planned, to make sure things were under control and on schedule—although the Madaris Construction Company had yet to miss a deadline, and certainly not on his watch.

And if he intended to hang around, there was no reason for him to remain cooped up in this hotel. First thing in the morning he would call Claire, the secretary he and Slade shared at the Madaris Construction Company, to get her to find him a place to stay. The more he thought about it, the more he liked the complex where Sam was living. He was certain there must be a unit there that could be leased on a short-term basis.

He smiled as he headed toward the bathroom for a shower. It didn't bother him in the least that he was doing some things he'd never done in the past in his hot pursuit of a woman. But then a man had to do what a man had to do, and since he believed it would be well worth it in the end, then so be it. The moment she had mentioned the words *wild fantasies,* he had known he would not be able to walk away until he discovered just what kind of wild fantasies she had in mind.

He was in the process of removing his shoes when his cell phone rang. A glance at the caller ID indicated the call was from Slade. He clicked on the line. "Hey, Slade, what's going on?"

"I thought I'd warn you that Mama Laverne has been asking about you. She dropped by the office today to visit with you."

Blade lifted a brow. She was always asking about him and every other son, grand and great-grand of hers. The old gal made it her business to try and keep up with everyone. She had probably planned to read him the riot act for not showing up for church that Sunday. "And?"

"And she's wondering why you're back in Oklahoma."

Blade leaned against the dresser in the bedroom. "What did you tell her?"

"That we have business there you had to take care of. I even showed her the model of the Mosley Building we have on display in the lobby. That may have satisfied her somewhat, but I suggest you give her a call to let her know you're all right. The older she gets the more she worries."

Blade chuckled. Slade was too nice to say that the older their great-grandmother got the more she meddled in their affairs. "Okay, I'll call her tomorrow. How's Skye doing?"

"My lady is doing fine."

Blade shook his head. His twin liked getting all mushy on him when it came to Skye. He was sounding like a whipped man. Like Luke, this marriage thing evidently agreed with him.

"Do you know how long you plan to stay in Oklahoma?" Slade asked, interrupting his thoughts.

Blade shrugged. "For another week or so."

He thought of Sam and then said, "Maybe longer. I want to be hands-on." He wasn't referring to the Mosley Building, but Slade didn't really need to know that.

"In fact, I plan on contacting Claire tomorrow to see if she can find me a bigger place," he added, giving Slade a heads-up on his plans. "It will be cheaper to lease something instead of remaining in a hotel, since I'll be making a number of trips back and forth periodically to check on things." He smiled. His reasoning sounded good even to his own ears.

"That might not be such a bad idea. It might save us a lot of money in the long run. Take care and I'll talk to you later."

"You, too."

"And don't forget to call Mama Laverne or you might be sorry."

"I'll call her." Blade hung up the phone thinking about Slade's comment about saving the company money. He chuckled. Saving the company money was the last thing on his mind. Getting Sam into his bed topped the list.

Sam couldn't help the smile that kept creeping across her face as she blow-dried her hair. You didn't have to be a rocket scientist to know that Blade thought he had her right where he wanted her—almost. The fact that he couldn't follow her inside the gated community might have set him back a bit, but there was no doubt in her mind that he intended to recover ground tomorrow over dinner. She would definitely be prepared.

A short while later, she got into bed and curled up under the covers. She hadn't gotten a lot done tonight because of Blade's visit, which meant she would have to get up and go into the office early. She had an appointment at ten with a woman who was divorcing her husband

and wanted full custody of the family dog. To avoid dwelling on what a circus the case might become, Sam shifted in bed, trying not to think about Blade—the man who seemingly was trying to monopolize all of her time.

She didn't have to close her eyes to recall how he'd looked standing in her office doorway or how she'd felt ogling him. Her office had been filled with so much sexual energy it was a wonder the two of them hadn't been electrocuted. She knew that she needed to mind her p's and q's at dinner the next day, and stay one step ahead of his game. He was a man on the prowl, determined to get inside her panties. And she was just as determined that he didn't.

She wondered if he would continue to send the flowers. Peyton had joked that her secret admirer must know her schedule, since no flowers had been delivered while she'd been away last week. It would have been easy for Blade to find out that information. Mac might have innocently mentioned it to him, just as she'd mentioned her where-abouts tonight. Or Luke could have been the one to spill the beans.

Sam sighed, thinking she missed the flowers and had gotten used to receiving them. The gesture seemed like Blade's M.O. Including a card with some mushy senti-mental line just wasn't his style. Evidently, he was trying to make sure he was always in her thoughts whenever she looked at the beautiful flower arrangement.

He hadn't mentioned that he was the one sending her flowers. He hadn't even paid much attention to the bouquet when he'd been in her office. If this was all a part of his version of the game of Seize and Conquer—which she was certain it was—then she intended to enjoy the flowers while they lasted.

She knew once he learned the truth—that she had been

stringing him along—he wouldn't be happy. There was a chance he might not want to speak to her ever again.

She pushed the thought to the back of her mind. She wasn't going to indulge in a guilt trip where Blade was concerned. All it took was remembering her wedding day to make her forget about having any sympathy for Blade. And then there was Vivian Randall, her college roommate. Ten years had passed, but at times it seemed just like yesterday that Sam had rushed to the campus emergency room, only to find out that it was too late—Vivian had died of an overdose of pills. She still felt guilty about Vivian's death, since it had been her medication—a drug Sam's family doctor had prescribed for her migraine headaches—that Vivian had taken when she committed suicide. And all because a guy she thought she was in love with had played her. He had hurt and humiliated her in the worst way.

Even under a pile of blankets, Sam still felt cold. She knew that exacting revenge wouldn't erase the memory of being embarrassed on her wedding day in front of five hundred guests, or what had happened to Vivian. But it gave her some satisfaction that at least one player would get his just deserts.

She shifted in bed when her phone rang. She reached to pick it up and saw from the caller ID that it was Frederick Damon Rowe, affectionately called FDR. She and Frederick were the same age, shared the same birthday, had finished law school at about the same time and had begun working at Di Meglio on the same day. Over time, they had become close friends.

FDR was a great guy. And unlike some of the other employees at the firm, it had never bothered him that her last name was Di Meglio. He treated her like anyone else and not the bosses' daughter.

"Hey, FDR, what's going on?"

They talked for a little while and she listened as he told her about a case he was working on. Although her parents approved of their close friendship, they had never tried to encourage a romantic relationship between them. Sam had always thought it was a little odd, since FDR was a very handsome man who had a lot going for him. In fact, she wouldn't be surprised if he made partner soon.

Later, after ending the call, she thought about what her brother had told her a few days ago. Angelo had claimed FDR was seeing someone and that it seemed to be serious. If that was true, why hadn't Frederick mentioned it to her? Why was he keeping secrets from her?

But she wasn't going to worry about that tonight. She had enough to deal with as she prepared for dinner with Blade Madaris tomorrow evening.

Chapter 7

"They're baaack…." said Priscilla jokingly, using the catchphrase from the *Poltergeist* movie sequel.

Sam glanced up at the beautiful bouquet of flowers that Priscilla placed on her desk. She couldn't help but lean back in her chair and laugh. For the past month Priscilla had been the one who'd delivered the flowers to her, at first complaining that the fragrance was too strong for the office. But last week, when Sam was out and the flowers didn't come, Priscilla had been the one complaining that she'd missed them, according to Mac and Peyton.

Priscilla had been with them for a couple of years, and at forty-one, she was more like a mother figure. She was a stickler for details and always maintained a professional demeanor, refusing to call them by their first names, even though she insisted they call her Priscilla. Sam had always thought that the single mother of eleven-year-old twin boys was very attractive. But in the two years that she'd been with them, she had never once mentioned anything about a man in her life.

"I heard you're nothing but a phony, Priscilla," Sam said, as she moved her chair closer to her desk. "Mac and Sam told me all about how you carried on when the flowers didn't come last week."

"Okay, Ms. Di Meglio, I admit I'd gotten used to them," Priscilla said, putting Sam's mail in her in-box. "You still have no idea who's sending them?"

A smile touched Sam's lips. "Maybe and maybe not. We'll just have to wait and see. Oh, I forgot to mention that when I saw FDR last week he told me to tell you hello."

"Oh," Priscilla said, her gaze quickly shifting away. "Well, I better get back to my desk. I have a lot to do before the end of the day."

Sam watched her secretary scurry out of her office. Had she imagined it or had Priscilla acted kind of weird at the mention of FDR? She shrugged, certain that she had just imagined it.

She studied the beautiful arrangement sitting on her desk. Every week the mix of flowers was different. She wondered if the choice had been the sender's, or just ones the florist had picked out. It didn't really matter, since every arrangement was breathtakingly beautiful and brightened up her week.

Sam glanced at her watch. Her first appointment of the day would be arriving in less than an hour.

Blade's meeting with Mosley lasted for a little more than an hour. The moment he walked out of the office building he was on the phone, returning his secretary's call. "Yes, Claire, what do you have for me?"

"I did what you asked and was able to find something

available in Windsor Park. The person I spoke with was extremely helpful. Once I mentioned your friend who's already living there, they were able to locate a vacant town house right next door. In fact, the two of you will practically share the same driveway, since your garages are connected. The place is completely furnished, with two bedrooms and…"

Blade didn't hear the rest of the details once Claire said how close his town house was to Sam's. He looked up into the Oklahoma sky and thought that someone up there definitely liked him. And to think he'd even missed church the past few Sundays.

"So, is this a place you want us to sign a lease for, Mr. Madaris?"

"Yes." He couldn't say the words quickly. "How soon can I move in?"

"Today if you like, once we finalize the paperwork, which can be done by fax. I spoke with the utility company and put them on hold until you told us to move forward. Now that you have, we can do so without delay. The keys to the unit and the paperwork will be delivered to your hotel before three o'clock. Would you like me to order groceries and have them delivered, as well?"

A smile touched his lips. "No, that won't be necessary, Claire. I'll be eating out most of the time while I'm here." That made him recall his dinner date, not that he'd forgotten.

"Will there be anything else, Mr. Madaris?"

"No, that's about all."

He hung up the phone, still smiling, and thinking now he was making progress in his goal to get Sam in his bed.

Felicia Laverne Madaris, matriarch of the Madaris family, leaned back in her chair and gazed at the woman sitting across from her. Dora had been her daughter-in-law the longest and was married to her oldest son, Milton. "So, Dora, what do you think? Is there another reason Blade is staying in Oklahoma City while all the women here are pining for him?"

Dora hunched her shoulders. "Who knows what that particular grandson of mine is up to? But I will tell you this—I pity any woman who gets mixed up with him, thinking he's looking for something serious."

Mama Laverne nodded in agreement and then said, "Mmm, I think he's hot on the tail of one of Mac's friends—the pretty one with all that curly hair. I saw him trying to talk to her at Mac and Luke's wedding, but the chile wouldn't give him the time of day." She chuckled. "I think she set him back a bit."

Dora chuckled in turn. "Smart girl."

"Yes, but if she's the reason he's back in Oklahoma, that means for the first time in his life he's actually running behind a woman instead of the other way around. The women here in Houston have made things easy for him, always at his beck and call. This Oklahoma girl might give him a run for his money, and I'd love to see that happen. I'm going to make it my business to find out more about her. She just might be the one."

Neither woman said anything for a long time while they sat sipping their cups of tea. "You're the first person I've mentioned this to, but I dreamed of fish again last night," Mama Laverne said.

Dora's eyes widened. "You think it's Christy?"

Mama Laverne understood why she would think that. Her granddaughter Christy had proudly proclaimed after the birth of her first child that she and her husband, Alex, wanted a lot more children, and it seemed that whenever anyone called or dropped by, the couple was always in bed.

Mama Laverne smiled and shook her head. "They might be working on a new addition, but not this time. I actually saw the image of a man sitting on a dock with a fishing rod in his hand, and he seemed pleased as pleased could be when he pulled in a whopper of a bass from the lake."

Dora's lips quirked into a smile. "Sounds like a mighty proud man who went fishing that day. Who was he?"

Mama Laverne didn't say anything for a minute. For the past month, her fish dreams have been coming steadily, and in a way it made her heart feel good to know that the Madaris family and their friends were multiplying and would continue to do so long after she was gone.

"Mama Laverne?"

Her feeble fingers tightened on the cup in her hand, and then she said in a voice that quirked with humor. "The man was Clayton."

Dora's eyes widened to twice their regular size. "Clayton?"

"Yes."

"That means…"

"Yes." Mama Laverne said the one thing Dora couldn't bring herself to say. "Yes, that means that Syneda is pregnant again, and heaven help us all."

Chapter 8

Blade crossed his arms over his chest as he leaned against his parked car. He couldn't hide the smile that touched his lips as he watched the woman who walked out of the two-story, redbrick building. Nor did he want to. He squinted against the sunlight and adjusted his eyes accordingly so he could see her better. She was definitely a beautiful sight to behold.

He hadn't known what to expect when he showed up at exactly five o'clock for their first—and what she probably considered their *only* date. Under normal circumstances he would have agreed with her. But he had a feeling that tonight would not end the way he wanted, though it definitely wouldn't be for lack of trying on his part. He wanted her in his bed, and his moving into Windsor Park greatly reduced the distance it would take to get her there.

She looked beautiful, as usual, wearing another business suit that showed off her legs. The red color high-lighted her complexion, and her curly hair flowing around her shoulders gave her a sexy appeal. He wondered how far he would go tonight. A better question was how far would she let him go? He had made reservations at a nice restaurant in Bricktown, one of the most popular areas of the city. He had requested a table in one of the cozy, secluded sections of the restaurant, with candlelight. After dinner he would bring her back here to get her car, and she would assume their night together would be over. Little did she know it would just be starting. He could just imagine what her reaction would be once she discovered he was now living next door to her.

Tipping the brim of his Stetson, he smiled when she approached, and said, "Sam."

"Blade. Have you been waiting long?"

"No. And even if I had been, you would have been well worth the wait."

Her mouth quirked at the corners and he knew at that moment that she'd probably heard that line before. That might be true, because he'd certainly delivered it over the years, but this time he'd actually meant what he'd said.

He opened the car door for her and inhaled her scent. She smelled feminine. She smelled like woman. And as he watched her slide onto the leather seat, he appreciated a glimpse of her thighs. He hoped that later tonight he would be getting more than a glimpse. In fact, he was anticipating seeing her naked.

"Thank you," she said, seconds before he closed her door.

"You're welcome."

He moved around the front of the car to open the door to the driver's side. Once settled with his seat belt in place, he glanced over at her and saw she was looking at him. He smiled. "Are you okay?"

She smiled back. "Yes."

Blade backed the car out of the parking lot, thinking she was smiling and that was a good thing.

Sam decided to stare out the window at the buildings they passed, although there was nothing different about them. She usually drove through these same streets every day on her way to the office. But she needed this time. Not to clear her head, because that wasn't possible as long as Blade was sitting in the seat next to her, but to affirm in her mind that going through with her plan was something she needed to do. It was something she *had* to do to the man who was most women's most ardent fantasy, and who could potentially become her own worst nightmare.

There was no doubt in her mind that over the next few hours she would be tempted as a woman in a way she'd never been tempted before. Blade had that ability. He had that skill. And she didn't have to be a genius to know that tonight he fully intended to use it.

"We should be there in a minute."

His words prompted her to glance over at him and ask, "Where are we going?"

"To Yates."

She nodded. She was impressed. "I heard it's a very nice place."

"You've never eaten there?"

"Surprisingly, no."

He looked pleased at that. "Then I'm glad your first time will be with me."

She shifted her gaze back out the window, thinking that in a way she was glad her first time would be with him, too.

"And you look nice."

She chuckled as she looked back at him. "You look nice yourself."

And she meant it more than he would ever know. When she had walked out of the building and seen him standing there, leaning against his car, waiting for her and looking like a man who knew what he wanted and had every intention of getting it, it had sent an intense shudder all the way up her spine.

"We're here."

She glanced out the windshield. Yes, they were.

The blood flowing through his veins felt warm as Blade glanced across the table at his companion. Sam had been quiet during most of dinner. He couldn't help wondering what she was thinking, what she was feeling, and if she had any idea how much he wanted her.

To be quite honest, he hadn't realized the extent, the degree, the depth of his desire for her until now. He had been in her presence for more than an hour, the longest amount of time he'd ever spent alone with her since they'd met. At least they were practically alone, since the restaurant had adhered to his request and seated them in a secluded area in the back, at a table set for two.

After mulling over the menu, they had decided on their order. While waiting for their meal to arrive they had indulged in a glass of white wine. She'd asked him questions about his work on the Mosley Building, which set the tone of their conversation, avoiding any personal subjects.

Once their food arrived, the conversation slowed—and almost ceased entirely. But what she didn't say, he could actually feel. That was something he had been aware of from the first time their eyes had met, at Mac and Luke's rehearsal dinner. Although she might not have wanted to give off those sensual vibes, she was doing so, anyway. They spoke to him and he automatically responded.

Like he was doing now.

He glanced over at her. As if she felt his gaze, she glanced up, and the moment their eyes connected he was literally robbed of his senses. The blood flowing through his body suddenly felt hot—to the boiling point.

"Dinner was wonderful, Blade. Thanks for bringing me here," she said in a soft voice, as if to break the intensity of the moment.

His gaze remained focused on her face. "You're welcome."

He had to fight the impulse to say he intended for there to be more of these dinners, but then he wondered why he would think such a thing. He was the hunter and she was his prey. Once she was caught there would be no reason for them to do this again. Their date tonight had a purpose and they both knew it. They were adults and were mature enough to handle whatever the outcome.

He wasn't looking for a long-term relationship or a serious involvement with any woman. He was a guy who wasn't interested in the house with the white picket fence or the wife who would greet him at the door each day when he came home from work. That was Slade, but that wasn't him.

"So, will you be having dessert tonight?"

Her question made him smile. "Yes, but not here."

She lifted an elegant brow and then tilted her head in a challenging pose when it became evident that she knew what he meant. "You think so?"

He chuckled softly. "I hope so."

And he truly meant that and couldn't believe he had done a complete turnaround in his approach to this woman. Usually he wasn't into playing games. However, Sam was definitely making him work hard for her. But then, he felt she was worth it.

"Maybe this is where I need to tell you that I plan on going home alone," she said, interrupting his thoughts.

For a moment he just stared at her, then nodded slowly. "Yes, but a lot can happen before you get there."

He watched her lower her lids in a way that had him wondering if perhaps her mind was engaging in the same sizzling hot, over-the-top, taboo kind of fantasies his mind was having right now.

He shifted in his seat and decided he needed to change the subject and do it quick. Otherwise his erection just might burst through his zipper. "Tell me about your family, Sam."

He could tell that his question had surprised her. He could also tell it seemed to relax her. She eased back in her chair. Once their dishes and wineglasses had been removed, they enjoyed a cup of coffee. Usually he didn't touch the stuff. He was hyper enough and didn't need a caffeine boost.

"What exactly do you want to know?"

"Anything you want to tell me." *So I can figure out what there is about you that makes me want you so much,* he thought to himself. *Right now I'm thinking what it would be like to take you on top of this table.*

"It might bore you."

"You could never bore me."

Sam chuckled at his response. "Don't say I didn't warn you."

She took a sip of her coffee and then said, "My paternal great-grandparents came to this country from Rome with their four sons and only the clothes on their backs. They worked hard, educated their sons and were proud when all four completed law school and went into practice together. And that was the birth of the Di Meglio law firm."

Sam paused for a moment to indulge in a few child-hood memories. As a little girl she remembered her grand-mother telling her the family story, and she could still hear the pride in her grandmother's voice. "Their first office was a place above my great-grandfather's restaurant in the Bronx. Then after they won their first big case, they opened offices in Manhattan." There was no need to mention the rumors that one of her grand-uncles had had Mafia ties.

She kept talking, mainly because Blade seemed truly interested in what she was saying—interested and in-trigued. She talked. He listened, while quietly sipping his coffee and looking attentively at her.

"My father met my mother in law school. I'm told they had a fiery relationship, couldn't agree on anything and argued case law most of the time." A grin touched the corners of her lips. "From what I hear they nearly drove their professors batty."

Blade burst out laughing.

"What's so funny?

"Your parents sound like my cousin Clayton and his wife, Syneda. They're both attorneys as well and can't agree on anything."

Sam smiled and pushed her hair back off her shoulders. "I met Clayton and Syneda last year during our handling of the Coroni case. Nice couple." She took a sip of her coffee and continued. "My parents had no contact with each other after law school, and then three years later they faced off in the courtroom. He was the prosecutor and she was the defense attorney. What the jurors saw was a hot-tempered Italian D.A. up against an African-American attorney with an attitude. She won. He lost. She went out that night to cele-brate. He went out to lick his wounds. They happened to both be at the same nightclub." Sam giggled. "Imagine that."

For a moment Blade could imagine it, especially if her mother had in her younger days looked anything like Sam. "Sounds like a stormy confrontation."

"I understand it was worse than that," she said, after taking another sip of her coffee. "They ended up leaving the bar together, presumably to help him get over losing the case—but in a way that only a woman can. I'm told it was supposed to be a one-night stand, but things didn't work out that way, and they've been together ever since. They have a rather close and loving relationship," she said with a huge smile on her face.

Blade couldn't help but smile back. "I know you have a brother. I recall meeting him at Luke and Mac's wedding."

"Yes, DeAngelo. But everyone calls him Angelo. He's thirty-two and he's also a lawyer. The Di Meglio law firm is still going strong, with my mother and father, my father's two brothers, their two sons, my brother and several associates."

"And you're not there?"

Sam shook her head. "No. I worked there for a while— two years, in fact, right out of law school. But I soon discovered there were too many Di Meglios. And as one of only two female attorneys, I was in the minority. My brothers and male cousins made sure I got the easy cases, nothing I could really sink my teeth into. I had three watchdogs instead of three fellow attorneys who respected my skill."

"So after two years you left New York and came here?" he asked, watching her expression closely. Throughout dinner he had been carefully observing her every time she spoke, practically hanging on every word she said. He could tell she was close to her family, probably as close to hers as he was to his.

"Yes, I came here," Sam said. "Mac, Peyton and I had been close friends in law school and had always talked about forming a partnership together, so we decided to fulfill our dream. And the rest is history."

She took yet another sip of her coffee and then glanced back at him. "Okay, it's your turn. Tell me about your family, although since Mac is married to Luke I know something about the Madarises already. Just to think you have an uncle who's married to Diamond Swain and is good friends with Sterling Hamilton is awesome."

Blade chuckled. He distinctly recalled the night his uncle Jake had made the announcement to the family. To say that they'd all been shocked was an understatement. Uncle Jake referred to his wife as his "diamond" and the family knew why. The well-known and much-beloved actress, Diamond Swain Madaris, was definitely a jewel to everyone who met her. And movie actor and producer, Sterling Hamilton was considered one of the family.

"Yes, it is. In fact, I think my entire family is awesome. My parents had four sons. You've met my twin, Slade, who is married to Skye. And as you know, they're expecting a baby."

"Yes, we're all excited."

He smiled. From what he'd heard, the entire family was excited. It seemed that having babies was becoming a favorite pastime for the Madarises and their friends. "I have two younger brothers. Quantum, who is twenty-six and completing his residency at a hospital in Houston, and Jantzen is twenty-three. Slade and I were able to recruit Jantzen into joining the family business as our PR and marketing director, and he's doing an awesome job."

They talked awhile longer as he told her more about his family. She had already met most of them at Mac's wedding, which made the conversation flow rather easily.

He liked how she remembered things that had happened at the wedding or at Mac's birthday party that made them both laugh.

"At Mac's party, you were with someone," said Blade.

Sam lifted her brow. She decided to respond truthfully, as she always did when a question came up about her and Frederick's relationship. "Yes, he's a lawyer in my family's law firm. Frederick Rowe. He still works there and I consider him a good friend."

"So there is nothing going on between the two of you?"

She held Blade's gaze for a moment and then said, "Why are you just getting around to asking me about Frederick? If you did think we were together that night, I see that didn't stop you from trying to hit on me."

He reached out and captured her hand when she placed it on the table. She felt herself trembling from head to toe when his fingertips brushed across her knuckles. "The reason I never got around to asking you about him was because I was able to find out that information from Luke. He said the guy was just a friend of yours."

"Then why did you ask me about him now?" She tried to ignore how the touch of his hand on hers was sending sparks of electricity up and down her spine. He was trying to seduce her, and heaven help her, but she was enjoying it and finding it hard to resist his charm.

"Because I wanted to hear you tell me," he said softly. His voice was like a stroke across her skin, sending even more sparks through her. "Before, I just had secondhand information, although I figured Luke knew what he was talking about. And the reason I still made a move on you that night was because I wanted you, and once Luke had assured me there was nothing between you and Frederick but a close friendship, I saw no reason to stand on the sidelines."

Just as she was sure he saw no reason not to continue stroking her hand. She was fully aware of what he was doing and why he was doing it. Electricity was coursing through her, and making her want things from him that she knew better than to crave.

She pulled her hand from his and casually glanced at her watch. She then looked up at him. "I hate to be a party pooper, but I'm a working girl and I've got an early appointment in the morning. I need to go home and get to bed."

Blade was sure it was the look of desire that appeared in his eyes that prompted her to add, "Alone."

He tilted his head to the side, studied her for a moment and then asked, "Do you really want to do that?"

She hesitated long enough for him to know she wasn't quite sure what she wanted to do about him, and as far as he was concerned that was a good thing. That meant he was making progress. He was an impatient man. And he didn't want to make progress, he wanted to make love—to her, nonstop, all night long. He wanted those long, sexy legs of hers wrapped tightly around him while he buried his body deep inside her. He wanted her so badly he could taste it. And he intended to taste her. That seemed simple enough, and as hot and sensual as it could get.

"Yes, that's what I want to do."

Her response, he thought, had been slow in coming. He wondered how she was going to handle knowing that he had arranged to be next door to her, never out of sight or out of mind. He was going to turn borrowing a cup of sugar into his favorite pastime. Sooner or later he would break down her defenses, and as her next-door neighbor, he would take pleasure in doing so.

Chapter 9

When Blade slowed to a stop at the traffic light, Sam couldn't help but look over at him, and not surprisingly, their eyes locked. Heat flooded her entire body and she wondered if he could feel it. He said nothing, but continued to stare. They got so caught up in the sexual chemistry transmitting between them that it took a blast from a car's horn to remind them where they were.

The sound also reminded her where they were going. Her car was still parked at the office and she planned get into it and drive home. And just as she'd told him, she would be going home alone.

Why did the thought of going home alone suddenly seem like such an awful choice, when she could have this sexy man go home with her? He had laid it on thick tonight, oozing sexiness all over the place and reminding her more than once that she hadn't had a man in her bed in close to four years. Blade was making her feel that certain parts of her body were overdue for a tune-up and some serious repair.

She chuckled to herself. She couldn't imagine him giving her a quick fix. He would take his time, probably make her beg, and then he would deliver in a way that would be far better than anything she could ever imagine.

But why imagine it when she could have the real thing?

She knew the answer to that question. Like all players, he needed to be taught a lesson, and she couldn't start letting her emotions get in the way. She couldn't forget that he was a womanizer who wanted one thing from her and *only* one thing. Once she had sex with him, he would move on to the next hard up and willing woman. He wouldn't care one iota that someone's heart would get broken.

Blade was an arrogant man, but not in an intolerable kind of way. She had been out with men who were a lot worse—men who wore the word *obnoxious* around their necks. But she could tell that Blade was a self-assured man—confident and comfortable with who he was. He wore his cockiness proudly, like a designer label.

He pulled into the parking lot, but instead of stopping beside her car, he circled the lot until he came to a secluded spot with very little lighting, under an arbor of low-hanging trees.

When he brought the car to a stop she glanced over at him. All it took was a look into his eyes to know his intention. "Tell me you're kidding," she said.

His smile was hot. The hottest thing she'd seen in a long time. He unbuckled his seat belt and slid his seat back. "I never kid when I'm about to make out with a woman."

She lifted a brow. "Make out?"

He reached over and, with a flick of his wrist, her seat

belt was unbuckled. "Yes, we'll start with a few kisses and go from there."

His arrogance was showing. "And you assume going from *there* will be easy for you?" she asked. She could deal with the kisses, and in fact was looking forward to them.

"I hope so. I want you, Samari Di Meglio. You give a whole new meaning to the word *desire*. I want you to the point that I ache." He drew in what sounded like an angry breath, and said, "Hell, this is the first time I've admitted that to a woman."

A smile curved her lips at the frustration she heard in his voice. "Wow, I'm flattered. A sensual confession. Got any more?"

"What? Sensual confessions?"

"Yes."

A smile touched his lips. "Not tonight." He leaned closer and whispered against her lips, "But I do have something else to give you."

She didn't have to ask what, and didn't have time to, anyway. Before she could draw in her next breath, he was there. And when his lips captured hers and he proceeded to slide his tongue into her mouth, while running his fingers through her hair, she couldn't do anything but close her eyes and moan.

Blade didn't have time to question why he was feeling so possessive toward this woman, and so needy. He refused to ponder why there was such an urgency to taste her and why she was becoming something he craved. Instead, he allowed his body and mind to tumble out of control while he feasted on her mouth, her lips, her tongue, on everything within his reach.

Her moans were like a symphony to his ears and propelled him to deepen the kiss. With each kiss she responded with a passion that matched his own. His stomach clenched each time her tongue stroked his with the same intensity he felt. Their movements were restricted by the confines of the car and the clothes they were wearing, and he could only imagine what it would be like to have her stretched out on a bed beneath him, totally naked.

The thought of that inflamed his passion caused a primitive hunger to stir within the depths of his masculinity. Emotions that he couldn't put a name to suffused him, enveloping all of his senses.

He was playing out one of his wildest fantasies with her. Making out in a parked car with the risk of getting caught gave him an adrenaline rush. Shudders of electricity coursed through his body. Under normal circumstances, he didn't take any risks with women. Caution had always been the name of the game. But at that moment, he couldn't think of anything else but enjoying her.

An alarm went off in his head at the thought that he was headed toward a danger zone, and he quickly pulled his mouth away and drew in a deep breath, taking in the scent of her sexual arousal. With moonlight coming in through the windshield, he could see her clearly. Her body had shifted and her back was pressed against the door. Her clothes no longer looked as neat as they had earlier. One part of her jacket nearly hung off her shoulder and a couple of the buttons on her blouse had come undone, revealing what looked like a red lace bra. Red lace? He'd seen red lace before, but why did seeing it on her have the lower part of his body throbbing?

And then there was her skirt, which had risen up her thigh and was barely covering her hips. Her long, beautiful legs were teasing him, making him see her as a delectable morsel to be eaten.

He quickly glanced out the window. He had parked in a dark and secluded area. It was the perfect spot to make out with a woman. He hadn't done anything like this since high school. Hell, he was a grown man, not a horny teenager.

But Samari Di Meglio was making him lose control. His desire for her was making him not think straight. Seeing her like this, with her dark, sultry eyes staring back at him and her moist lips parted, he felt the sexual tension inside him become almost unbearable.

A sexual hunger tore into him—more intense than before. He ignored whatever had triggered the alarm inside his head, and lowered his mouth to hers again. A sensation filled with horrific need ripped through him the moment their mouths connected. She moaned and sank against him as he shifted his body deeper into the arms she had opened to him.

More sensations raced through him when his hand made contact with her thigh. He felt her respond to his touch as she arched her back to get closer. He couldn't do everything he wanted to do to her in the car right now, but what he would do, what he intended to carry out, would be done in such in a way that she would always remember this place, this time tonight, with him.

Sam felt a sense of loss when Blade slowly pulled his mouth away. She drew in a deep breath, but before she could summon any more of a response than that, she felt his hand continue its trek up her thigh. At the same time his lips brushed lightly across the bare skin above the top of her blouse.

What he was doing with his lips and hands was causing

heat to course through her veins in a way that had sensations spiking in other areas of her body. She'd heard about people making out in cars, mostly in the backseat, but she had never done it. Although she was intent on making players pay for their behavior, she drew the line on just how far she would go in her quest for revenge. She enjoyed setting them up, teasing them mercilessly, fueling their fire and then dousing them with cold water. Telling them exactly where they could go—and none too nicely.

For some reason she had made Blade an exception. She was granting him liberties she'd never given any other man—player or otherwise. But she was convinced there had to be a good reason for this madness, and before it was all over she would regain her sanity.

She believed the reason he'd become her weakness was because he was making her feel things she'd never felt before. It could also have been because he evoked the wild, risqué fantasies that she had kept hidden for years. They had been locked away, buried, until recently, when she became enraptured by her erotic dreams. Lately, he'd played a starring role in them. It was as if he'd found the key to her innermost sexual fantasies, secrets that she had always wanted to explore. And now she was on the verge of living out her sexual desires.

He lifted his head and met her gaze, and she saw the naked hunger in the depths of the eyes staring back at her. He held fast to her gaze while his fingers inched farther and farther up her thigh, moving toward the juncture of her legs. Within seconds, his fingers had reached their mark and his hand flattened and gently sank into her, as if staking a claim.

She felt the heat of his palm against the crotch of her wet panties, and the contact launched a surge of sexual heat that burned through her. Her breathing intensified while her heart thumped loudly in her chest.

"Remember our conversation earlier tonight about dessert?" he asked in a deep, husky tone. The timbre was so sensual that she felt her pelvis clench.

Yes, she remembered. And their verbal exchange, every single word they had spoken, his innuendo, were still vividly on her mind.

"I remember," she said, barely able to get the words past her lips as heat flooded her belly.

She felt the moment he gripped the hem of her skirt and began inching it up with his free hand, the moment the air surrounding them began cooling her exposed flesh. Now was the time to stop him, to tell him that what he was about to do was totally crazy, insane. She needed to rein him in, take control and remind him they were adults and not hot-and-bothered teenagers with overactive hormones. But her mind and her body dismissed every argument that her brain was trying to make.

Instead, her primal sexual urge overwhelmed any rational thoughts. She couldn't do anything at that moment but remain still. And the idea made the area under the palm of his hand that much wetter. From the look of the dark eyes staring intensely at her, she knew he was aware of it. The smile that touched his lips, corner to corner, confirmed it.

And then she watched as he lowered his head. Not to her lips, nor to her breasts, but to the area between her thighs.

"Blade!"

She screamed his name the moment she felt his palm being replaced by his mouth, and he began flicking the tip of his tongue against the moist spot in the crotch of her panties. It didn't seem to bother him that they were practically drenched. The only thing he appeared to care about was savoring the taste of her.

That thought sent a flood of pleasure through her. He gripped her hips and used his teeth to move aside her barely there panties, then proceeded to insert the hot tip of his tongue inside her.

Her body responded immediately to the invasion. Even the leather behind her back seemed to burn at that moment. Sharp, piercing, hot strokes of pleasure shot through every part of her. When he worked her legs over his shoulders and delved his tongue even deeper inside of her, he literally stole her breath.

How had she lived twenty-eight years and never experience something like this? She forced herself to breathe, and when his lips joined his tongue and skated over sensitive flesh, he lapped her right into an orgasm. Shudders began consuming her and she grabbed hold of his head, to keep him in place.

His tongue and lips continued to stroke, caress and consume her as if it was his due, his every right to send passion blazing through her. And as her body continued to shudder and convulse, he held tight to her hips, refusing to release his grip as he continued to use his mouth to give her pleasure.

She screamed his name once more when everything within her body exploded, sending sharp shards of ecstasy spiraling through her. Instead of releasing her, he spread her legs farther and continued to sip her as if she were the finest of wines. His foreplay sent bone-deep sensations all the way to her womb, making her quiver from the inside out.

Her body felt suspended in midair and her senses were wrung tight as her womanly core became drenched with her juices. At that moment she did something she'd never done before—she purred with intense satisfaction. Searing waves of pleasure continued to overtake her, and she closed her eyes while drowning in pure rapture.

* * *

Blade didn't pull back his tongue until he felt the last of Sam's spasms subside. He licked his lips, thinking that he'd never gone down on a woman like that before, with a hunger that seemed unquenchable. Her taste had tempted him. It had teased and taunted him mercilessly. Even now, the flavor of her womanly fluid had seeped into his tongue, saturated his lips and made the thick veins of his erection pulsate like crazy.

Before he eased his head away from her, he lifted his gaze and met her eyes, which seemed dazed, hazy, stunned. Surely she'd had a man make love to her in that way before. The look in her eyes, her flushed face, took his breath away. He reached out and gently stroked his hand through her hair, which had come undone and was tumbling around her shoulders, making her look downright sexy and sated.

He let his fingers glide through the strands, while fighting the throbbing of his aroused body part. The interior of the car had her intimate scent. The more he inhaled it, the more he wanted of it. Not only did he want to taste her again, fill his mouth with her flavor, but he wanted to sink his shaft into her, feel the wetness that he'd tasted.

He lowered his mouth and kissed her, knowing she could taste the essence of herself on his lips and tongue. The thought of her doing so sent molten blood surging through his veins, and drove his senses wild, so much so he thought he would explode. But he couldn't stop kissing her. He couldn't curb the urgency of his tongue as it took hold of hers, stroking, melding, tangling. This was definitely an R-rated kiss if ever there was one.

Finally, he released her mouth and drew in a deep breath as he leaned back against his seat. He wanted to do a lot more than just kiss her, but he knew the confines of the car wouldn't allow it.

"Blade…"

He shifted to meet her gaze. Her eyes were still hazy with a look of sensuality, and her breathy voice seemed throaty and constrained. "Yes, Sam?"

"I have a sensual confession of my own to make," she whispered, in a tone saturated with the aftereffects of her orgasm.

He moved closer to her. "What's your confession?"

"What you did to me down there…no one…ever."

He released a hard, guttural breath as his mind translated what she was saying. He had suspected as much, but her confession confirmed it. She had just admitted that no man had ever done to her what he'd just done. A fierce sense of sexual pride arose in him as he shifted his body to lean closer to her lips, connecting them with his again.

He began devouring her mouth once more, enjoying sexual pleasure everywhere his tongue touched. When she pushed him away, he literally groaned in protest.

"I thought I saw a light, Blade."

He glanced out the window and saw the headlights of what looked like a security patrol car headed their way. He pulled her up on the seat. "Come on. We need to get out of here."

Blade watched as Sam quickly eased up in her seat. He turned on his headlights to give the impression he was about to pull away, and when the patrol car circled the parking lot and left without approaching them, he released a deep breath.

He glanced back over at Sam and saw her straightening her clothes, tugging her skirt down her thighs. Then she ran fingers through her hair and glanced over at him.

Not sure what she was about to say, and really not wanting to risk that it would be something he didn't want to hear, he leaned over and kissed her again. He then pulled back, looked into her eyes and whispered, "We'll talk about it tomorrow."

He appreciated that she merely nodded as he backed out of the parking space. It didn't take long to reach where her car was parked. As soon as he pulled up beside it, she opened the door and jumped out.

"Sam!" he called after her.

Instead of slowing down she tossed over her shoulder the same line he'd just said. "We'll talk tomorrow."

He watched as she quickly got into her car, and when her red sports car sped off across the parking lot, he was right behind her.

Sam's fingers tightened on her steering wheel as she drove through the streets and away from downtown. How did tonight happen? She was supposed to have been the one with the upper hand. But somehow Blade had turned the tables on her, caught her at a weak moment and taken advantage of the fact that she had lowered her guard.

She squeezed her legs together in an attempt to stop the tingling sensation that was still there, actually pulsating out of control. His mouth ought to be outlawed. She drew in a quick breath and then thought, *Umm, maybe not.*

She shook her head. She wouldn't want his mouth outlawed, definitely not with the lingering sensations she was feeling now. Once she got home and calmed her enflamed nerves by drinking a cup of herbal tea, she would be able to recover her shattered brain cells and recoup her senses. At least now she was aware just what she was up against, and the next time she would be fully prepared.

To be honest, a part of her, though—definitely not the area between her legs—was hoping there wouldn't be a next time. Fool that she was, she had even confessed to him that it had been her first time.

"That was real smart, Samari," she muttered angrily to herself as she hit the button to roll down her car window. The cool night air blowing in her face was what she needed right now.

Sam glanced into the rearview mirror and saw the object of her distraction was following her home again tonight. She couldn't do anything but smile, thinking that at least she would have the upper hand in something. He evidently assumed he had primed her for the next phase of her seduction, and that she was so hot and bothered that she would tell the attendant at the security gate to let him through. It wouldn't surprise her if Blade was already wearing a condom in anticipation.

When she came to a traffic light her thoughts went back to what had happened in his parked car. Talk about something that had definitely been wild and risqué. And to make matters worse, she had been so absorbed in what he'd been doing to her that she hadn't given much thought to where they were parked. Frank, who usually worked from nine at night to nine the next morning, had a habit of driving around the parking lot as part of his security duties. What if he had caught them in a compromising position? Talk about major embarrassment.

She frowned when she saw that Blade was still following behind her as she turned into the driveway toward the security gate. He actually thought she would be gullible enough to tell the guard that it would be okay to let him through. The corners of her lips curved in a wicked smile. She would take great pleasure in bursting his arrogant bubble. She brought her car to a stop. The attendant recognized her and the security arm was lifted.

As she drove through, she glanced back in the rearview

mirror. When she saw Blade stopping at the station, she smiled as she kept on going. He would probably claim that he was with her, but the attendant on duty would not let him through under any circumstances without her consent, which she hadn't given. That would serve Blade right, for assuming he had the upper hand after what had happened tonight.

She had just hit the switch inside her car to open her garage door when she noticed the headlights coming toward her cul-de-sac. She blinked upon recognizing the dark sedan. There was no way. No how. But when the car pulled into the driveway next to hers, she knew for certain it was Blade.

Everything before her turned red as she quickly switched off her ignition and got out of her vehicle at the same moment he did. He had the audacity, the sheer gall, to smile at her.

"Out kind of late, aren't you, Sam?" Blade said, leaning against his car as he watched her approach with a look on her face that could only be described as furious.

"What are you doing here?" She all but flung out the words.

He shrugged easily before saying, "This place was empty so I decided to lease it while I'm in town."

She stared at him for a moment before the full impact of his words seemed to sink in. He could tell the moment they did by the look in her eyes. They had sharpened to slivered glass. "Why would you do such a thing?" she all but snapped.

He gave her a faint smile and said, "I like having you within easy reach."

Sam burst through her front door and slammed it shut behind her. She threw her purse on the sofa in a fury. Her

Italian temper was in full bloom. She began pacing the floor, calling herself all kinds of fools ten times over. Every cell in her body, even the ones between her legs that had been throbbing earlier, were now vibrating in anger.

How dare Blade assume he could move next door to her because, as he'd put it, he liked having her within easy reach. The nerve of the man! After he'd spouted those words she had gotten so angry that instead of giving him the response on the tip of her tongue, she had literally turned and stomped off.

Tonight he had proved that he was no different than all the rest of the players out there. He would do whatever it took to get what he wanted, because his needs and wants were all that mattered.

She headed for the kitchen to make a cup of tea, although she doubted anything would be able to calm her down right now. She hoped that Blade realized his actions constituted all-out war on her part, and that by the time she was finished with him, he would regret ever having crossed her path.

Chapter 10

The sunlight shining through the window roused Blade from sleep. He glanced around the room, thinking his ever efficient secretary had come through with shining colors, as usual. Claire had taken care of every single detail. She had already hired a cleaning service that had come in yesterday afternoon and made sure clean linens were on the bed.

When he had checked out of the hotel, she'd hired a service to transport his belongings from the hotel to the town house. His clothes were hanging up in the closet and his toiletries were in the bathroom. And the refrigerator was stocked with bottles of water and his favorite beer.

When he'd walked through the door last night after his confrontation with Sam in the driveway, he had needed a beer. In fact, he could have actually used something stronger. To say she'd been upset with him was an understatement. He would give her time to cool off, time to realize that being next door to him would benefit the both of them.

After what had happened between them in the parked car, what could possess her to continue playing her hard-to-get game was beyond him. How long would it take for her to concede that he'd gotten her already? At least partly. What they'd shared last night was a sexual act whether she wanted to admit it or not. So the way he saw it, they might as well go ahead and finished what they'd started.

When he heard a car door slam, he swung his legs over the side of the bed and walked over to the window. He saw Sam putting something in the trunk of her car.

He rubbed his hand down his face and wondered what time it was, figuring it had to be before eight in the morning. The clock on the wall confirmed his suspicions. He then remembered Sam had mentioned last night that she had an early appointment at the office.

She was wearing the kind of business suit that he was beginning to recognize as her personal style. She looked professional, yet her short skirt showed off her long, gorgeous legs in a very sexy way. Today's suit was a lime-green, and like all the others he'd seen her wear, she looked damn good in it. Her hair was down and flowed around her shoulders. A breeze was blowing and he watched as it ruffled her curls, making her hair billow like soft chiffon around her face.

It was a face he had stared into last night, watching the afterglow of her orgasm. The orgasm he had given to her. He took pride in his skill as a lover, making it his business to assure that every woman he slept with experienced sexual pleasure.

He was not a selfish man by any means, and never left a woman's bed until she was contented and purring like a satisfied kitten. But last night he'd wanted to do more than merely make Sam purr. He'd wanted to satisfy a primal urge, the sexual triumph of seeing his woman explode in unadulterated passion.

His woman.

His breathing literally stopped when he realized what had crossed his mind. He was startled at the mere thought he would consider any woman his. Blade flinched. That had certainly been a slip of the mind, a temporary loss of his senses. He enjoyed too many women to settle on just one. It wasn't in his makeup to love just one woman.

He inhaled a deep breath. He had to be rational now. The novelty of having made out in the car was messing with him, filling his head with foolish thoughts and making him think things he had no business thinking. Whatever had possessed him to make out with her in a parked car was beyond him, but he knew he would do it again if the opportunity presented itself.

His gaze focused on Sam. She had gone back inside to get her briefcase, and was putting it in the backseat. When she leaned over, her skirt inched up and he got a glimpse of those same thighs that he'd been between last night. As he stared some more, he saw her lean over so far that he caught sight of her shapely backside, as well as a glimpse of her panties.

He wiped his hand across his forehead, feeling the heat. Going to bed with an erection larger than Texas would probably do that to you. He couldn't remember the last time he'd been in such a state.

Blade wasn't sure how long he stood there gazing down at her, and was surprised she hadn't seemed to realize she was being watched. Maybe she had and was deliberately ignoring him.

Had she deliberately flashed him?

She finally got into her car and drove off, and he stood there until she was no longer in sight. It was only then that he moved away from the window to go back to bed, with a hard-on that was practically killing him. He wouldn't be totally satisfied until the day Sam was in this bed with him.

Sam's mouth thinned as she kept on driving. She had been very much aware that Blade had been standing at his bedroom window watching her, but she had refused to turn around and give him the satisfaction of acknowledging his presence.

But what she had done, and what she would continue to do every chance she got, was to give him an eyeful of what he would not be getting. That was the reason she had opened the back door to place her briefcase on the seat, leaning over more than she'd needed to.

A smile touched her lips. He thought living next door to her would put him in heaven, but she intended to make it a living hell. And when he finally came over to her house, panting like a dog that needed to get laid, she would tell him just what she thought of him, and let him know he was the last man she wanted to sleep with.

Her cell phone rang when she got to the traffic light. She clicked it on without checking the caller ID. "Yes?"

"I thought I'd call to let you know our parents aren't too happy with you right now."

Sam rolled her eyes at her brother's warning. "What did I do now, Angelo?"

"You didn't make any headway with Cash. They like him."

Sam rolled her eyes. "They liked Guy, as well. Big deal."

Angelo chuckled. "Yeah, well, this one has political aspirations."

"So did Guy. And Cash didn't rack up any points with me."

"Tell that to the folks. By the way, what's up with FDR? He's been acting rather strange lately. Taking trips out of town on weekends and being evasive about where he's going."

Sam put on her turn signal as she exited the highway. Remembering her brother's suspicions that FDR was seeing someone and trying to keep it a secret, she figured whoever it was probably lived in another city. "FDR's a big boy and can take care of himself. He probably feels he has a lot on his plate, trying hard to make partner. He won't be a shoo-in like someone I know."

"Hey, I work hard. I'm good at what I do."

"Whatever." She switched to another radio station. She knew Angelo was right. He was a good attorney and a hard worker. And like her cousins, the other Di Meglios working at the firm, they were earning their way up the ladder and not living on easy street. Her father and uncles made sure of it.

"Okay, I'll give you that. You *are* a hard worker. The only thing you're lax about is making a move on a certain woman," she said smartly.

"What are you talking about, Sam?"

"Mmm, I'll let your figure it out. Goodbye, Angelo."

She clicked off the phone, wondering when her brother would finally acknowledge that he had a thing for Peyton.

Blade cradled the phone between his shoulder and ear as he studied the paper that had been faxed to him earlier. "This is going to be a real nice facility when it's completed, Trevor. Slade and I appreciate the business."

Trevor had chosen Madaris Construction to turn a huge

empty warehouse he had purchased on the outskirts of Houston into a tactical training facility.

"And no, there shouldn't be a problem with it being operational within eight months. I'm returning to Houston next week and look forward to meeting with you then."

A few moments later Blade ended the call, and smiled as he studied the preliminary drawings he held in his hand. As he'd told Trevor, the facility he envisioned, the one Slade had designed, would be an imposing structure and serve Trevor's purpose. Blade would make sure it was built to specifications, perfect in every way. He had already surveyed the location where Trevor wanted the building erected, and felt the area was ideal. This was one project that Blade looked forward to returning to Houston to oversee, once his work in Oklahoma City with the Mosley project was finished.

Folding the papers, he vividly recalled Madaris Construction's first major project. The opportunity came from Trevor's brother-in-law, Mitch Farrell, on the recommendation of Uncle Jake, who was one of the partners in the venture. The Madaris Building and Office Park had been a dream come true and their success in handling the project had opened doors for the company.

But business wasn't what was on Blade's mind as he tossed the drawings onto the desk and walked over to the window, the one facing the back of the property. From where he stood he could see a recreation park, similar to the one he'd designed for the condominium complex he and Slade had developed in Houston.

His thoughts shifted to Sam. He would be the first to admit that he found the situation with Sam out of character for him. But to be honest, he hadn't really been in character since the day he'd laid eyes on her. He refused to think it had to do with anything more than his desire to have her in his bed.

The thought of making love to her—especially getting a taste of what she had to offer—was constantly on his mind. Luckily, he'd kept busy making the necessary phone calls to assure the Mosley project remained on schedule, but more than once throughout the day his thoughts had drifted and he had replayed what had happened in the parked car the night before.

He shook his head, thinking heaven help him if his great-grandmother discovered the true reason he was hanging around Oklahoma City. She had her own ideas about how her grands' and great-grands' lives should pan out. She thought there was a woman out there for him, one who would get him to settle down, a woman who would make him want a meaningful relationship.

He had tried telling her that such a woman didn't exist, and it wasn't meant for every man and woman to marry. But that didn't keep her from dropping hints whenever she could, making him aware of her desire to see her grands and great-grands tie the knot. He wasn't stupid. He knew she'd been working behind the scenes on him for years. With Slade and Luke in wedded bliss, you would think she would be happy.

Blade was hoping she saw him as a lost cause and would move on to Reese, who was the next oldest great-grand. Reese was considered a loner, so Blade wasn't sure how he felt about getting married. Reese was especially close to La'Kenna James. They had been best friends since college and the two claimed that's all they were. And since Kenna and Reese often dated others, the family had no reason to believe otherwise. But Blade had seen them together at Luke and Mac's wedding. He had noticed the way Reese looked at Kenna, and wondered if something was about to change with his cousin's status.

He glanced at his watch. He was through for the day.

Luke had called earlier and invited him to dinner, since Reese was in town. There was no doubt in Blade's mind that the best way to handle Sam was to give her the time and space she needed to think about last night. Sensual memories were a good thing. But if she thought she'd be able to ignore him, then she had another think coming.

"Is there a reason why you're giving those computer keys a beat down?"

Sam glanced up and couldn't help but smile. Peyton stood in the doorway with her arms crossed, staring at her with a frown on her face. Sam knew that standing in front of her was a tough cookie. Peyton had grown up on Chicago's South Side and had returned there to work as an attorney after law school. Of the three, Peyton was the one they considered the quiet storm, but she would be the first to put up a good argument if one was needed.

Peyton was also someone who would listen, study and weigh every aspect of a case, focusing on the facts, without being emotional. She believed in fighting for the little guy. Sam would be the first to admit that their relationship in law school had gotten off to a rocky start because they had come from such different backgrounds. Peyton had seen her as the spoiled little rich kid, and she had seen Peyton as someone who still had a chip on her shoulder because of what she hadn't had while growing up, as if it were Sam's fault. Mac had fit nicely in between, and after getting to really know each other, they had forged a friendship that Sam knew would always be there, no matter what.

"Actually—" Sam leaned back in her chair "—beating on these computer keys is better than finding Blade Madaris and beating up on him."

Evidently Peyton thought her statement amusing, if the

smile that replaced her frown was anything to go by. She walked into the room and dropped into the chair across from Sam's desk. "Is he causing problems?"

Sam rolled her eyes. "Like the flowers aren't enough."

Peyton lifted her eyebrow in surprise. "He's the one who's been sending you those flowers?"

Sam nodded. "Yes, although he hasn't admitted it. I haven't brought it up and neither has he. But it's a typical player move to try and break down a woman's defenses. The flowers started coming not long after Mac's birthday party, where Blade tried hitting on me several times. And a few nights ago when Mac and I met him and Luke after work at Carlton's, he conveniently dropped the hint that his aunt had opened a florist shop."

Peyton grinned. "So, he's trying to work you, is he?"

"So he thinks," Sam said, shaking her head.

"I take it that dinner with him last night didn't go well?" Peyton asked.

Sam wondered if Peyton detected the blush that she was trying to hide. Dinner had been great. It was the dessert after dinner she'd been trying to forget.

"Dinner was fine," she said truthfully. "It was when I got home that still has me pissed."

"Pissed about what?"

"He's leased the vacant town house next door."

Peyton's eyes widened as she sat up straight in her chair. "You're kidding."

"Wish I was. He even told me the reason when I asked him why he'd done it. He said to keep me within reach."

Peyton shook her head. "I don't know whether you should be flattered or scared."

Sam stared at her. "Scared?"

Her friend nodded. "If it was anyone else, I would say

it sounds like he's stalking you. But I've met Luke's family and they all seem sane."

Sam laughed. "However, you and I both know that in every family there's a loony tune. But seriously, I think of Blade's antics as more of him making a nuisance of himself than a threat."

"Then maybe you *should* be flattered. I've heard stories about him. I have cousins living in Houston and his reputation there is legendary. Blade Madaris is used to having anything and anyone he wants. The women love him. Good eye candy is hard to find these days and you have to admit he's rather pleasing to the eyes."

"Yes, he is pleasing to the eyes," Sam couldn't help but admit.

"If he did lease that house just to keep you within reach, it's probably a first for him to give any woman that much attention. Hmm, makes me wonder."

"About what?"

"How you're going to deal with him. Blade appears to be a man pretty sure of himself, and he goes after what he wants. Moving next door proves that he wants you."

"He won't have me." She knew that had to be a sore spot with him. Men who assumed they could have any woman they wanted, and play them however they felt like playing them, without concern for their feelings and emotions, were used to having things their way.

"So, what are you going to do about him living next door?"

Peyton's question interrupted Sam's thoughts, and she couldn't help but smile at the plan she'd decided on earlier. "I intend to drive him crazy. Take every opportunity to remind him of what he doesn't have and what he won't be getting. Handle him like I handle all players. I think he needs to be taught a lesson."

Peyton frowned. "Haven't you gotten enough of going after players to teach them a lesson, Sam? One of these days it's going to backfire on you again. Do I need to remind you about Belton LaSalle?"

Just hearing the man's name sent shivers down Sam's spine. LaSalle had been a player of the worse kind. He had pursued her for weeks after meeting her in a bar where she, Peyton and Mac had been enjoying after-hours drinks. He had walked in that night with the word *player* all but plastered on his forehead.

Sam had decided that Belton should be taught a lesson. She didn't want to think about what might have happened that night if Mac and Peyton hadn't been at the same restaurant and seen LaSalle slip something into her drink when her back was turned. They had immediately called the police, who had arrested Belton there on the spot. Belton had been sentenced five years for possession of GHB, the date-rape drug.

Not wanting to talk or think about Belton LaSalle any longer, Sam changed the subject and discussed the woman she had met with earlier that day: one who wanted to sue the local newspaper for failing to print her husband's obituary. She was certain more people would have shown up for the service had they known.

"Where's Mac?" Sam asked a few moments later, when Peyton stood to leave for her three-o'clock appointment.

"She left early today. Her brother-in-law Reese is in town and she wanted to prepare dinner."

Sam nodded, remembering Mac had mentioned that Reese would be arriving. She wondered if Blade would be having dinner with Mac and Luke. Sam certainly hoped so. The last thing she wanted was for him to make his way over to her place and knock on her door. It would be just like him to find some excuse to aggravate her.

Besides, she needed time to put her plans for him into motion. She wanted him to think she had come around and was open to having an affair. And when he thought he had her just where he wanted her, she would let him know that he was the one who had been used.

There was nothing like seeing the look on a player's face when he was ready to sizzle, only to have her defuse the flame. She liked being a tease and proving to them that some women were immune to their doggish charms.

"Peyton, what do you have planned for the weekend?" she asked. Tomorrow was Friday and the last thing she needed was to run into Blade over the weekend. And with him living next door there was a strong possibility that would happen. Besides, she needed distance to think of a good plan for him.

"Nothing. Why?"

"How would you like to go with me for the weekend to that new resort in Sparks? I heard it has a real nice spa, and it will be my treat."

Peyton studied her a second and then asked. "Any reason you want to get out of Dodge?"

Sam rolled her eyes. "For Pete's sake, stop asking questions. Do you want to go or not?"

Peyton smiled. "Yes, I'll go, but it doesn't have to be your treat, Di Meglio."

Sam waved one hand in the air. "Whatever. I'll bring my bags in tomorrow and we can leave right after work. I'll call to make the reservation."

After Peyton left her office, Sam leaned back in her chair, feeling more relaxed. She had found something to do for the weekend and didn't have to worry about crossing paths with Blade.

Chapter 11

Late Sunday night the sound of a woman humming woke Blade up. At first he thought he'd been dreaming, but now he was wide-awake and could still hear the sound. He flipped on his back, perked up his ears and wondered where the melody was coming from.

Easing out of bed and grabbing his robe, he glanced around his room. He didn't believe in ghosts, so the thought of this place being haunted didn't enter his mind. He began walking toward where the sound was coming from.

He opened the French doors leading to the balcony and stepped out in his bare feet on the cool ceramic tile. He glanced to his right and had a good view of Sam's balcony. Because of the way the townhomes were designed, the only thing that separated the two was a brick planter, which afforded only a semblance of privacy between the two homes. But all he had to do was push a few plants aside to see into the screened-in area off her bedroom.

She had installed a hot tub and she was outside in it. Her head was thrown back and her eyes were closed and she looked relaxed. She was humming the song that had awakened him.

Although he hadn't checked the time, he figured it to be close to midnight, since it had been after ten o'clock when he'd left Luke and Mac's place. When he'd arrived home he'd assumed Sam had returned from her weekend getaway and had turned in for the night, since all the lights were out at her place.

During dinner on Friday night Mac had mentioned that Sam and Peyton had gone away for the weekend to a resort in a town called Sparks. He figured that had been Sam's way of putting distance between them.

Now she was back and he was wide-awake and feeling like a Peeping Tom. He'd never had a reason to stand in the shadows to watch a woman in a hot tub before, but he was doing so now, as all kinds of sensations formed deep in his belly.

Blade wasn't sure how long he stood there, but it was long enough to focus on the way her head lay against the back of the tub, and how her beautiful face seemed to glow in the moonlight. Her hair was tied up on top of her head, exposing the long, graceful curve of her neck and throat.

Bubbles were swirling all around her and he didn't have to strain his eyes to know she was naked in the hot tub. That much was evident by the way the bubbly water splashed on her chest, and on occasion a plump, bare breast would be exposed when she shifted positions. He felt the lower part of his body get hard and was about to open his mouth to let her know he was there, and to ask if he could perhaps join her, when she spoke.

"Enjoying the peep show, Blade?"

She hadn't even opened her eyes, which immediately let him know she'd been expecting him and had known all along he was there. She had intentionally been humming to lure him out of his bed. Okay, so she'd gotten him, and his mind was suddenly filled with a number of ways he would like to get her. Several positions came to mind, but the one he liked best was doggie style.

A shudder rippled through him, all the way to his groin, when he visualized it in his mind. He clenched his jaw, trying to suppress the heat consuming his body. He finally decided to answer truthfully. "Yes, I'm enjoying it, immensely. But I would enjoy it even better if I could see a lot more of you."

"That can be arranged."

His eyes strained as he watched her. What he hadn't expected was her easing out of the water to stand up. And just as he'd assumed, she was naked and her body was simply beautiful. She was so flawless that he could hear his heart weep and could feel his erection beating its head against his zipper in agony.

She possessed what had to be the most perfect pair of breasts—firm, luscious, shapely. Her nipples seemed to be calling out for his mouth. He forced his gaze to move lower, to her flat stomach and the water that was glistening off her gold belly ring. And then he saw the small tattoo of an eagle on the side of her hip.

Blade pulled in a deep breath as his gaze moved to the juncture of her thighs. *Sweet mercy.* He muttered deep in his throat as he fixed his eyes on her womanly charm, perfectly shaped with a Brazilian wax. He licked his lips, remembering the kiss he had placed there, and how his tongue had felt sliding around the smooth surface before going deep inside of her.

He could have sworn she had tasted of cinnamon and spice that night, and even now the flavor of her still clung to his tongue and wouldn't go away. Her feminine heat was emitting a scent that was being absorbed into his nostrils, his skin and every damn inch of him.

He released his breath when she got out of the tub, showing a nice curvy and delectable backside. Her long, beautiful legs glistened with water and were gorgeous and as shapely as a pair of legs could be. As soon as her feet, which were as beautiful as the rest of her, touched the tile floor, he noticed a toe ring.

She crossed the floor to where she'd placed a towel across a chair, and worked every curve of her body as she strutted her stuff. A lump formed in his throat as she swayed her hips, lifted her breasts and all but glided sensuously to her destination. A model on a runway could not have done any better. He nearly moaned in agony when she reached for the towel, flapped it open and then draped it around her body, covering up all those parts he'd enjoyed seeing.

"Show's over, Blade."

His gaze moved to her face. "Why did you even bother?"

She threw her head back and laughed. "So you'll have a chance to see what you'll never get."

She was teasing him, toying with his jewels, and he didn't like it one damn bit. "Would you like to bet on that? Two can play your game, Sam."

He could tell from her expression that she didn't like the sound of that.

"What do you have in mind? Torment me. Tease me. Tantalize me with no promise of release?" he asked.

"All of the above."

Now it was his time to chuckle. "Don't mess with a

man who's at the top of his game, especially if that man is so hard up for you that he can't think straight." He was giving her fair warning. It was the right thing to do.

He watched her features and knew she was trying to make a decision about something. "Maybe you're right. All we're doing is causing each other agony, which is a waste of time and energy."

His erection throbbed in anticipation. Now she was making sense.

"But I'm not sure you can handle me, Blade. I'm not a woman who can be easily pleased."

It was on the tip of his tongue to remind her that pleasing her hadn't been too difficult the other night. "There's not a woman walking this earth that I can't please."

"So you say."

"So I know. Give me one night with you to prove it."

He saw indecision etched on her face. "I'll think about it."

He couldn't help but smile. "Yes, you do that. But in the meantime, have breakfast with me in the morning."

She shook her head. "I have an early appointment at the office."

"What about lunch?"

"I plan to work through lunch."

He refused to give up. "Dinner?"

He waited to see if she would come up with another excuse, and then she surprised him by saying, "Dinner will be fine, but it has to be here. It was your treat the last time. It's only fair that it will be mine this time."

He nodded, wondering what her "treat" consisted of. "What time?"

"Will six o'clock work?"

"Yes."

"Fine. I'll see you here at six."

She was about to open the French doors to her bedroom when he stopped her. "Wait! Do you need me to bring anything?"

She looked at him for a moment, then tossed her head to send the hair that had been atop her head falling to her shoulders. She stood there, looking not only like a seductive creature, but one who was wild and too sexy for words.

"Yes, you can bring something."

The look in her eyes was scorching every part of him. "What?"

"Plenty of condoms."

He couldn't think. His mouth dropped, and before he could pick it up, she slid inside the house and closed the door behind her. And while he stood there in a daze, with a hard-on that was like nobody's business, the lights on her balcony went off and cast him in total darkness.

Sam couldn't help the smile on her face as she slid into bed an hour later. By her parting words, Blade could only assume that there would be some action after dinner at her place. But he was so wrong. She planned to tempt him and tease him, but she had no intentions of delivering. In the end she would frustrate him, annoy the hell out of him and make him mad. Then she would ask him to leave and take his condoms with him.

Oh, well.

Tomorrow night she would pretend she had softened and was just as hot as he was, but not quite ready to go all the way. She would lie about some hang-ups she had and see what kind of cure he would concoct for them. Most players thought they were love doctors who had their own brand of medication for whatever ailment a woman had. She wondered if Blade knew how to mend broken hearts. The ones he'd probably caused many women.

She had known the exact moment he had stepped out onto the balcony. She had been aware of when he had begun watching her through the planter. Although she hadn't wanted it to, her body had responded to him in a way it had never responded to another man. She would have to be on her toes tomorrow, making sure she was the one in charge at all times. He'd already discovered her weakness, and she had to make sure he didn't have any more tricks up his sleeve. If she could keep his head from between her legs, she would be fine. She simply refused to become another woman he could easily seduce.

She flipped over on her back in bed and stared up at the ceiling. Now was not a good time to question her judgment in handling Blade. He was a man who liked sex, and to dangle it in front of him with no intention of giving in just might push him over the edge. What would he do if that were to happen? Other than wanting to wring her neck, she couldn't think of a single thing. He wasn't a violent man who would be driven to such an act. He would walk away, pissed as hell, and would not want to have anything to do with her again. Players did have their pride and didn't like any conquest to get the best of them. They didn't like to fail.

But he would fail. She would be Blade's ultimate downfall.

Blade woke up the next morning in the best of moods, with Sam's words ringing in his ears. When he'd asked her what he could bring, she had simply said, "Plenty of condoms."

He wondered what plenty meant. A dozen? Hell, he'd bring two dozen just in case, although he couldn't imagine going through that many in a single night. He hadn't done anything like that before, but there was a first time for everything. His thoughts shifted to the other night. Now *that* had been her first time, by her own admission.

Of course, she'd alluded to the possibility that there wouldn't be any action because he just might not be able to please her. He looked forward to proving her wrong and enjoying every inch of her luscious body in the process.

He was heading to the bathroom to take a shower when his phone rang. He checked the caller ID and saw that it was his cousin Felicia. Smiling, he clicked on the line. "What's up with you on this cheerful Monday, Fe?"

"Nothing much. I'm helping Diamond with Rasheed's party and doing invitations. Usually you don't bring anyone, but I thought I'd play it safe and check to make sure nothing has changed."

She was right. He never brought anyone to a Madaris family function. He wouldn't dare. First, there wasn't a woman alive he could bring who wouldn't think she was the anointed one. And if he was to show up with a woman, his family would assume he was making a statement. He liked scoping out the eligible single women invited to family parties. Over the years, he'd scored quite a number of hits. He then thought of Sam and conceded he'd also made one or two misses.

"Thanks for asking, but I'm doing the solo thing as usual," he said, ignoring Sam's face, which kept popping up in his mind. There was no way he would consider taking her to a family function, regardless of how bad he wanted her in his bed.

"All right, but if you change your mind let me know."

He chuckled. "Trust me. I won't be changing my mind."

"Well, I'll let you go," Felicia said. "When do you plan to return to Houston?"

"Probably next week." He thought about his hot dinner date later this evening and then added, "But it depends on how much I get accomplished while I'm here."

After hanging up the phone, he glanced at his watch. He didn't have a whole lot to do today. There was a conference call at eleven and a meeting with J. W. Mosley at three. Then he would eagerly return home for the dinner date he had with Sam. There was no way he wouldn't be on time, and there was no way he wouldn't have plenty of condoms, which meant he needed to make a pit stop at the drugstore. He'd brought only so many with him, since he hadn't expected to be this lucky.

And while he was out and about he might as well pick up a little gift for Sam to set the mood. He'd noticed a florist shop not far from Windsor Park. Sam looked to be the kind of woman who would appreciate getting a bunch of flowers.

He smiled as he headed to the bathroom to take that shower. Yes, a beautiful floral arrangement should do the trick. Normally he didn't do the flowers thing, but he would try anything to get in her good favor.

Hopefully the end result would be him in her bed.

Chapter 12

"I heard Blade moved into the place next door to you. What's up with that?" Mac asked as she slid into the chair across from Sam's desk.

Sam turned away from her computer and gave her a faint smile. "You and I both know what's up with that. He's up—probably most of the time—and figured being close is just another way to get me into his bed."

Mac nodded, knowing what she said was probably right. "I've never known Blade to work this hard for a woman. You might have become an obsession with him."

Sam shrugged. "As long as it's a healthy one I don't have any problem, because it's coming to an end soon."

Mac leaned forward in her chair. "He's not going to like it if he discovers you've set him up, teased him with no intention of delivering."

"He'll get over it."

"And if he doesn't?"

"Then it's his concern and not mine."

Before Mac could respond to that, there was a knock on the door. "Come in," Sam said.

Patsy Ackerman, the young woman who worked for them part-time as a paralegal, stepped in. "Here are those reports you wanted to look over for the Collins case."

Sam smiled at her as she accepted the folders. "Thanks. Now I have to make time to read them before our court date in a few weeks."

Patsy nodded and then glanced at the flowers on Sam's desk. "You got more flowers. They're pretty."

Sam studied the arrangement and couldn't help but agree. "Yes, they are pretty, aren't they?"

"And you still don't know who's sending them?"

Sam lifted a brow, wondering how Patsy knew the flowers were being sent by an unknown admirer. "No, it's still a secret," she replied honestly, seeing no reason not to.

Moments after Patsy had left, Mac silently stared at Sam. "What?" Sam asked, seeing the concerned look on her friend's face.

"I hope you know what you're doing. Blade's a player, true enough, but he's also a Madaris. They don't like being crossed."

Sam frowned. "Then maybe he needs to learn how to keep a certain part of his anatomy in his pants."

"Maybe so, but be forewarned. If you're trying to teach him a lesson, your self-control just might be tested, as well."

She didn't doubt that. It was tested each and every time she breathed the same air as Blade. Each and every time she remembered what he'd done to her that night in the parked car. She couldn't look at his mouth and lips without remembering, without feeling a tingling sensation at the juncture of her thighs, and without her panties getting wet.

"I can handle Blade, Mac."

Mac drew in a deep breath and said, "A Madaris man can be lethal when he has one thing on his mind, so for your sake I hope that you *can* handle him."

The knock sounded on Sam's door at exactly six o'clock, even though she hadn't expected Blade to be late. But she hadn't expected him to be standing there with a huge bouquet of flowers—more beautiful than all the others he'd sent her—and wearing a Stetson that shadowed his eyes and did everything to emphasize those oh-so-sexy lips of his. She thought he looked good in a pair of jeans and white shirt and his signature blazer. He smelled good, too, with whatever cologne he was wearing.

She couldn't help but smile when he stepped inside her house, thinking that all those other floral arrangements, although beautiful, hadn't done anything for her, but for some reason these did. Maybe the reason was because there was no secrecy shrouded in these flowers. With these, he was finally admitting that she was definitely the object of his seduction.

"These are for you," he said, tossing his Stetson on her coffee table with a perfect aim before handing her the flowers.

"They're beautiful, Blade. But then they always are. Thank you."

He gave her a funny look and shrugged his masculine shoulders. "You're welcome."

She turned to put the flowers in a vase and set them on the table. She felt his gaze roam over her body, taking in her short denim skirt and the white halter top stretched tightly across her breasts, which she wore without a bra. She had seen the outfit on a mannequin in the store today and had known it would be perfect for tonight. It was just the thing to get a man's erection throbbing. It was designed to get him hot and definitely bothered.

Sam turned back around and her gaze automatically went to his zipper, although she couldn't have missed the massive bulge even if she had wanted to. He was huge and appeared as hard as a rock. He was as aroused as any man could be, and he wasn't trying to hide it. She doubted he could have hidden the colossal protrusion even if he'd wanted to do so. She hadn't counted on blood pulsating rapidly through her veins upon seeing him in that state and realizing the degree of his desire for her.

And just like she was checking out every single aspect of him, he was checking her out, as well. His gaze moved all over her, from head to toe, but paused for more than a second on her breasts. And then, as if his eyes sent some kind of erotic message, the nipples of her breasts started feeling sensitive, almost achy against the material of her top. She also felt the tips swell under his unwavering gaze.

If she'd been any other woman, into casual sex just for the hell of it—and if he'd been any other man, and not a player whose philosophy was to always bed and never wed women—she would have seriously considered being his sexual playmate for a while. She'd never thought about doing such a thing before, but he would have been a temptation she might have given in to.

"I hope you're hungry," she heard herself saying, as his gaze continued to scan her up and down.

His eyes returned to her face and he smiled. She forced herself not to melt right there on the spot at how sexy his smile looked, while he stood there with his hands shoved into his pockets, staring at her as if he wanted to eat her alive. He'd nearly done so before and the memory sent sensuous shivers up her spine.

"Yes, I'm hungry," he said, breaking into her thoughts. "So, what's for dinner?"

Now that he'd asked… Sam sauntered across the room to Blade, deliberately swaying her hips in the process. She saw red-hot desire in the depths of his dark eyes. And his erection seemed to swell even more.

She reached up and placed her palms on his shirt and brought her body flush against his. She felt his hand go immediately to her backside and was well aware of him inching up the back of her skirt.

She looked up into his eyes, smiled and said in what she hoped was a sexy voice, "Me. So let's start cooking."

She then pulled his mouth down to hers.

If this was an appetizer, he didn't want to imagine what the main course was, Blade thought as he tightened his hold around Sam's waist. He hadn't expected this, for her to give herself to him on a silver platter, to let him know he would be feasting on her tonight.

She wasn't just kissing him, she was whipping up something so delicious that he couldn't do anything but groan in delight. Her tongue was working magic on every part of his mouth, not leaving any place untouched as she explored from crevice to crevice.

Her tongue was tangling around his and was feeding at his mouth with an intensity and hunger that let him know they had mutually greedy appetites tonight. Unable to help himself, he took the kiss deeper, and his hand roamed over her backside, pressing her closer to his hard form. He wanted her to feel him, wanted her to know just how hot he was for her.

To his surprise, he was the one who finally pulled his mouth away, not because he couldn't handle any more of her kisses, but because he was ready to move from the appetizer right on to the main course. She stared at him, and he studied her kiss-swollen lips and couldn't help wondering what she was thinking.

Sam couldn't believe that the kiss she and Blade had just shared had nearly blown her away. She was supposed to have been in control, but the moment his tongue began tangling with hers, and when he pressed her center close to his and the throbbing of his erection increased, sending vibrations of pleasure shooting to all parts of her body, she had gotten lost in a way she'd never gotten lost in a kiss before.

He stepped back and her eyes became glued to him when he removed his jacket and tossed it aside. Next came his shirt, and she gathered that he intended to strip right in her living room and wasn't wasting any time. She wouldn't stop him yet. She would take this as far as she could. Besides, she wanted to see him naked. After tonight it would probably be her only chance to see him in the raw.

She tossed her hair back along with the notion that such a thing bothered her. Blade Madaris was due his due, and she was going to be the woman who would make sure he got it.

But she couldn't help the knot that formed in her throat when his hands went to the zipper of his jeans. She'd said she was his dinner, and he wasn't wasting any time digging in. Maybe she should stop him, after all, before things got too out of hand, especially while she still had some control of her senses. Once he undressed, she wasn't sure just where things would go.

But she didn't stop him. She was afraid she might miss seeing something if she did. That sounded so awful, but it was the honest to goodness truth. So she stood there and watched as he leaned over to remove his boots and socks and then kicked them aside. He then slid his belt out of the pant loops before easing his jeans, along with his black silk boxers, down his legs. By removing those two pieces of clothing she saw just what she'd been waiting to see, in all its entire glorious and swollen splendor.

His shaft was huge. It was more than enough to fill her hands. She doubted it would even fit into her mouth, and she was having serious misgivings about her ability to get it inside of her—not that such a thing was going to happen.

But still, there was nothing wrong with getting an appreciative eyeful. And she had to admit it was definitely an impressive sight, painstakingly erect amid a groin area covered in dark curly hair. Whoever said that when you've seen one you've seen them all evidently hadn't seen this one.

She shifted her gaze to study the rest of him, fully unclothed, beautifully naked with sculpted arms and shoulders, and gorgeous abs. He had muscles all over, and his body was both defined and refined from head to toe. He was truly a work of art.

"Come here, Samari."

She couldn't explain it, but things happened to her whenever he said her full name. The sound of it coming from those incredible sexy lips not only seemed to caress her skin, it also made goose bumps appear all over, and sent prickling sensations throughout her body.

A voice inside her head cautioned her—warned her that this was where she should call everything off. Urged her to reveal to him that it had been all fun and games, and that she wasn't interested in taking things any further. But the truth was she *was* interested, if for no other reason than to test her resolve. Besides, she might as well get something out of this before sending him on his way.

She felt herself moving, drawn to him in a way she'd never been drawn to a man before, yet at the same time determined that this night would end no differently than with any other player she'd dealt with.

Keeping her eyes fixed on his, she kept walking and then came to a stop directly in front of him. She watched as his gaze lowered from her eyes to the top of her blouse, seeming to linger on her swollen nipples. If there was any doubt in his mind of her reaction to him, her breasts were telling it all, sending the message he needed to hear.

He then returned his gaze to her face. "Do you have any idea just how long I've wanted to get inside of you?" he asked in a voice that set her juices flowing. "When I saw you at the rehearsal dinner I wanted to suggest then that we forget everything and go somewhere and make love."

She noticed he'd said "make love" and not "have sex." She didn't think that players knew the meaning of making love, and that the only thing they thought about was having sex with women. She'd seen the look of interest in his eyes that night and figured he'd planned to make her the next notch on his bedpost—his flavor of the hour. And the next day, at the wedding, she figured he would hit on some other woman. That's how players operated.

"Take off your top so I can see your breasts, Sam."

She swallowed. She had a feeling that wasn't all he wanted to do with them, and before she could talk herself out of doing so, she lifted her halter top over her head and tossed it aside. His gaze zeroed in on her breasts and she could feel them swell even more before his eyes.

Suddenly, as if he had every right to do so, he reached out and cupped her breasts in his hands as he leaned forward. Before she could draw her next breath he used his tongue to lick a wet circle around the hardened tip of one, and then drew a nipple into his mouth and began sucking. Every pull on the swollen bud sent sensations rippling throughout her body.

Searing heat seemed to thrum between her legs and she released a deep moan and squeezed her eyes shut. She'd never gone this far in her game of revenge, never had been tempted to do so. But Blade was doing more than just tempting her, he was reminding her in every possible way that she was a woman, a woman with needs. A tight feeling erupted in her chest at the thought that for the first time in her life she wanted a man.

His mouth finally released her breasts and she felt the sense of loss, but he eased downward to nibble on her belly and she opened her eyes to find he had dropped to his knees in front of her. He was definitely getting serious, and she immediately knew where all this was leading. She also remembered her one weakness when it came to him.

"Blade, I—"

Whatever words she'd been about to say ended in a moan when his fingers found their way inside her panties and touched her achy flesh. She felt weak in the knees and all but slumped across him. He tugged down her skirt and she knew she shouldn't let him go any further. And when he proceeded to remove her panties and toss them aside, she couldn't muster the strength or the will to stop him.

But she knew whatever she did with him, she would have to do with caution. Blade's lovemaking had a way of getting her so wrapped up in pleasure that she would forget everything except how he made her feel. And the one thing she could not forget was that he could not go all the way with her. At some point she had to end things and ask him to leave.

But not now, she thought when she felt the tip of his nose rubbing against her feminine charms. He was muttering things she couldn't entirely understand, but she could make out the words *sweet, hot, delicious.*

And before she could strain her ears to make out anything else, she literally gasped when he suddenly used his arms to widen her legs, and at the exact same moment jabbed his tongue inside of her.

"Blade!"

He didn't respond. Not that she'd expected him to. Neither did he stop what he was doing, nor had she truly expected that, either. She grabbed ahold of his shoulders when his mouth became relentless in what he was doing to her—more relentless and hungrier than the night in the parked car. It was as if he was intent on consuming her alive.

Passion and lust made her womanly flesh throb even more and made sensations sweep through her body. She threw her head back while he held tightly to her thighs and his tongue penetrated even deeper.

Her moans became cries, her groans became gasps and her heart began racing as if it would never, ever slow down. And just when she thought he couldn't possibly torture her any more, his tongue delved even deeper and made moves, some incredible thrusting motions that nearly had her screaming.

Suddenly an orgasm hit and it hit her hard, slamming into her with the strength of a tractor trailer. Her hands left his shoulders and grabbed the sides of his head, not to pull him away but to hold him in place. She could tell that he was a man intent on finishing what he'd started, and didn't plan on going anywhere until the last spasm left her body.

It was then that she pushed him backward, sending him

tumbling to the floor, and she quickly proceeded to crouch down on top of him. Before he could say a single word, she became the aggressor and captured his mouth in hers, tasting herself on his lips and tongue.

Her flavor mingling with his did something to her. It made something snap inside of her as she continued to take control of his mouth. She was very much aware of his erection poking her belly.

She released his mouth and leaned downward, capturing his erection in her hand, and proceeded to feather it with kisses before taking her tongue and licking it as she would a lollypop.

"Damn, woman, what are you doing to me?" He choked out the words while his body exploded and he groaned out her name. When his shudders subsided, he grabbed hold of her hair and gave it a fierce tug.

"Ouch!" She released him, and the moment she did so, he caught her off guard and shifted positions so that she was the one on her back and he was towering over her.

"I got to get inside you, Samari. Now!"

He had spread her legs with practiced ease, and then suddenly, before she could react, she felt the hard thickness of his manhood enter her, stretching her wide in the process, and she flinched in pain. It was then that she realized just how far out of hand things had gotten. He was halfway inside of her. "Stop!"

That single word startled Blade and he froze. He didn't go any farther, but neither did he pull out. He stared down at her with lust-laden eyes, as if trying to figure out why she'd told him to stop. He blinked, and then as if it dawned on him, he pulled out of her and reached for his jacket, which he'd toss on the floor nearby.

Before she could say anything, he told her, "Sorry about that. I can't believe I forgot to put on a condom."

She watched as he shook his jacket, and a dozen or more foil-wrapped condom packets went flying everywhere, all over her floor. She was amazed at the number and couldn't help wondering just how many he'd planned to use on her. As if the question going through her mind showed in her expression, he laughed. "When it comes to you I've discovered I have a huge appetite."

She could only stare, and tried to force out of her mind just how good he'd felt inside of her for that brief period of time. Her womb was literally weeping at the thought that he wouldn't be back. When he had invaded her, her muscles had clamped down hard on him like a vise.

She shut her eyes at the memory, but quickly opened them when she felt his hands grab hold of her thighs again. Already he had put on a condom and was ready. And so was her body, although she didn't want it to be. More than anything she wanted him back inside of her, too, but she knew that couldn't happen. She pulled herself up into a sitting position. "Blade, wait. We need to talk."

He looked at her, surprised. "Talk?"

"Yes."

Confusion replaced the surprised look in his eyes. "Now?"

She nodded. "Yes."

"You're kidding, right?"

She pulled in a deep breath that was filled with the aroma of sex. She could certainly understand why he thought she was kidding. They were on the floor, naked, with condoms spread all around. And he had a huge erection, poised and ready for action, with his hands planted on her thighs with the intent of spreading her legs. He'd been there before, so he knew she was wet and ready—just waiting for his return.

She met his gaze and shook her head. "No, I'm not kidding."

She watched him swallow and then saw how he released a deep breath. "Is it because I forgot the condom? Look, I'm really sorry about that. That's not the way I usually operate, and nothing like that has ever happened to me before. When it comes to making out with a woman I'm usually in better control. I can't explain what the hell happened."

She could, and easily. Like her, he had gotten caught up in the moment, wrapped up in the most intense kind of pleasure. Their bodies had reacted and had left their minds behind.

"It has nothing to do with the condom," she said, pulling away from him, and grateful when he let go of her thighs. What she was about to say wouldn't be pretty. She intended to make it sound worse than it was. He would get pissed. She broke eye contact with him to reach for her skirt, blouse and panties.

"Then if it's not about the condoms, what is it? Why aren't we finishing what we've started?"

She felt her heart thud against her chest at the sound of the disappointment in his voice. She stood and slid into her skirt and pulled the halter top over her head. She tossed her panties back down, since they were wet.

She then met his gaze again. Cleared her throat and said, "I invited you over here, but I didn't intend for us to have sex, Blade."

He sat back on his haunches. The dark brown eyes staring back at her narrowed. "Of course you did. Did you not tell me when I arrived that *you* would be my dinner?"

She tossed her hair over her shoulders and deliberately gave him a haughty look. "Yes, I told you that. But when I did so, I had no intention of going through with any such plan."

"Then why did you lead me to believe that you would?"

She lifted her chin. "To teach you a lesson. You're a player. A man who thinks he can have any woman he wants, and I wanted to prove there're some women who find you resistible. I am one of them. Sorry you couldn't break through my *defenses*."

She saw the flash of anger that appeared in his eyes when her words sank in. He slowly got to his feet and she tried not to concentrate on the fact that her words hadn't deflated his erection any.

"Are you standing here telling me that you're nothing but a tease? That you deliberately invited me over here to set me up? That you dressed that way to make me want you, and did everything you did to me knowing that you wouldn't deliver?" he asked, with confusion and fury in his voice.

She pushed aside any feelings of guilt that plagued her. "Yes, that's what I'm saying."

Her response sounded flippant, totally lacking in remorse, and her expression gave the appearance of a woman who didn't have a shameful bone in her body.

He covered his face, as if he was awakening from a bad dream—a very bad dream. "But why, Sam?"

She crossed her arms over her chest. Again she fought back any feelings of guilt. There was something about the look in his eyes that was totally unexpected. That look was something she would have to think about later, but definitely not now.

"The reason is simple. You're a player and I'm a player hater. Because of men like you I was made a fool of on *my* wedding day, in front of over five hundred guests, when two women showed up claiming to be my fiancé's baby mamas. And I lost a good friend in college—my roommate. She committed suicide after a guy she thought she loved made a fool of her."

Those eyes that had been flashing fire before were blazing now. "You're punishing me because of what some other guys did?"

"Yes, but don't think you're the only one. There have been others before who got the same treatment from me."

"And you're still alive to brag about it?"

A sneer touched her lips. "Evidently being a tease doesn't mean a death sentence."

Instead of responding, Blade gathered up his clothes and angrily began putting them on. Like her, he didn't bother with his underwear. She watched as he balled up his briefs and put them in his pocket. He then headed for the door.

"Wait! What about all these condoms?"

He turned and glanced at her in a way she wished he hadn't. If looks could kill then she would definitely be dead. "Flush them down the damn toilet for all I care. And just for your information, Sam, I don't have sex with women who don't know the score. I've never misled a woman by making promises I didn't intend to keep. The women I sleep with know I'm not into long-term relationships, and for whatever reason, they prefer things that way."

He paused and then said in a somewhat softer tone, "I regret what happened on your wedding day. What your fiancé did to you was unforgivable in my book. And as for your friend who committed suicide, believe it or not, the same thing happened to my cousin Dex's best friend, Greg. He fell in love with a girl in college and she played him and he took his own life. So men aren't the only ones who are players. Just like all women aren't alike, all men aren't the same, either."

Sam pulled in a deep breath. Instead of feeling a surge of satisfaction at what she'd just done to Blade, a part of her felt pangs of regret. "Look, Blade—"

"No!" he snarled. "*You* look, Sam. You got your damn pound of flesh. You got your laughs at my expense, so let's end it there. We know where we stand with each other now. Personally, I don't think you're a nice person, and although it's unlikely our paths will never cross, I suggest we try to avoid each other whenever possible."

She lifted her chin. "Fine. And you can stop sending me those flowers."

He glared back at her. "I have no idea what you're talking about. I've never sent *you* or *any* woman flowers, other than the women in my family."

He then threw his head back and laughed. "And I'm such a fool that today was the first time I've ever given a woman I'm interested in flowers. For some reason I thought you were special. Damn, was I wrong. You can flush them down the toilet along with the condoms."

Muttering an obscenity that Sam was grateful she couldn't hear, Blade opened the door and walked out, slamming it shut behind him.

Blade let himself into his town house as rage blasted from every pore in his body. In all his thirty-four years, nothing like this had ever happened to him before. And the woman had had the damn nerve, the gall, to blame him for something he'd had nothing to do with.

Admittedly, he was a player. He enjoyed women. He liked variety when it came to making love, and so far there hadn't been a woman out there capable of giving him what he wanted, what he needed and desired, all in one single package. Hell, considering his fantasies, he doubted it was possible for any one woman to fulfill his needs.

He didn't make excuses for doing what he did, but he of all people respected women. He had enough of them in his family and had been taught from an early age how women were to be treated. He'd never held a gun to their heads to make them sleep with him, so what gave Sam the right to come off thinking she was justified in seeking revenge on behalf of women who'd ever been hurt by him?

He ignored the blinking message light on his answering machine as he walked through his living room toward the kitchen. He needed a beer. In all honesty, he needed something stronger, but he would settle for what he had.

Moments later he was leaning against the kitchen counter, after taking a huge swallow of his beer. The cold brew had flowed down his throat, but other than that, the drink hadn't affected him. He was staring down at the floor as his anger continued to boil.

By her own admission she was a player hater? He had heard about those kinds of women, but had been lucky not to have encountered one until now. How could he have been so stupid, so gullible? So damn horny for a woman that he hadn't seen the signs? How had he allowed her to get under his skin to the point that he had been chasing her for the past ten months like a fool?

And how in the hell had he allowed her to make a difference when no other woman had?

Damn! She was probably next door having a good old-fashioned laugh.

He slammed the beer bottle on the counter, almost spilling the contents on his hands and the countertop. And just to think that all the while he had been getting dressed to go over to her place for dinner, he'd barely been able to put his clothes on without thinking about when he would be taking them off with her, how his naked body would lie on top of hers, slide deep inside of her—as deep as he could go—giving her the ride of her life.

But things hadn't gone quite the way he'd wanted. Although he had slid inside of her. At least he had tried to. She had been pretty damn tight and he had enjoyed the feel of her muscles clamping around him as he tried pushing deeper, determined to be deeply embedded in her, before she'd stopped him. And he'd assumed that was because he wasn't wearing a condom.

He couldn't believe such a thing had happened. This was the first time he'd been skin to skin with any woman, and the feel of being inside of her without being sheathed in latex had every muscle in his body pulsating, even now. She probably hadn't realized it, but he had managed to stroke her at least once before pulling out.

But that was the thing. Even after realizing he wasn't wearing a condom, he hadn't wanted to pull out. He had wanted to stay in, ease deeper inside of her, feel her wetness claim him, her feminine juices saturate his erection, and press into her deeper and deeper.

She hadn't minded when he'd spread her luscious thighs wide. And she hadn't minded being taken—or almost taken—right there in her living room. He liked a woman who didn't believe lovemaking had to be confined to the bedroom. Where was it written that the bedroom was the only place two people could make love? The thought of that was so damn boring.

Hell, he'd had lots of plans for Sam tonight. The moment he'd walked into her house and saw that her place was just like his, a number of erotic scenarios had danced through his mind. He had thought about taking her on the kitchen table, in the sauna and in that damned hot tub she had tempted him with last night.

But things didn't quite work out that way. Instead, after getting him all hot and bothered, she had sent him packing with a damn smirk on her face. What she'd pulled

An Important Message from the Publisher

Dear Reader,

Because you've chosen to read one of our fine novels, I'd like to say "thank you"! And, as a special way to say thank you, I'm offering to send you two more Kimani™ Romance novels and two surprise gifts – absolutely FREE! These books will keep it real with true-to-life African American characters that turn up the heat and sizzle with passion.

Please enjoy the free books and gifts with our compliments...

Glenda Howard

For Kimani Press

Peel off Seal and Place Inside...

We'd like to send you two free books to introduce you to Kimani™ Romance books. These novels feature strong, sexy women, and African-American heroes that are charming, loving and true. Our authors fill each page with exceptional dialogue, exciting plot twists, and enough sizzling romance to keep you riveted until the very end!

KIMANI ROMANCE ... LOVE'S ULTIMATE DESTINATION

Your two books have a combined cover price of $13.98, but are yours **FREE!** We'll even send you two wonderful surprise gifts. You can't lose!

YES!

I have placed my Editor's "thank you" Free Gifts seal in the space provided at right. Please send me 2 FREE books, and my 2 FREE Mystery Gifts. I understand that I am under no obligation to purchase anything further, as explained on the back of this card.

PLACE FREE GIFTS SEAL HERE

About how many NEW paperback fiction books have you purchased in the past 3 months?

❏ 0-2
EZQE

❏ 3-6
EZQQ

❏ 7 or more
EZQ2

168/368 XDL

FIRST NAME	LAST NAME

ADDRESS

APT.#	CITY

STATE/PROV.	ZIP/POSTAL CODE

Thank You!

BUSINESS REPLY MAIL
FIRST-CLASS MAIL   PERMIT NO. 717   BUFFALO, NY

POSTAGE WILL BE PAID BY ADDRESSEE

**THE READER SERVICE
PO BOX 1867
BUFFALO NY 14240-9952**

tonight was unforgivable in his book, and just as he'd told her, it would be best for the both of them if they made it a point to avoid each other.

Chapter 13

"You okay, Blade?"

Blade glanced across the table at his cousin Reese. There was no way he would tell him that no, he wasn't okay. He'd gone to bed mad and had awakened that morning even madder. What was worse, he had gone to bed with a hard-on and had awakened with a bigger hard-on. It had taken a couple of cold showers to make his erection go down. The mere thought of how Sam had deliberately played him was something he had yet to get over, and he doubted if he ever would.

"Blade?"

He blinked and noticed both Luke and Reese were staring at him. "Yes?"

"I asked if something was wrong. You don't seem like yourself today," Reese said.

He shrugged. "You're imagining things."

The three of them had met for breakfast, and afterward,

they would return to Luke's ranch and help him with moving some furniture around. Mac had decided she wanted to redecorate, and now with the three additional bedrooms, a massive family room and a spacious kitchen that he and Slade's crew had added on six months ago, what used to be a small ranch house had become a sprawling home with a lot of room for a larger family. It wouldn't surprise Blade, when Mama Laverne talked about fish again, that the fishing rod would be aimed straight at Luke and Mac.

He glanced over at Luke to find him staring at him. "You sure you're okay, Blade?" he asked.

"I'm positive."

"Then where were you last night?" Luke asked. "Slade was trying to reach you."

Blade chuckled. "I wasn't lost. I was out. And when I returned I didn't check my messages. I called him this morning." He took a sip of his coffee and asked, "Is there a law that says I have to be home at all times?"

"No."

"Okay, then."

"Kind of touchy today, aren't you? If I didn't know better I would think you needed to get laid or something," Reese said with a grin on his face.

Blade didn't see a damn thing funny about it, mainly because he *did* need to get laid—and in a bad way. He'd never gone without sex this long and all because of one woman. How screwed up was that?

He opened his mouth, ready to give his cousin the scathing response he deserved, but Luke interrupted, eager to keep the peace. "The rodeo school is looking good, Blade."

Blade's frown turned into a smile. He always appreciated compliments about the work that he and Slade's company did, and Luke of all people knew it. "Thanks. According to Townsend, the last coat of paint will be hitting the walls next week. The only thing left will be landscaping. Any idea when the horses will arrive? I want the corral and the new barn ready before they're delivered."

Just the mention of horses got Luke talking, and Blade was grateful for the distraction. He could nod and feign interest while his mind wandered to other things—namely Samari Di Meglio.

He had gotten very little sleep last night. The worst thing he could have done was to let her mouth touch him. Even now he was getting excruciatingly hard just thinking about it. Women had gone down on him before, but never in the way she had. It was quite obvious she was a novice at that sort of thing. He could even believe that she'd never done it before. Her lack of experience had showed, but it hadn't been felt. As far as he was concerned, no pro could have done it better. There had been something about the way she had taken him in her hands, and later with her mouth, and applied the perfect amount of pressure and—

"Blade, you're daydreaming again."

He met Luke's gaze. "Am I?"

"Yes. Reese has been asking you a question for the last five minutes."

Of course, he knew Luke was exaggerating. He cut his eyes over to Reese. "Sorry. What was your question?"

Reese grinned again and Blade was tempted to knock that silly smirk off his lips. "I asked if you were headed back to Houston for the party Jake and Diamond are hosting for Rasheed and his wife this weekend."

"Yes, I'll be there."

He would leave for Houston on Friday. The women in Houston knew how to treat a man. They didn't play games or seek revenge. They weren't teases. They weren't player haters. "What about you?" he asked Reese. "When do you take over Trevor's old job?"

Reese smiled. "In a couple of months. Trevor is finalizing the projects he started. And yes, I'm headed back to Houston. In fact, I'm leaving here on Thursday to swing by Austin to get Kenna. She's going to the party with me."

Blade nodded and didn't say anything, but after taking a sip of his coffee, he decided to ask, "Has it ever occurred to you that if you ever get married, your wife probably won't take too kindly to the fact that your best friend is a woman?"

Reese leaned back in his chair. "Nope, mainly because I'd never marry a woman who didn't get along with Kenna. Would you marry someone who didn't get along with Tanner and Wyatt?"

Blade frowned. It wasn't the same and Reese damn well knew it. "Since I don't ever plan to marry I can't answer that question," he said.

"Well, I do plan to marry one of these days, although no time soon, and I would never consider marrying someone who couldn't accept my relationship with Kenna," Reese said. "And vice versa. She would never marry someone who could not accept her relationship with me."

Blade shook his head and decided to play devil's advocate. "And you know this for certain?"

"Yes. We've discussed it. Everyone has a best friend. I'm a man who just happens to have one that's a woman. No big deal."

In Blade's book it was a big deal. But if Reese and Kenna were convinced it wasn't, then who was he to argue? He glanced over at Luke. "Are you ready for us to leave and get started on your place?"

Luke nodded. "Yes. I promised Mac that when she got

home this evening I'd have at least one room finished.
And you never make Mac a promise you don't intend to
keep."

Sam had a drowsy look on her face from a sleepless
night when she walked into the office. The first person she
saw after passing through Security was Patsy, who was
leaving the building.

The young woman smiled at Sam. "More flowers came
for you today and there's a card with them," she said excitedly. "I saw the florist bring them in."

Sam gave her a slight smile and nodded as she made
her way toward the reception area. Priscilla glanced up
when she saw her and smiled. "More flowers arrived
today, Ms. Di Meglio, and there's a card with them."

"Thank you, Priscilla," she said as she made her way
down the hall toward her office. Everyone was more interested in her secret admirer than she was. In fact, she was
still trying to get over Blade's statement last night that he
hadn't been sending them. All this time she'd actually
thought he was.

Thoughts of Blade were still in her mind and had been
since last night. After he'd left her place she had picked
up every condom packet off the floor and placed them in
a drawer in her bedroom. She had actually counted
them—thirty in all. Had he honestly thought he would use
even half that number?

She rolled her eyes, thinking, yes, he probably had. If
he would have had his way, he would have humped her
all night and she would have enjoyed every minute of it.

She drew in a deep breath at her sensual confession.
Chances were she would have gone to sleep totally
relaxed, sated and satisfied. Instead, she had slid between
the sheets tense, annoyed and obsessing about what she

could have had—and all in the name of revenge. Whoever said getting even was sweet hadn't met the likes of Blade Madaris.

She opened the door to her office and her gaze immediately went to the huge arrangement sitting in the middle of her desk. These flowers were more beautiful than all the others had been, and whoever was sending them certainly had great taste. But the ones Blade had given her last night had these beat.

She walked around the desk and pulled out the drawer to put her purse inside. Then glanced up to see Peyton and Mac standing in the doorway. "We heard the flowers came with a card this time," Mac said with a huge grin on her face.

Sam rolled her sleepy eyes. "Evidently the entire office has heard about it," she said, sitting down behind her desk and leaning back in her chair, thinking she could certainly use a good eight hours' worth of sleep.

"Boy, you look tired," Peyton said, laughing. "Didn't you get any sleep last night?"

Sam glared at her friend. "Don't mess with me, Mahoney. I'm so *not* in a good mood."

Mac crossed her arms over her chest. "And why aren't you in a good mood, Sam? I thought you had a date with Blade. Didn't things go the way you had planned?"

Sam refused to answer that. Instead she snatched the card off the flowers. "I know the only reason the two of you are here is because you're dying to know who's been sending me flowers."

"Like you don't already know," Peyton said smartly, as she stepped into the office and took a chair across from Sam's desk.

"I thought I knew, but I found out last night it wasn't Blade."

Mac rolled her eyes. "You actually thought they were

from him?" she said, closing the door and then taking the chair next to the one Peyton occupied. "According to Luke, Blade never gives women flowers," she added.

Sam decided not to say anything about the fact that he had given her a beautiful arrangement last night. Instead she opened the small envelope and pulled out the card and read it.

I've been sending you flowers to enjoy while you can, because starting today your days are numbered. An old friend.

Sam reread the card, certain that what she'd read was meant to be a joke. But she couldn't stop the uneasy feeling that was running through her mind and the sweaty palms of her hands. She dropped the card on her desk and glanced over at Peyton and Mac in shock.

"Sam, are you all right?" Peyton asked, getting out of her chair. "What did the card say?"

Sam opened her mouth to speak but couldn't. Instead she shoved it toward them. Mac picked up the card. Mac and Peyton read it together and she could hear the expletives coming from Peyton's mouth.

"What the f— is going on? Who the hell is making a threat like this? Is this some kind of sick joke?"

"Peyton, calm down," Mac said, as her eyes remained glued to Sam. "Sam, do you have any idea who could have been sending you these flowers?"

Sam, still unable to speak, only shook her head. She didn't have a clue. She watched as Mac then picked up the phone on her desk and began dialing. "Yes, Detective Adams, this is Mackenzie Standfield Madaris, and you're needed over to my office immediately."

* * *

Luke handed the bottles of beer to Reese and Blade. "Thanks, guys, you deserve these. I didn't know Mac had so much stuff to move from the attic."

The phone rang and Luke reached over, checked the caller ID, smiled and picked it up. "Hello, sweetheart."

Blade and Reese watched as the smile on his face turned to anger. "When?" Then moments later he asked, "Did you call the police?"

Luke pulled in a deep breath as he stood up, already grabbing his car keys from his jeans pocket. "That's fine, I'm on my way." He hung up the phone.

"What's going on, Luke?" Reese asked, with concern in his voice.

"That was Mac. The person who's been sending Sam flowers for the past six weeks finally sent a card with them today, with a death threat."

"What!" Blade was out of the chair, almost knocking it over. "Are these the same flowers Sam thought I was sending her?"

Luke raised a brow as he grabbed his Stetson off the hat rack. "I wasn't aware she thought *you* were the one sending those flowers."

"She mentioned it last night and I assured her they weren't from me," Blade said, hot on Luke's heels as he headed for the door. Reese quickly followed Blade.

"Well, according to Mac, the card Sam got with the delivery today wasn't pretty, and said something about her days being numbered," Luke said over his shoulder as he headed for the truck. "And the two of you don't have to go with me. Hopefully, I won't be long."

"I'm going," Reese said, already opening the door and climbing inside the backseat of Luke's truck.

"And don't think for one minute I'm not going, too,"

Blade all but snarled, feeling more protective of a woman than he'd ever felt before. The same woman he'd convinced himself just last night that he didn't want to cross paths with ever again. "If it involves Sam, then I'm going."

Luke glanced over at him and nodded. "Fine."

Blade took in a deep breath as he opened the door and got in the front seat. Why he felt the need to see for himself that Sam was okay, he wasn't sure. He would figure out the reason why later.

Chapter 14

During the last thirty minutes, Sam's attitude had gone from shock to anger and then fury, evident from her use of some of Peyton's colorful expletives, which at one point had begun flowing from her mouth as if they were an everyday part of her vocabulary.

Now she had calmed down—somewhat. She had managed to prove that her temper at its best would put even her father to shame. How dare someone send her flowers for six weeks, only to inform her that now her days were numbered? The man had to be a lowlife, a scoundrel, an asshole.

"And you're sure you have no idea who could have sent you these flowers or why they want to threaten your life, Ms. Di Meglio?"

Sam glanced across the room. For a while she'd forgotten the detective had been sitting in the extra chair Priscilla had brought into her office. She'd also forgotten that

Mac and Peyton were still in her office, as well. Everyone was sitting there and staring at her.

She drew in a deep breath and returned the detective's intense gaze. She had met him a year and a half ago, when he had been investigating the trouble involving Mac. "No, Detective Adams, I have no idea who's behind those flowers and—"

At that moment her office door flew open and Sam saw Blade standing in front of her, bigger than life. Over his shoulder, she could see Luke and Reese standing behind him. The look on Blade's face was fierce, almost lethal. Detective Adams had been quick, and was already on his feet with his gun drawn.

"Wait!" three female voices said at once, although Sam's was the loudest.

It was only when Luke pushed passed Blade that Detective Adams recognized him and put his gun back in his holster and straightened his jacket. "I would suggest you knock the next time," Adams said, offering Luke his hand.

Luke grinned as he shook hands with the man. "It wasn't my idea to burst in like that. That's my cousin Blade. He's sort of a hothead at times. And this is my brother Reese."

Sam sat back down in her chair, trying to get her heart rate back to normal, as she stared across the room at Blade. She'd known he was with Luke when Mac had called, because Mac had mentioned it. But considering everything, she hadn't expected him to come.

Her gaze moved past him to Reese. She'd only seen him a few times since the wedding, and she thought there was no mistaking him and Luke for brothers, since they favored each other quite a bit. Like Luke, Reese was a very handsome man.

But no one, she thought, letting her gaze shift back to

Blade, was more handsome than the man staring back at her, even when he was mad. And yes, he was mad, but she couldn't tell if he was angry at her or the situation that she found herself in.

"I was just asking Ms. Di Meglio a few questions so I can decide how to proceed, since she prefers that I not alert the police yet. So for now, I'm working this case privately."

"Why don't you want the police involved?" Blade asked her, as if he had every right to know.

It was on the tip of her tongue to tell him it was none of his business what she did, but for some reason she couldn't do that. "I prefer that my parents not know about this," she said. "And for now, until we find out if there is a legitimate threat, I want as few people to know about it as possible."

He nodded and then leaned against a wall. There was a knock on the door and Priscilla brought in more chairs and left, closing the door behind her.

Everyone sat except for Blade. It seemed he preferred standing, bracing himself against the wall, directly in her line of vision. She tried focusing her eyes on Detective Adams instead of on him.

"Now then, we can continue," Detective Adams said. "And before we do I need to make sure you're comfortable with everyone here."

She drew in a deep breath. Although Blade was probably the last person she should have felt comfortable with, considering their history, she said, "Yes, I'm fine."

"All right then. I was asking if you have any idea who could have sent you those flowers with the card."

She shook her head. "I have no idea."

"And just how long have you been getting the flowers?" he then asked.

"About six weeks. They were delivered once a week, every Wednesday."

"Uh, they arrived a day early this week," Detective Adams said, as if making an observation.

Sam glanced over at Blade. The card had been passed around and now he was reading it. She could feel the anger raging in him. It was hard to believe his rage was directed toward her assailant and not her.

"So why didn't you contact the police when the flowers started coming?"

She shifted her gaze from Blade back to Detective Adams, who was watching her closely. "I saw no reason to."

"And why not?"

She frowned. The man was asking a lot of questions and she had to remind herself that he was merely doing his job. She met his inquisitive gaze. "Because I thought I knew who was sending them."

"And who did you think was sending them?"

"Really, Detective Adams," she said, giving him an exasperated look. "Do you need to know all that?"

"If you want me to help you stay alive."

"Yes, but—"

"I'm the one she thought was sending her the flowers," Blade said, in a voice that was deep and controlled.

Sam glanced over at him, as did everyone else in the room, including Detective Adams. He studied Blade and it was easy to tell he was sizing him up, seeing him in a whole new light. Now as a possible suspect.

"But you didn't send them?" the detective asked, his penetrating stare trained directly on Blade.

Blade stared right back. His eyes were just as unwavering. "No, I didn't send them."

"And you have no idea who did?"

"No," he stated firmly.

Detective Adams nodded before glancing back at Sam. "Do you have any reason not to believe him?"

Sam looked at Blade and studied his features, got caught up in the eyes staring back at her. Although he'd come, he was still mad. He hadn't gotten over the stunt she'd pulled last night. And in a way she probably had hurt him. Probably not emotionally, but for most men their ego was just as real as any living thing. It could easily get bruised. And then there was male pride that could be just as easily wounded. She had pretty much trampled on both. She had tried to play him the way he'd played others. Sooner or later he would try getting back at her, she had no doubt of that. But he wouldn't try it this way. He wouldn't stoop that low.

"Ms. Di Meglio?"

She blinked and looked back at Detective Adams. "Yes?"

"I asked if you had any reason not to believe Mr. Madaris." He smiled, remembering there were three of them in the room, and added, "Blade Madaris."

She shook her head. "No, there's no reason not to believe him." She then chuckled and said, "He might think he wants to wring my neck about now, but he would never intentionally hurt me."

"And you know that for sure?"

She pulled in a deep breath, refusing to acknowledge Blade's presence, and responded to the detective's question. "Yes, I know that for certain."

The muscles in Blade's neck knotted, and it had taken all he had not to hit something after reading the card that had come with the flowers. Who in the hell had sent it to her? Evidently it was the same person who'd been sending her the other flowers for six weeks. A secret admirer, so she'd thought. She had been damn wrong about that. And she had been wrong in assuming it had been him.

Detective Adams was still asking her some routine questions. She was answering them, but already Blade's mind was focused on what she wasn't telling the officer. As far as he was concerned, there were a number of men who could have put her at the top of their shit list, if what she'd claimed last night was true. She was a player hater who took pride in seeking revenge. In his book that wasn't a reason to want to bump her off, but there were a lot of people walking around who were not playing with a full deck.

Detective Adams stood and closed his writing pad. "I plan to contact the florist. I know you said the flowers were ordered over the Internet. Still, there's a way for us to track a credit-card payment."

"So what should she do now?" Mac asked.

"Watch her back," the detective replied quickly. "I know you already have a security team set up here and that's good. You might want them to make sure no one gets through unless they have appointments, and I suggest that you don't work late for a while. Leave when everyone else leaves, and if you do work late have one of the security guards walk you to your car. And you might want to—"

"Hold up. Time out," Blade interrupted. "There may be a lunatic on the loose, trying to kill her and for now it's going to be business as usual?"

Detective Adams turned to Blade. "Basically yes, since she refuses to have us make a big deal out of it. We can't get fingerprints off the card, since practically everyone's hand has been on it."

Detective Adams then turned to Sam. "Where do you live?"

"Windsor Park."

It was obvious from his expression that he was familiar with the complex and impressed. "That's a good place to live. It's a gated community, almost like a fortress. I don't know the last time anyone from the police department had to respond to a crime there. They have an excellent security system set up. The president would be safe there without the Secret Service, they're that good."

"Yes, but she isn't in that gated community twenty-four hours a day," Peyton said. "She will be pretty secure here and at home, but what about the distance in between?"

Detective Adams shrugged his shoulders. "If she doesn't want police protection, I suggest she hire a body-guard."

Moments after Detective Adams left, everyone in Sam's office sat around staring at the vase of flowers on her desk. How could something so beautiful carry such an ugly message?

Still, the flowers were pretty, a mix of fresh roses, sun-flowers, lilies, daisy poms and other varieties Sam couldn't name, and all beautifully arranged inside a green glass vase. There was nothing about the flowers that would indicate the person who'd sent them was devious rather than thoughtful.

Sam checked her watch and then pushed back from her desk to stand. She didn't want to look at the flowers any longer. "I'm going out to grab some lunch," she said.

Five pairs of eyes shifted to her and stared. She put her arms across her chest. "Don't any of you even think it."

"And what do you think we're thinking?" Luke asked.

She lifted her chin. "That one of you, possibly all of you, intend to be my shadow."

"And you have a problem with that?" Blade asked.

Sam's gaze slowly moved to him. He was glaring at her and she glared right back. She couldn't help the cynical smile that touched her lips. "What's in this for you, Blade? We're not exactly bosom buddies. In fact, the last time we talked we decided that we don't even like each other, especially after last night."

Too late she'd realized she had said the wrong thing, and quickly wondered why she'd said it at all. She had wanted to strike out at something and he was an easy target. The dark eyes staring at her became darker and his jaw tightened. His hands were opening and closing in tight fists, and she wondered if he'd decided to wring her neck, after all.

He slowly turned to the others and said in a rather calm voice, "Excuse us a moment. Sam and I need to have a private conversation."

It was on the tip on her tongue to say no, they didn't need to have anything, but then she changed her mind. It was best to get it over and done with now. She'd thought last night was the end of things, but apparently it wasn't.

None of the others, she noted, seemed inclined to hang back. Luke, however, leaned over and whispered in Blade's ear, but loud enough for everyone to hear, "Hey, man. Go easy on her. Remember, until they catch this guy you're still a suspect."

Blade's eyes sharpened, but hers rolled. She was glad when Mac all but shoved him out the door. When the door closed behind them, Sam decided to sit back down in her chair. If Blade wanted to stand during their confrontation, that was his business.

"So, what do we have to talk about?" she asked.

He didn't say anything for a long while. He just stood there and stared at her.

"Well, I'm waiting and I don't have all day, Blade."

She knew she was goading him again, deliberately being a pain in the ass. But for some reason she couldn't help it. He wasn't supposed to be here. Last night should have been the last she'd seen of him, at least for a good while. He was a player and she had played him. He was supposed to hate her guts. He should be spitting on the ground she walked on, or better yet, sticking pins in a voodoo doll that bore her likeness.

But instead he was here. He had all but burst into her office like a madman, as if he was a former lover or even her current one. The entire time Detective Adams sat asking her questions, he'd stood across the room, propped against the wall with his eyes glued to her.

"Why didn't you tell Detective Adams everything, Sam?"

She logged off her computer and then turned and looked at him. "Everything like what?"

He crossed his arms over his chest. "Like how you like getting your kicks as a player hater by playing guys. Did you ever think doing that kind of crap might catch up to you one day? Did it ever cross your mind that somewhere along the way you might have pissed some guy off big-time?"

She rolled her eyes, something she'd found herself doing a lot around him. "Hey, Blade, it's not that serious. Does every woman you dump come gunning for you?"

He came around the desk and pulled back her chair and then pinned her in with his arms braced on both sides. He leaned down, in her face, and nailed her with his gaze, as if he wanted to make sure he had her absolute attention.

"How many times do I have to tell you that the women

I get involved with know the score?" he said in a clipped tone. "I don't play those kinds of games with women. They know what I want from them. They also know what I don't want, which is a commitment of any kind. And if they somehow get it into their heads that they can change me along the way, then it's their fault for thinking it and not mine. Not all players are dogs, so don't blame me for what some other guy did to you, Sam. I don't appreciate it and I won't accept it."

A caustic comeback was just on the tip of her tongue. She thought about telling him that she didn't give a damn what he didn't appreciate or accept, but something stopped her. Maybe it was because she realized just how close those sexy and kissable lips of his were to hers. It could have been his heated breath that warmed her skin. Or maybe it was the memory of those lips on her breasts, her belly, between her legs, inside of her, that suddenly made a shudder run through her body. Whatever the reason, it didn't matter, because she was sure that he felt it, as well. He'd once said her body had the ability to send him vibes. Evidently it was doing so now. There was a change in his eyes, in his breathing and in the way he looked at her. At that moment she knew that she was his main focus.

She tried to shift her body in the chair and wished she hadn't when her knee accidentally brushed against his crotch. She felt his erection—hard and massive. Her throat tightened and she tried to look away, but found she couldn't. The gaze holding hers was intense, almost daring her to avert her eyes even a fraction. And she couldn't. Instead she sat there, staring as intently into his eyes as he was staring into hers. She felt the heat rise between her legs, wetting her panties, sending fierce sensations all the way to her womb.

And then she remembered just how it felt to have him inside of her. Although he hadn't gone in all the way, he had gone in deep and far enough for her to commit to memory what he'd felt like. At that moment, that was what her mind was dredging up. The feel of him inside of her, how her inner muscles had clamped hold of him, ready to pull everything out of him.

It would be so easy to just go ahead and reach out and unzip his pants, and pull out his aroused body part, shift her position in the chair, prop her legs on her desk if she had to, and lead him inside of her, to finish what they'd started last night. She could just imagine him gripping her hips with his hands, leaning forward, flexing his lower body to push all the way to her womb. She'd never been taken in her office before, although she'd fantasized about it several times. And he'd always been the man she figured that she would be crazy enough to risk doing such a thing with.

If the chair got to be too uncomfortable, he could always move her to the desk, spread her legs, get on top of her and pump his way inside of her. He could hold her body immobile while he thrust back and forth like nobody's business, and make her come all over the place, all over him. And likewise, he would come, too. She could just imagine the feel of his hot semen shooting inside of her.

She clenched her thighs together, wondering if a woman could have an orgasm in broad daylight just thinking about what a man could do to her. She heard herself moan and realized from the look in Blade's eyes that he'd heard it, as well. Before she could pull in her next breath he responded to her moan with a guttural growl, just seconds before slamming his mouth down on hers.

* * *

He didn't mean to kiss her. In fact, he had decided after last night that he wouldn't come within ten feet of her again. But there was something about Samari Di Meglio that got to him on a level no other woman could. She had done more than just get under his skin. She had gotten into other places in his body, as well. Places he didn't want to think about now.

Instead he wanted to concentrate on this—the taste of her, the feel of her tongue tangling with his. The sensations that having his mouth locked with hers were invoking within him—those were the things he wanted to focus on. Those were the things so clearly on his mind.

She was a hard nut to crack since she still refused to acknowledge or believe that no matter what she said, her body always told a different story. He'd known the moment she had wanted him, the moment her panties had begun getting wet. He didn't have to touch them to know it had happened. Her body had emitted a sensuous scent, an aroused scent, one he had come to know and recognize. It was a scent that pushed him to want to take things to another level, such as taste her in the most intimate way. Get inside her body and this time stay there, without any damn interruptions, whether he was wearing a condom or not.

He heard the warning bells going off in his head. They were flashing like crazy, making all kinds of loud noise. But he would deal with all that later. Right now, the only thing he wanted to deal with was this. The tastiest woman he'd ever had the pleasure of devouring.

The soft knock on the door broke them apart. He pulled back reluctantly and breathed in deeply. Then a frown covered his face. Whoever was at that door had better have a good reason for interrupting them.

"What?" he called out, and none to nicely.

The door slid open and Luke poked his head in. He glanced at both of them and Blade was certain he could clearly see Sam's kiss-swollen lips and his still-wet mouth. And Luke had the damn nerve to smile.

"Sorry for the interruption, but I'm just checking to make sure that the two of you are still alive in here, and haven't done each other in." His smile widened when he added, "It was Mac and Peyton's idea. They were worried."

Blade moved toward the window, deciding to let Sam respond to that. "As you can see, we're fine. However, we're still discussing a few things," she said.

"Okay, I'll let them know. Priscilla ordered pizza and it should be here in a few minutes. It's best eaten when it's hot."

"Fine. We'll be out shortly," Sam said.

Luke nodded and then closed the door.

Sam glanced across the room. Blade had been standing at the window, gazing out, but when Luke closed the door he had turned around with his hands in his pockets and was staring at her. She pulled in a deep breath. "I thought we settled things between us last night, Blade," she heard herself say in a shaky voice. That had been some kiss. Her body was still tingling all over from it.

Emotions she didn't want to deal with, emotions she wished would stay locked where she had kept them, were rising to the surface. She tried forcing them back under lock and key and discovered she couldn't.

"I thought so, too," he said. But for some reason she didn't think he was as confused by what had happened as she was.

"You said you wanted to talk," she reminded him.

She watched as he slowly walked back to her desk and

sat on the edge of it. Then he said, "I'm sure you have your reasons for not telling Adams everything. I don't have a full understanding of what those reasons are, but what I do know is that there are two women beyond that door who will do anything, even put their lives on the line if they had to, in order to protect you. Do you want that?"

No, she didn't. She didn't even want to think of her own life being on the line, although after reading that card she had to face the reality that there was a strong possibility it was. "No, that's not what I want," she finally said, reaching for the business card Detective Adams had left her. It was a business owned by a friend of his. She picked it up. Rowdy's Security Service. She shook her head. Security service was just another name for bodyguards.

"And do you want to do that?" he asked, glancing at the card she held. "Hire someone to be around you twenty-four hours a day?"

She glanced up at him. "No, but do you have a better idea? And I meant what I said about not wanting my parents to know. They would call in the darn National Guard if they thought for one moment my life was in danger."

Blade nodded. "You might eventually have to tell them what's going on."

"I'll cross that bridge when I come to it," she said, tossing the business card back on her desk.

Blade looked at her. "And to answer your question, yes, I think I have a better idea, and I want you to hear me out. Okay?"

She wasn't sure what his idea would be, but she was willing to listen. "Okay."

He stood, paced a few times and then turned back to her. "The way I see it, you're probably safe at work and at home. Any danger you'll face will be traveling between both places."

"Kind of."

He lifted a brow. "Kind of?"

"Yes. I do go places other than work and home, Blade. I go grocery shopping. I get my hair done once a week. I get my nails done and occasionally a pedicure. Also, when I need to, I get a wax job and—"

She stopped talking. Clamped her mouth shut. Too late she realized she'd given him too much information, especially since he knew firsthand about her Brazilian wax job in an up-close-and-personal sort of way. She cleared her throat. "Uh, you get the picture."

He met her gaze. "Yeah, I *got* the picture."

Probably more than he should have, she thought. "So as you can see I do have a life."

"And I'm sure you want to keep that life, so I propose that when you're not home or at work that we hang out."

She lifted a brow. "Hang out?"

"Yes. Since we live next door to each other, it will be easy for me to drop you off at work each day and come back and pick you up in the evenings. I can also make sure you get to all your errands."

Blood rushed through her ears upon hearing his offer. Her first impulse was to tell him where he could take his offer, almost certain that there was an ulterior motive. But then she decided to not be so quick to jump to conclusions.

"Why, Blade? Why would you waste your time doing that? You're an intelligent man, so I'm sure you know what I pulled last night was meant to break all ties between us."

He shrugged. "Breaking all ties between us is easier said than done, Sam, especially since your best friend happens to be my cousin's wife, and her husband is a man who is as close to me as a brother. When they worry about something, then I worry."

She narrowed her gaze. "So you're willing to put up with me so they won't have to worry?"

"That's the gist of it. There cannot and never will be anything between us. I think we both know that."

She glared at him. Did he have to be so brutally honest? In a way it was for the best, since they both knew where they stood. But if that was the case, then what was that kiss all about a few moments ago? He had taken her mouth like always. Nothing had changed there. Not even her response to him. Or the fact that she wouldn't mind too much if he decided to take her right now. She wasn't sure why she had this fantasy about being taken on her desk, but she did.

She shook her head, not believing the path her thoughts had taken. This was not a good day. It had started off bad and now it had ended badly. She needed a glass of wine. She needed to spend time in her sauna. A relaxing soak in her hot tub sounded real nice. She needed Blade to move away from her desk. He was too close. He definitely didn't need to be within arm's length of her again. And she certainly didn't need to see up close how aroused he still was.

She cleared her throat. "Fine, if you want to play baby-sitter, then knock yourself out."

She could tell by the expression on his face he would probably like the pleasure of knocking her out instead, given how flip her response was. But he wouldn't. Blade was not a violent man. He might be pretty pissed off with her, but he would not hurt her. She really and truly believed that.

And, she thought, glancing over at her flowers—or

rather she hoped—that the person who'd sent them wouldn't hurt her, either. She was hoping that whoever he was, he was just trying to mess with her, scare her out of her wits. He had signed the card "an old friend." She tried to remember how many players she had humiliated over the years. Now she would be racking her brain for the rest of the day and probably all night, trying to figure out who it could be.

"Ready to go? I left my car at Luke and Mac's place, which is just as well, since I'll be using yours," Blade said, breaking into her thoughts.

"Whatever. We'll take this a day at a time. I'm hoping this is all a bad joke and that nothing comes out of it."

"Trust me," he said, opening the door and then leading her out. "I'm hoping the very same thing."

The man picked up the phone on the first ring. "Is there a problem?"

"The flowers were delivered with a card this time."

He rolled his eyes. "I'm well aware of that," he said, trying to keep his voice calm. The woman was getting on his nerves. "You said you understood why I have to do what I'm doing, and that I had your full support. Are you changing your mind now?"

"No."

He smiled. "Good. And I'll have something special for you when I see you again. And remember, no matter what, we're in this thing together. All I want to do is shake her up a little bit, scare her some. Once that's over, our life together can begin."

The lie coming from his lips was bittersweet. First, he would take care of Samari Di Meglio, and then *she* would be next. He couldn't risk anyone ever finding out he was the mastermind behind everything. He had waited years for this opportunity.

"Love you," he said, repeating another lie in a deep, husky bedroom voice, trying to remind her of what had happened between them the last time they'd been together, and how good things were between them when she did what he asked.

"Love you, too."

He knew she did, and he would play it for all it was worth to get the results he wanted.

Chapter 15

"I can't believe I ate so much pizza."

Blade started the car and couldn't help looking down at Sam's legs. Not for the first time he thought they were definitely a luscious pair. He had been between them three times and there was still unfinished business. He still didn't know how they would feel pinned around his back while he was locked inside her body, rocking them toward one hell of an orgasm. He felt his lower body swell just thinking about it.

He tracked his gaze from her legs up to her face and saw that her eyes were close. And as if she felt him looking at her, she opened them and glanced over at him. She lifted a brow. "Well?"

He swallowed. "Well what?"

She rolled her eyes. "Can you believe I ate so much pizza?"

He couldn't help but chuckle. Hell, yeah, he could

believe it, since he was watching each and every time she slid a slice into her mouth, recalling how she had used that same mouth on him. "Yes, I can believe it. I saw you." He would tell her that much. "Evidently you were hungry."

She nodded. "I was. I skipped breakfast and figured I'd get a bite to eat later. As you know, that didn't happen."

Yes, he knew.

When she closed her eyes again he backed out of the parking lot. They rode in silence, and when he came to the first traffic light, he glanced back over at her. Her eyes were still closed, so he lowered his gaze to her thighs. Her skirt had inched up when she'd buckled her seat belt. He liked seeing her thighs, but definitely needed to say something to her about wearing those short skirts.

He chuckled to himself, thinking he really didn't have the right to tell her how to dress, and knowing Sam, she wouldn't hesitate to let him know it. It wasn't as if they were involved or anything.

Then what the hell was he doing becoming her chauffeur? Her personal bodyguard? Frankly, he didn't have a problem with the latter, he thought as he drove the car through traffic. If anyone needed to guard her body it might as well be him. Not that he could lay claim to it or anything. It was just the principle of the thing. He smiled, wondering just what that principle was.

"What's with the smile?"

He glanced over at her. She had awakened from her nap. "Nothing important." Then to change the subject he asked, "And what time do you plan on going into the office tomorrow?"

He watched as she drew in a deep breath before running her hands through her hair, to take advantage of the breeze that was coming in through the window.

"Good thing you asked," she said. "I have an eight-o'clock appointment. Will that be a problem for you?"

He didn't want to tell her he usually didn't get up before eight. So instead he lied. "No, that won't be a problem. Will you need to stop somewhere for breakfast before you get to the office?"

She shook her head. "No, I usually prepare my own breakfast."

He nodded, thinking it would be nice, since he was driving her into the office, if she invited him to join her for breakfast. When time passed and she didn't issue an invitation, he figured he wouldn't be getting one.

When he came to another traffic light he glanced over at her and saw she'd closed her eyes again. Evidently, she hadn't gotten any more sleep last night than he had.

At that moment, he couldn't help but wonder just what kind of relationship she had with her parents. She'd mentioned that they had attended Luke and Mac's wedding, but then so had more than five hundred other people. Besides, he had spent his time checking out the single women and not older married couples.

However, he did recall seeing Sam's brother, although the two of them hadn't been officially introduced. What he had seen was the way the man had watched Peyton every chance he got. He wasn't the only one who'd noticed. Of course, Wyatt and Tanner had been checking Peyton out for themselves, had picked up on his territorial actions and figured it was best to keep their distance. Sam's brother didn't look like a person anyone would want to tangle with over a woman.

When he made the turn into the complex, he noticed Sam's eyes were open and she glanced around. "We're home already?"

A hot, tingling sensation shot through his midsection

with her response. She made it sound as if they were a couple who were going to the same place, to eat together, tangle between the sheets and eventually fall asleep together. It was hard to explain, but playing house with her didn't sound so bad.

"Yes, we're almost there," he said, "just as soon as we get through Security."

A short while later, as they drove toward the area where their town houses were located, slowing down almost to a crawl for the speed bumps, Blade glanced over at her. "You aren't planning on going back out any more tonight, are you?"

"No, I'm in. I need to get all the sleep I can."

So did he, but he had a feeling sleep wouldn't come easily again tonight.

"Thanks for bringing me home, Blade, and you didn't have to walk me to the door."

He came and stood beside her, much too close for her peace of mind. "Yes, I did. And I'm going to check out the inside, as well," he said in that throaty voice that gave her goose bumps.

"Do you really think that's necessary?" she couldn't help but say as she worked her key into the lock.

"Considering everything that's happened today, yes, I do."

She decided not to argue with him. Instead, after opening the door she moved aside to let him enter first. She walked in behind him and closed the door, watching as he moved around checking the rooms downstairs. She had tossed her purse on the table when he walked into her kitchen and dining-room area. When he returned and headed up the stairs, she felt a tightening in her stomach. She wasn't sure how she felt about him being in her bedroom. That was really invading her personal space. Kicking off her heels, she quickly moved to follow him.

"Really, Blade, is all this necessary?"

He barely glanced over his shoulder. "You asked me that before and I told you that it was."

When they made it to the landing he glanced around. "Did you know the design of your town house is identical to mine?"

"I figured it would be."

He kept walking, looking into the bedrooms he passed. "How do you like having a sauna?" he asked.

"It's nice." Then she frowned. "If someone is in here, then our talking out loud has taken away the element of surprise. I hope you know that."

Instead of responding he shrugged his muscular shoulders and kept walking. When he got to her bedroom he paused in the doorway and glanced around. She couldn't help wondering what he was thinking, with all the shades of pink and gray. She loved the decor of her bedroom and had bought the furnishings using the money from the first case she'd won. All the pieces of her furniture, including her California-king-size four-poster bed, had been hand crafted by a furniture designer out of North Carolina named Dwight Chesley.

"Nice bedroom."

She looked up at Blade. "Thanks, but I'm sure if you've seen one, you've seen them all," she said, making light of his compliment.

"For some reason this one is different."

She forced herself not to say it was probably the first bed belonging to a woman that he hadn't been in, but decided not to do so. It was getting late and she was tired. The day had been overwhelming to say the least.

Instead she said, "Now that you've satisfied your cu-

riosity, I'll walk you to the door." And instead of waiting
for him to move, she began walking back down the hall
and then down the stairs. He didn't immediately follow
her and she could only assume that he felt the need to
check out her master bath, as well. When he finally joined
her downstairs, she was waiting beside the front door.

"I input my phone number on your landline under *B*,"
he said. "Hand me your cell phone for a second."

Rolling her eyes, she moved to the sofa to get it out of
her purse, and walked back over and handed it to him. She
watched as he entered his name and phone numbers—
both for his cell phone and landline—into her Black-
Berry. He then handed it back to her.

"Now I need your numbers," he said, taking his phone
out the pocket of his jacket. She gave them to him and
moments later he returned his own BlackBerry to his
pocket.

He met her gaze. "I guess I don't have to tell you to be
careful opening the door for anyone you really don't know."

She forced her eyes not to roll. "No, you don't have to
tell me, although you've done it anyway."

He frowned and crossed his arms over his chest. "You
like having a smart mouth, don't you?"

"I don't know. Do I?"

His frown deepened. "Keep it up and I'm going to get
pissed."

She couldn't help but inwardly smile at that. "Mmm,
what else is new, Blade? Same place—" she looked at her
watch "—and almost the same time. Seems like your
mood is a repeat of last night."

When she saw anger flicker in his eyes, she drew in a
deep breath and then said, "Look, sorry I brought up
anything about last night. I'm not in a good mood right
now. I'm tired, sleepy, aggravated and—"

"Trying to make the best of a difficult situation."

She was. And the fact that he knew it almost was too much for her. All day she'd tried being strong, but now she felt vulnerable. Knowing there was someone out there who wanted to do her harm had her stomach in knots, and it had taken everything she had to fight back her fears. She was a Di Meglio, she had come from a long line of Italians and Africans who were mighty and invincible. Brave to a fault. Not a coward among them and she was determined not to be the first.

"If you want to get to the office by eight, then we need to leave here no later than seven-thirty," he said.

She nodded. "I'll be ready. And I'm doing breakfast if you'd like to drop in. It will be ready around six-thirty."

"Thanks, but fair warning. I'm not a morning person, Sam."

She shook her head and glanced down as a chuckle erupted from her throat. She glanced back up at him and smiled. "Neither am I, but I can do a good job at faking it."

The smile that touched his lips—those incredible lips—she thought, was refreshing. His eyes held hers for the longest time and then he reached out and touched her cheeks. The fingertips touching her skin felt warm, soothing…caring. She inhaled deeply at the thought that there was a slight possibility that he did care. He might not want to, but he did anyway. Otherwise, he would not be here now. She couldn't help but find that interesting.

"Try to get some rest," he said. He leaned closer and brushed a kiss across her lips and whispered, "Good night."

"Good night, Blade."

When she opened the door to let him out, a private security patrol car was driving by, making its rounds.

Seeing the patrol car made her feel safe and secure. As she watched Blade walk down her steps and head next door to his own place, she suddenly felt so terribly lonely.

Blade pulled off his jacket and tossed it aside, then picked up the phone to retrieve his messages after seeing the light blinking. He checked the first number and saw the call had been from Alex. He hit the speed-dial button to return the call.

"Alex, this is Blade. Did you try reaching me?"

"You're not picking up on your cell phone. What's up with that?"

Blade pulled in a deep breath. "I was in a meeting," he said, thinking of the time he'd spent in Sam's office while Detective Adams had asked her questions. "What's going on?"

"I never got the chance to thank you for helping out at A.C.'s birthday party last month."

A.C. was the nickname for Alex and Christy's daughter, Alexandria Christina, who had turned two last month. Alex and Christy had asked him to be the cameraman at the party when the one they'd hired became ill. Blade hadn't minded filling in, since it had been better than playing lifeguard at the kiddy pool as he'd done the previous year.

Blade smiled. "No problem, although I wouldn't want to do it again anytime soon."

Alex chuckled. "Does that mean I can't pass your name on to Sir Drake? His daughter will be celebrating her first birthday soon and I'm sure they'll want a bunch of pictures."

"Hey, don't do me any favors."

Alex laughed. "Will we see you this weekend at Jake and Diamond's party?"

Blade rubbed a hand over his face. In his haste to volunteer as Sam's bodyguard, he'd forgotten all about the fact that he was supposed to return to Houston this weekend for the party Jake and Diamond were hosting for Rasheed. He would have to think of what to do about Sam while he was gone. He couldn't talk her into going to the ranch with Mac and Luke, since they'd made plans to attend the party in Houston, as well. The Madarises liked to party, and enjoyed any excuse for a family gathering.

"Yes, I plan to come."

"I'll see you then, and again thanks for taking care of the pictures at A.C.'s party. You took some real good shots and all of them came out great. I owe you one for agreeing to do it on such short notice," Alex said, regaining Blade's attention.

"I might be collecting on that IOU sooner than you think," he said. "A woman I know is getting flowers."

Alex laughed. "And?"

"She doesn't know who's sending them."

"I'm sure they aren't coming from you. And I can't imagine you getting jealous about someone sending a woman you're messing around with flowers, since jealousy isn't one of your attributes. Sounds like she has a secret admirer. Why do you care? What's the problem?"

He glanced out the window at the lake. It was just beginning to get dark and there was a breeze in the air that was stirring the waters. "The problem is that her secret admirer threatened to kill her."

"Damn. That doesn't sound good. Who is this woman?"

"Samari Di Meglio. She's one of Mac's law partners."

"I've met Sam. A nice person. She's also a looker."

Blade smiled. Since he knew just how much Alex loved and adored his wife, he knew his comment was nothing more than a compliment. "Yes, she is."

"Call me tomorrow so we can talk about it. And by the way, in case you hadn't heard, Mama Laverne dreamed about fish again."

Blade rolled his eyes toward the ceiling. "What's going on with her? Why can't she have normal dreams like everybody else?"

Alex laughed. "Depends on what you consider normal dreams. Hell, I would hate for her to start having any of yours."

Blade couldn't help but chuckle at the thought of that, and quickly concluded that Alex was right. He would hate for the old gal to start having any of his dreams. They would turn her gray hair grayer. Hell, she just might wake up the next morning completely bald.

"And just so you know, all eyes are on Clayton and Syneda."

Blade almost got weak in the knees at that announcement. "I hope you're bullshitting me, Alex."

"Sorry, but I'm not."

Blade shook his head. Clayton and Syneda, the attorneys in the family, and a power couple if there ever was one, already had a daughter, eight-year-old Remington, who was definitely a handful, and that was putting it mildly. The thought of adding another child to their already chaotic household was a bit much.

Moments after his conversation with Alex ended, Blade returned calls to his brothers Slade and Jantzen. Both wanted to give him the scoop about the stork possibly visiting Clayton and Syneda again, just in case he hadn't heard.

It was close to eleven when he finally headed upstairs to take a shower and try to get some sleep. He'd seen security patrolling the area when he'd left Sam's place, and he felt good about it. He also felt good that he was right next door if she needed him.

Sometime tomorrow he would call and talk to Alex and tell him what he knew. Alex was a former FBI agent who owned a private investigation firm and was good at what he did. Hell, Alex wasn't just good. His ability to solve cases was legendary.

If anyone could find out who the person was behind the threat to Sam's life there was no doubt in Blade's mind it was Alex.

Chapter 16

Daylight was just beginning to break when Sam finished her shower. After toweling dry she slipped into her robe to go downstairs to start a pot of coffee.

Even after all the drama of yesterday, she had been able to get some sleep. She was certain the glass of wine she'd had before finally going upstairs to shower and dress for bed had helped.

As strange as it seemed, she had felt a measure of comfort knowing Blade had been in her bedroom. The man had a way of being a part of her fantasies whether she wanted him to be or not.

With the coffee brewing she was about to head back upstairs, when she remembered she had left her purse on the sofa, and that when Blade had returned her Black-Berry after inputting his phone number, she'd noticed that she had missed a call. She had totally forgotten about it until now.

Taking her BlackBerry from her purse, she saw the missed call had come from Peyton's private number at the office. Sam pressed the button to listen.

"Sam, this is Peyton. After you guys left I hung back to get some work done and happened to be here when your eight-o'clock appointment called to cancel. I thought I'd let you know so you wouldn't get up so early to come into the office. After everything that happened today, you need your rest. In fact, if you want to just take the whole day off and chill, then do so. Mac and I can handle things here. Love you. Bye."

After Sam ended the voice-mail message she breathed a deep sigh. She wished she'd checked her messages last night and then she wouldn't be up so early this morning. Oh, well, since she was already up, she might as well stay up, and she just might take Peyton's advice and work from home today and get some rest.

Then she remembered Blade. It was too late to call and let him know about her change in plans. He would be knocking on her door for breakfast in about a half hour. Since she was up, she might as well prepare breakfast as planned. Besides, she was hungry. All the activity in her dreams last night had made her ravenous.

She headed upstairs to get dressed and tried to suppress the thought running through her mind that she was actually looking forward to seeing Blade.

A scowl covered Blade's face as he locked his front door to head over to Sam's place. It was quiet, barely daybreak. Yet when he'd glanced out his bedroom window at the park, he'd seen a number of people who were up and walking or jogging. Hell, why anyone in their right mind would be up at this time of morning was beyond him.

He glanced at his watch. It was a minute shy of six-thirty. He had gotten some sleep last night, but not a whole lot. After he'd taken his shower and gotten into bed, he'd received more phone calls from family members. Now that the word was out that Clayton and Syneda were expecting, everyone was making bets as to where this child might have possibly been conceived. It was a family joke that Remington was conceived in an elevator. There was no telling with this one, since from what he gathered, Clayton and Syneda had an active and adventurous sex life.

Some wondered whether the baby would be a boy or girl. Frankly, he thought Remington was all the daughter Clayton could handle. But others in the family felt that it would serve Clayton right to have another girl, given his playboy bachelor days. Blade chuckled, his sense of humor returning for the first time since learning of the threat to Sam's life.

He glanced around before walking up the steps to her front door. This particular cul-de-sac was quiet. Most of the people had money and could afford the exclusive lifestyle. Even though Windsor Park was supposed to be one of the safest neighborhoods in the city, he still intended to be very cautious, and hoped that Sam would do the same. She might think this was no big deal, but he wouldn't make that mistake.

He figured the reason he was so hell-bent on keeping her safe was that there was still unfinished business between them. And although she assumed that the stunt she'd pulled Monday night was the end of things between them, he had no intention of letting her walk away so easily. She needed to understand that a Madaris man wasn't someone to toy with. And when all this was over, he would deal with her in his own way.

After knocking on her door, he didn't have long to wait for it to open. His eyes slid over her, noticing just how good she looked barefoot and in a pair of cutoff jeans and a tank top. She was definitely not dressed for work.

"I hope you're not thinking of wearing that to the office," he said, trying to keep his eyes from staring at her cleavage, peeking out from the vee of her tank top. She had nice breasts and it didn't take much for him to be reminded of how they looked and tasted.

"Of course not. I decided to work at home today," she said, walking away and leaving him standing in the doorway.

He slowly ran his hands down his face. She had decided to work at home? Had he known, he could have gotten at least three or four more hours of sleep. "Excuse me," he said, walking over the threshold and closing the door behind him with a little more force than necessary. "But did you not tell me you had to be in the office at eight this morning?"

She turned around and he realized that she had noticed the frown on his face. "Yes, I did tell you that. However, Peyton called and left a message on my phone last night that my eight-o'clock appointment had canceled. Only problem is that I didn't retrieve the message until a short while ago. I figured since you were probably already up, the least I could do was go ahead and fix you breakfast."

Then, as if that settled it, she tossed her curly hair over her shoulders, turned back around and continued walking toward the kitchen.

The man really was a grouch in the mornings, Sam thought, as she returned to the kitchen to finish preparing breakfast. She hoped he was hungry, since she had cooked a lot of food, and had even made biscuits from scratch. According to Mac, Luke ate a big meal in the morning, so Sam could only assume most men did.

She was standing at the stove frying bacon when she heard Blade enter the kitchen. She decided not to turn around just yet. Let him continue to stew quietly. One of the first things she noticed when she'd opened the door was just how good he looked. This was the first time she had seen him wearing casual clothes. His jeans actually looked well-worn—even had a rip in the knee—although she wasn't sure if the tear was from a designer or the real thing. His T-shirt, which fit him like a muscle shirt, was a walking advertisement for his construction company. And he still had that just-woke-up look, which was sexy as hell.

"Need help with anything?"

Now, that question made her turn around. When did a man offer to help in the kitchen? She knew from experience that her father always conveniently disappeared when it was time to do the dishes. And her brother was just as bad.

"What can you do?" she asked.

"Just about anything you can."

Now, that was a challenge if ever she'd heard one. The Di Meglio men avoided the kitchen every chance they got, but the women definitely knew their way around it, even blindfolded. "You think so?"

He leaned against one of the kitchen counters and crossed his legs at the ankle. "I'm sure there are some dishes you could probably make better than me, but I'm confident that I can hold my own."

Sam turned and removed the frying pan from the stove before turning back to him. She took the bacon out of the frying pan and placed it on a platter. "You want to explain how that came about?"

She glanced up at the exact moment a smile touched his lips. "Easily," he said. "Felicia Laverne Madaris, my great-grandmother. She made sure all her sons, grandsons and great-grandsons knew their way around the kitchen, regardless of whether we wanted to or not. Some of us fared better than others, but all of us have our specialties. Luke has his casseroles and Slade is the best when it comes to preparing a well-balanced meal any time of day."

She nodded. "And what's your specialty?"

He smiled broadly, which gave Sam a sensation like a shot to the bottom of her belly. "I can handle just about anything," he said in a deep, husky tone. "But my specialty is desserts."

She felt the heat settle between her legs and felt the tips of her breasts harden against her top. She swallowed deeply, wondering if he could gauge her body's reaction to his words. *Desserts.* That would always be a hot topic for them. She couldn't hear the word without thinking of a parked car, being physically aroused and having oral sex.

She looked away from him and began cleaning the frying pan before putting it in the dishwasher. She knew she had to say something or the heat between them would steam up her kitchen.

"Ahh, if you still want to help, you can go ahead and set the table," she said.

"Sure thing."

She could hear the sound of his footsteps across the kitchen floor, then him opening her cabinets, removing dishes, glasses and eating utensils. She then went to the refrigerator to take out the orange juice. The blast of cool air was just what she needed, but it did nothing to alleviate the tingling sensation that was still pulsing between her legs. She probably needed a cold shower to get rid of that. He hadn't been in her house more than ten minutes—ten nerve-racking minutes—and already her body was betraying her.

She inhaled a deep breath as she closed her refrigerator door. She would get through breakfast with him this morning, even if it killed her.

Blade was convinced that this was one breakfast he wouldn't survive, since Sam's outfit was practically killing him. Talk about being hot. He'd always thought she had gorgeous legs, but he was really starting to go crazy over those luscious brown thighs. And when she bent over to put the frying pan in the dishwasher, he had actually seen her rounded cheeks. Of course, there was the memory of having gone halfway inside her that was driving him crazy, making his erection throb uncontrollably.

Deciding it was best to shift his gaze elsewhere to get his sex-obsessed thoughts under control, he looked at her china and studied the pattern. Not that he really cared, but it was better than standing there and drooling over her. He thought the design was pretty, just like her. His great-grandmother once said you could tell a lot about a woman by the dishes she used.

He studied the plate in his hand. It was a cool green. He could see that the smooth, transparent surface of the china was made with fine craftsmanship and beauty. And those were the same qualities he saw in her.

"How are things coming over there?"

He glanced at her. His eyes traced her body, from her painted toes to the tousled hair on her head. She was curvy, downright luscious looking. Her beauty was enough to steal his breath and make him proud he was a man. He was determined more than ever to finish what they'd started two nights ago.

Sexual tension was building between them and he knew she could feel it just as he could. She was standing in the middle of the kitchen with platters in her hand, looking both sexy and domestic. He looked surprised when he saw how much food was on the platters. Had she expected to feed an army?

"Everything is all set," he said, finally finding his voice as he placed the last fork down beside a plate. He glanced at the table set for two and thought he hadn't done a bad job.

She walked over to him and put one of the warm platters in the middle of the table, then looked up at him. "I'm impressed. The table looks nice."

"Thanks."

"There's a half bath around the corner if you want to wash up," she said.

"All right."

He headed to the bathroom, wondering how he would get through this meal. Somehow he would, and then he would leave and go back to his place and get the sleep he'd been cheated out of.

Sam's eyes lingered on Blade as he left the kitchen. It was only then that she released a deep breath and let her fingers relax enough to set the other platter down on the table. She didn't have to ask herself what there was about being in the same room with him that made her feel this way. The man oozed sexiness in a way no other man could. And it didn't help matters when she looked into his eyes, or caught him staring at her. It was at those times that she could vividly recall intimate moments between them, sensual confessions they had shared.

She quickly walked back to the refrigerator to get the bottle of orange juice. The best thing to do was to keep him occupied with idle chitchat, she thought, and once breakfast was over, he would leave and she would get to work reading the case files that Patsy had dropped off last week.

She glanced up when Blade returned. "You drink orange juice, right?"

"Yes. And over breakfast I need to talk to you about a couple of things."

She arched an eyebrow. "What?"

"The threat on your life."

She chuckled lightly as she came back to the table. She sat down after filling their glasses with juice. "Getting tired of your babysitting gig already?"

He took the chair across from her. "No. I just don't like not knowing who and what we're dealing with. That's why I talked to Alex."

She paused and reached for a slice of bacon. "Alex?"

"Yes, Alex Maxwell. Remember him?"

She nodded. "Yes. I don't want to think what could have happened to Mac if he hadn't figured things out," she said.

"Alex has agreed to help us, but I need you to be up front with him and tell him everything, Sam. You need to tell him about all those guys you didn't mention to Detective Adams. He will need names."

"The only reason I didn't mention anything about them to Detective Adams is because I don't think there's a connection."

"Maybe not, but we need to let Alex check things out and decide that."

"And he's willing to help?" she asked.

"Yes, he's willing to help investigate."

What Blade didn't tell her and what he himself hadn't wanted to dwell on was the reason Alex was willing to do it. It was simple. Alex was doing it because he'd asked him to. They were family and if Blade had come to him with concerns about Sam's safety, then that pretty much sealed it. Although Alex hadn't said anything, he knew Sam wasn't like those other women Blade had messed around with. For some reason, Sam meant something to him.

"But what if this was just a joke? And someone is doing what Detective Adams said, just trying to ruffle my feathers?" Sam asked, breaking into his thoughts.

As far as Blade was concerned Sam's questions were timely and necessary. He still wasn't ready to think about his relationship with Sam. He wasn't even ready to consider the possibility that they even had a relationship. And he was certain that she would be the first to deny one existed.

He leaned back in his chair. "And do you really think that?"

She slowly chewed her bacon. "I honestly don't know what to think, Blade."

The frustration in her voice touched him. He was tempted to get up and pull her into his arms and hold her, whisper in her ear that as long as there was life in his body, nothing would ever happen to her.

He took in a sharp breath. He was confused at how he was thinking, shocked by how he was feeling. He grabbed his glass of orange juice and almost finished it in one swallow. It would have been better had it been a glass of cold beer.

"I think the worst thing we can do is to not do anything and assume that note is the end of it and we won't hear from him again. Whether this guy plans to take things further or not doesn't matter." His tone then turned somewhat angry. "I want to know who he is regardless. I don't want him to get away with what he's done."

And he won't get away with it, Blade thought, as he continued to eat. Whoever the guy was, he had gone too far and Blade was determined to let him know it.

"You said you had a couple of things to discuss with me. That's one. What's the other?"

He glanced over at Sam. And suddenly his mouth almost went dry when she licked a crumb off her lip with her tongue. He straightened in his chair when he felt his erection straining against his zipper.

"I want to talk to you about this weekend," he said.

She raised a brow. "This weekend?"

"Yes. I'm leaving town for the weekend, heading back to Houston."

"Oh."

"I'm attending that party Jake and Diamond are hosting for Sheikh Rasheed Valdemon and his bride. I want you to come with me."

A look came across her face. He could tell she was surprised by what he'd said. Hell, he could understand that, since he was surprised by what he'd said, as well. For him to bring a woman to a family function was something he would hear about for the rest of his life. It would set a precedent. It would start all kinds of speculations. It would give his great-grandmother the idea that she should start looking for a dress to wear to his wedding. Hell, it would set off all those rumors he'd rather not deal with. But for some reason he wanted Sam with him. If only so he could continue to protect her. If he left her here he would only worry, so it stood to reason that she should come with him. It made perfect sense.

Evidently it didn't make perfect sense to her, if the

expression on her face was anything to go by. "Do you have a problem going to Houston with me this weekend?" he asked her.

"Yes."

Her response had been quick and he wasn't sure just how much he liked that. "Why?"

She set her fork down. "Because for some reason you've gotten it into your head that I can't look out for myself, Blade. I am well aware that I need to be cautious until I find out who sent those flowers and that note. But I refuse to become dependent on a man. I appreciate you being here and wanting to make sure I'm okay, but we agreed it was only so that Peyton, Mac and Luke wouldn't worry. I don't think we should get carried away with anything."

Too late, he thought. They had already gotten carried away. He had done some things with her he hadn't done with any other woman, and being inside her body without a condom was just one of them. And the crazy thing about it, as strange as it sounded and as unwise as he knew it was, his shaft was bursting to get back inside of her, just that same way.

"Want some more juice?" Sam asked when she noticed his glass was empty.

"Yes. Thanks."

Sam lifted the pitcher off the table and poured him a glass. She wondered how and why he'd made an offer like that. Take her to Houston with him? And just where was she supposed to stay when she got there? She knew he had a condo, but did he actually expect them to stay under the same roof? All night? And what would his family think if they did?

And why was every muscle in her body, every fiber, oozing with a need that was as intense as anything she'd ever experienced? The sensations running through her had her almost to the breaking point, but she still refused to give in. She was a tough nut to crack—stubborn to a fault. A die-hard Di Meglio.

But as she sat there and watched Blade butter his toast, she knew she was in deep trouble.

Chapter 17

"Since you prepared breakfast I'll clean up the kitchen," Blade said as he stood to start clearing the table.

Sam stoodm as well. "That's not necessary. It's the least I can do, since you got out of bed early for nothing."

"No problem," he said, walking toward the sink with dishes in his hand. "Any inconvenience was repaid two-fold. You outdid yourself with breakfast." And he really meant it. He'd never eaten eggs so fluffy and she'd even baked homemade biscuits.

"There's no way I'm going to let you clean all this up by yourself, Blade," she said when she reached his side.

He turned to face her. Stared into her eyes and said, "Yes, you are, because I need the space right now."

Sam swallowed as she noted the look in his eyes. It was hot, full of lust. So much that it nearly took her breath away. She took a step back. "In that case maybe you should leave. I can handle things here."

"No. Let me do this. Just leave me alone for a while. I'm sure there are other things you have to do."

"Yes, I did bring some files home with me."

"Then how about going and read them."

A furious expression crossed her face. "Now look here, Blade. You don't tell me what to do."

"No, *you* look here, Sam," he said, lowering his gaze downward toward his crotch.

She followed the direction of his eyes and gave a sharp gasp. He had a massive erection, bigger than she'd ever seen before, and it was pressing hard again his zipper.

Her gaze slowly returned to his face, then roamed over it. His eyes were like dark orbs glinting with fire, his nostrils were flaring and his lips were tight.

"It was hard as hell getting through breakfast with you sitting there," he said in a low and husky tone. "Watching you eat. Seeing you chew your food and lick the syrup off your biscuits. Remembering."

She drew in a deep breath and knew exactly what he'd remembered…her going down on him. "I think I'll go up to my office and read those case files after all," she said, slowly backing away. "Thanks for cleaning up, and you can let yourself out when you're through."

Her heart skipped several beats as she quickly walked out of the kitchen.

Instead of going into her office to read, Sam decided to stretch out on her bed. She had opened the blinds to let in some sunlight and had turned on the radio so that soft music played in the background. Then she tried focusing on the case file she'd grabbed out of her briefcase, and not on the man downstairs in her kitchen.

An hour or so later, she could no longer concentrate

on what she was reading, and dropped the papers as her head fell back on the mattress in frustration. Did Blade think he was the only one who'd had a hard time eating this morning? Well, he didn't know the half of it. If he was watching her, did he not notice her watching him? She'd felt like a fool sitting there staring at his mouth each time he put a cup of coffee or a glass of juice to his lips.

And talk about licking something. What about the time her gaze had followed him when he'd stuck his tongue out to lick jelly from the corner of his mouth? Didn't he realize seeing that had been a real turn-on for her?

She flipped on her back and stared up at the ceiling. In all her twenty-eight years she'd never encountered the likes of a man like Blade Madaris. He could be angry with her one minute and then give her a look that said he wanted to make passionate love to her the next.

If they continued on like this, allowing sexual tension and lust, not to mention anger, to rule their senses, then where would that lead? She knew the answer to that question without thinking about it: right to the nearest bedroom to work it out.

With all the planning she'd done, her elaborate scheme, she still hadn't gotten rid of him. Blade Madaris was like the Energizer Bunny that keeps going and going and going. She closed her eyes and groaned when she felt a twitch between her legs.

She opened her eyes and decided to think logically about the situation. The first thing she needed to know and understand was why he was there. After what she'd done Monday night she would think he'd be miles away from her, jumping for joy at the thought that someone wanted to bump her off. Instead, he was staying close and had re-arranged his schedule to become her bodyguard.

She glanced at the clock on her nightstand. It had been

more than an hour since breakfast. Why was it taking him so long to tidy up the kitchen? She eased to the side of the bed, thinking that perhaps he'd left already and just hadn't told her that he was leaving. After all, she *had* told him to let himself out when he finished cleaning the kitchen.

But regardless of what she'd said, the decent thing for him to have done was to let her know he was leaving, if for no other reason than she could reset the security alarm. Slipping into her flats, she made her way down the hall and quietly walked down the stairs.

When she reached the bottom floor she walked through to the kitchen and found it spotless. Even the stainless-steel appliances had been wiped clean and were gleaming. She left her kitchen and headed for her front door to reset her alarm. She stopped and stared as butterflies fluttered in her lower belly. Blade was there, stretched out on her sofa, asleep.

The first thought that came to mind was why hadn't he gone back to his place and slept on his own sofa? And then she knew. As much as they didn't fully understand it, there was this pull that kept yanking them back together no matter how upset, angry and frustrated they got with each other. She had tried brushing him off, dissing him, setting him up for humiliation and deliberately getting on his nerves, and he was still here.

And it was time that at least one of them found out why.

She figured she should wake him, but decided against it. They would talk when he woke up on his own. Right now, she just wanted to look at him while he slept.

His breathing was deep and even and his chest moved with every breath. He was lying flat on his back with one leg thrown to the side, nearly hanging off the sofa. His zipper was facing her and she could tell he was no longer as aroused as he had been before, but still big. He had taken off his shoes but had kept his socks on.

Her gaze moved back to his face. His lower jaw seemed more prominent today. Probably because of the slight shadow covering it, which indicated he hadn't taken the time to shave before coming over. And his lips, those lips she enjoyed looking at so much, seemed to move slightly with every breath he took.

She also slept on her back and had once read an article that said people who sleep on their backs were confident and ready to tackle life. It also said they were vain and happy with their physical appearance and were always up for trying something new, both in and out of bed. Hmm, now that was definitely a thought.

Just watching him lying there filled her with a sense of desire she hadn't known possible. The man was smoldering with sensuality of the fieriest kind. There was nothing about him that didn't turn her on, whether he was in clothes or out of them.

Taking a deep breath, she was about to turn around when she heard him groan. She looked back at his face and saw his eyes were still closed, but there was an odd expression on his face, as if he'd gotten swept up in some sort of dream. He moaned again, and as she slid her gaze lower, she saw his T-shirt had risen to uncover a little of his tummy. The hair covering the area was curly and appeared soft to the touch. Her eyes moved a little lower and his erection began to swell right before her eyes.

From her studies in college, she recalled that according to Freud's theories, the reason people dreamed was to release hidden urges and secret desires they weren't allowed to express in real life.

She swallowed, and wondered just what kind of dream Blade was having when he groaned again, a grunt that almost sounded like a growl this time. She knew she should leave him, let him do whatever it was he was doing in private, and turned away. However, the moment she did so, he groaned out her name in a fevered pitch. "Samari."

She turned around quickly and stared at him. His eyes were still closed, but an intense look of pleasure covered his face. And she knew at that moment that whatever dream he was having, she was part of it.

Chapter 18

*I*n the deep, dark recesses of his slumber, Blade pulled at Sam's hair, held tight to her curls when he slowly entered her, hoping and praying that they could finish what they started this time. If she told him to stop he didn't know what he would do.

Very carefully he began entering her, feeling her body stretch to accommodate his entry, experiencing the sexual pleasure of her muscles clamping him tightly. He paused a moment to give her body time to adjust to his size and glanced up at the stars. They were outside on his balcony, back in Houston. He had taken the spread off of his bed, along with some pillows, to sleep out in the open. And make love.

They'd had a glass of wine, but that was not what was driving their desire. It was passion of the deepest kind, a need to know each other this way, to finally push aside the mistrust and anger. It was time for both of them to

*realize there was a reason for this bond between them.
They could continue to fight it, deny it and not claim it.
But the truth of the matter was this was meant to be.*

*He looked down into her face and felt something he'd
never felt before, saw something in her eyes he'd never
seen, and he knew this time their union would be complete. There would be no interruptions.*

*He spread her legs farther apart as he felt his shaft go
deeper and deeper inside of her, almost to the hilt. He
hadn't put on a condom, so they were skin to skin, flesh
to flesh, and just the thought of it almost made him come.*

*He kept going, spreading her legs even farther, and
then he—*

"Wake up, Blade."

He drew in a sharp breath and felt his body being
shaken. He tried to hold on to the dream but felt it drifting
away, out of his reach and out of his touch. He moaned
in despair, not wanting to believe that once again he had
not finished the task he'd set out to do. Refusing to accept
that someone had the damn nerve to interrupt his dream,
he opened his eyes wide. And there she was, the object
of his obsession, the cause of his current state of frustration, looking down at him with a smile curving her lips
from corner to corner.

"You were dreaming," she said, as if that explained
everything.

With a deep, guttural groan to mask his curse, he
turned his head away from her for a second, trying to get
his bearings, to hide his disappointment, and wondering
just how much of his dream she'd heard. Slade swore that
he talked in his sleep, telling things better left unknown.

Blade sighed as he turned his head and looked back up
at her, and then moving carefully, he pulled himself up in
a sitting position as he rubbed his hands across his face.

He then looked up at her again and flinched when he saw that damn smile was still on her face.

"How long have I been sleeping?" he asked, working the kinks from his neck.

"I have no idea, since I wasn't aware you'd gone to sleep until I came downstairs to check on things. I thought you had left."

"Started to," he replied. "But couldn't make it to the front door. I collapsed on your sofa. Sorry about that."

"No problem."

He tried to move his legs, which felt as if they were still asleep. "Did you finish reading that file?" he asked.

"Not all of it. There's only so much legal stuff I can take in one sitting."

"Oh." He wished she wouldn't stand there like that, so close to him. She still had on those cutoffs and a tank top. She looked fresh and smelled good. And just to think that in his dream he had come close to getting what she had refused him in reality. Close but not close enough, deep but not deep enough.

He pulled in a deep breath and figured he'd better get out of there before doing something real stupid. Like reaching out and grabbing her thighs, unzipping her shorts and tasting her all over.

"I guess I better go now," he said, getting up from the sofa, causing her to take a step back.

"Call me if you need to go somewhere. Give me a ring even if you decide on takeout for lunch. I want to be here if anybody shows up," he added, throwing the sentences over his shoulder as he headed for the door.

"I don't like being bossed around, Blade."

He turned before reaching for the doorknob. If she was trying to pick a fight with him, now was not the time to do it. Twice he had left her house in a sexually deprived state. The last thing she would want today was to deliberately provoke him.

"Let it go, Sam. I'm not in a good mood. Just do what I ask."

"No, I won't do what you ask. My father's name is Antonio DeAngelo Di Meglio and not Blade Madaris."

Blade glanced down at the floor and counted to ten. He even muttered a few choice words. When he felt enough time had elapsed, he glanced back over at her. He studied her and saw the stubbornness etched in her face, and he saw something else, too—deep sexual frustration.

His heart began beating deeply within his chest. He knew the signs and should have picked up on them sooner. Their predicament was basically the same. They needed to get laid, but not with just anybody, only with each other.

Always with just each other.

He sucked in a deep breath, thinking how possessive that sounded. How final and absolute. He'd never thought about final and absolute with a woman in his entire life. All of a sudden a realization struck and it hit hard. If his feet hadn't been planted firmly on the floor he probably would have been knocked over. He was feeling strong emotions toward a woman.

But this wasn't just any woman. This was a woman who had proved she was different—difficult and different. Evidently that's what he needed. And that's what he'd been waiting for without knowing it.

He could vividly remember the night they'd met and all the times they'd seen each other since then. He had tried his luck with her, but instead of giving up, he had become almost obsessed with having her. He had convinced himself she was just another notch to add to his bedpost, and that his attraction to her was only sexual.

Now, ten months later, he hadn't added her to his bed-post yet, mainly because she could never be just another notch. She was the one he had singled out without real-izing he was doing so. The one woman he hadn't gotten out of his mind since first seeing her. She was the woman who constantly invaded his dreams. The one who'd trig-gered an urgency within him that no other woman could match.

Over the years, he had been told, preached and even lectured to about what to expect when a Madaris man knew he had found the woman for him. The one he was meant to share his life with, his soul mate. And the one thing he'd always been told was that she would be differ-ent.

The one standing across the room glaring at him was different, all right. As fiery as they came and with an attitude that he would have to work on. And then there was that temper of hers from her Italian side of the family. He would let her keep it, just encourage her to tone it down some.

At that precise moment it was crystal clear why he'd been chasing her from the start, even after she'd dissed him a few times. Why he had looked for any excuse to come back to Oklahoma City to see her. Why he was living next door to her now. Why he had become her watchdog, determined to keep her safe. Why he had asked Alex to find out who was trying to hurt her. And why he had given up three hours of sleep this morning.

The reasons were as clear as the nose on his face. She was meant to be his. She *was* his. And he loved her with all the heated passion that was flowing through his body, all the torrid sensations that he felt—both sexual and non-sexual.

She would never believe the emotions he was feeling.

Very few people who knew him would. He would have to show her rather than tell her, and eventually she would understand. He would make damn sure of it. But he definitely wouldn't share his feelings with her yet. If he gave her an inkling of how he felt she would refuse to believe it, and would think it was his way of getting revenge. There was no doubt in his mind that she would put up a wall between them so high it might take him years to climb over it.

"Do you have a problem?"

Her words pulled him out of his daze. "A problem?" he asked.

"Yes, you're just standing there staring at me like you have a problem."

If she only knew. He leaned back against the door. "My only problem is that you have too much of a smart mouth."

She narrowed her eyes, stiffened her spine and placed her hands on her hips. "You want to try and change it?"

He could tell she was poised, ready for a fight. She had no idea the type of battle they were about to wage. It was probably a good thing she didn't know, he thought. "Yes, I want to try and change it. I would love teaching that mouth of yours about respect."

He saw the fiery blaze deepen in her eyes and his lips couldn't help but twitch in response. The heat was certainly on now.

She laughed. "Do you honestly think you can take me on?"

A sensuous smile touched both corners of his lips when he said, "I'm going to damn well try."

He began walking toward her and he had to admire her for standing her ground, not moving an inch, keeping her hands on her hips and tilting her chin up, which was fine with him. It gave him a better angle for his mouth to connect to hers.

When he got close she said, "Enough of this, Blade. I want you to leave."

He kept smiling. "No you don't. If I left that would be like you admitting defeat, and I don't think you want to do that."

She lifted her chin an inch higher. "I'll never admit defeat."

"I didn't think you would."

And then before she could blink, he reached out and gently grabbed a fistful of her hair and pulled her face closer and slanted his mouth across hers. He was doing something about her smart mouth, just as he'd warned her he would. He was teaching her about respect in the most sensuous way.

Sam knew the best way to get out of his grasp was to use her knee to kick Blade in the groin. She hadn't taken all those self-defense classes growing up for nothing. But at that moment when Blade slid his tongue inside her mouth, any thought of doing physical harm to him flew out the window.

Instead she grabbed hold of his shoulders and pushed her mouth even closer. His taste was invading her senses as it did each and every time their mouths locked. She enjoyed kissing him. She enjoyed him kissing her. And the touch of his tongue on all parts of her mouth was causing her to groan back in her throat. It enticed her to participate in this sensual mouth play any way she could.

So she did.

Her tongue became embroiled in a heated duel, tangling with his, swirling from one side of his mouth to the other. It was as if they couldn't taste enough, touch enough or get close enough. Her body was humming in pleasure, telling her this was what it needed, but it was only the tip of the iceberg. It didn't come close. Deeper intimacy was what her body craved and what she longed for. And to prove the point—as if her body had a mind of its own—her middle pressed against his aroused member and her erect nipples poked hard into his chest. Her body prodded him to press his tongue even deeper inside her mouth, move it around in a frantic pace and lick and suck everything it touched.

He suddenly pulled his mouth from hers and stared down at her face as he drew in a much needed breath and gave her the chance to do the same. "Do you understand about respect now?" he asked in a thick, raspy voice.

She held his gaze. "No. You're going to have to do a lot better than that," she challenged.

A growl emanated from deep in his throat and the expression on his face became one of intense determination. The look in his eyes—hot, hungry and devouring—sent shudders through her body and had her shivering. "Then I guess I'll need to take things to another level," he said in a voice raw with sexual need.

He didn't wait for a comment. Instead, he simply reached out and ripped the tank top off her body, tossing it somewhere behind him. A furious look crossed her face. "Damn it, Blade. That's going to cost you."

He gave her a haughty smile. "Send me the bill."

His gaze then went from her face to her chest to see what his handiwork had unveiled. Beautiful and plump breasts with the most gorgeous dark tips he'd ever witnessed. He'd thought that before when he'd seen them and thought the same thing now. He'd been around enough to know that no two women had the same breasts. Shapes, sizes, textures and tastes varied. But he could stand there and say that hers were in a class by themselves. They were made for his hands and mouth alone.

"Give me my top back."

Her request pulled his gaze back up to her face. "I don't know why you'd want your top when you're about to lose your bottoms. But I think I want to hear you beg me to take them off of you."

Sam glared at him. "Don't hold your breath because I don't beg."

Blade shrugged. "There's a first time for everything."

And before she could open her mouth to give him a scathing retort, he tumbled her back onto the sofa.

Chapter 19

Blade's game plan was to seduce her body and then conquer her heart. And ignoring Sam's shrieks of rage, he captured her mouth the moment her back touched the sofa cushions.

First she had been the object of his seduction, then the object of his obsession. Later, the object of his protection, and now she was the cause of his frustration.

But he was about to remedy that.

Nothing was going to stop him, not even the angry look that was flashing in her eyes when he lifted his mouth. She was a hellion. There was no other way to describe her, and he loved every inch of her. He smiled at the thought that he could confess to such a thing and *feel* like smiling.

"I'm going to count to ten, Blade, and you better be off me before I get to the last number," she said through gritted teeth.

He wouldn't tell her not to waste her breath. He had

her pinned down on the sofa with her breasts bare. That wasn't good enough for him, especially when he remembered how she'd looked on the floor Monday night, totally naked as he'd been.

He could vividly recall her curvy body and sliding between those long, gorgeous legs.

"One."

And how good it felt to be pressed between such a luscious pair of thighs.

"Two."

And then he glanced down at her chest.

"Three."

Those were the sexy twin mounds that he had enjoyed tasting.

"Four."

He recalled almost making her come just from having his mouth on them, sucking them like crazy and licking them all over.

"Five."

Blade dipped his head and captured a torrid nipple in his mouth, sucked it in like a whirlwind and then began licking it with his tongue like candy.

"Six."

He smiled, thinking that the sound of the number six hadn't been as blistering as the others. He noticed her breathing had changed. It was now faster and she had begun wriggling under his body. He began sucking on her nipple a little harder, as if he was trying to draw something out of it. He heard her moans turn into cries, not of pain but of pleasure. He knew that was the case when she captured his head in her hands to hold him to her breasts.

His mouth switched to the other nipple, and he didn't waste time before giving it the same attention and torment—the same pleasure. She had stopped counting.

Instead what he heard pouring from her mouth were moans of the most sensuous kind. And now she was writhing beneath him. His ears perked up when she said his name.

"Blade."

He smiled. That was a start. She was coming around nicely and he intended to keep her coming—literally.

Keeping his mouth glued to her breasts, he slowly inched his hand downward and smoothly began easing her zipper open. Her body tensed for only a second and then she began writhing again.

And then she said, "Blade! Please!"

His fingers made their way inside the opening, moved past the silken material of her panties and slid to the crotch that shielded her womanly charms. The moment his fingers touched her, soaked in her wetness, he began stroking her.

Her feminine scent filled the air and her moans became groans as he continued to work his fingers while still not letting up on her breasts. And then she cried out his name again, bucked against him, tightened her thighs to capture his hand, and thrust out her chest so her nipple wedged deeper into his mouth.

He felt her muscles clench his fingers, and wished it was his erection that was being taken. He lifted his mouth from her breasts to stare into her face. Her orgasm was so intense and the look on her face was totally beautiful. Her eyes were tightly shut and her lips slightly parted, and she was breathing through her mouth in short gasps.

One day she would learn to keep her mouth closed, he thought, inching his lips toward hers and sliding his tongue inside the opening. She latched onto it, tangled with it, mated with it. And while his fingers continued to work her, she exploded into yet another orgasm.

He pulled his mouth away to let her scream. He wanted to hear it. He needed to hear it. And at that moment, hearing the sound sent desire racing through him in a way it had never done before. Mainly because that scream had come from the woman he loved—the only woman that mattered, the woman who had captured his heart.

His woman.

With her eyes tightly shut, Sam felt drained, totally spent and shocked. Two orgasms back to back! She would not have believed such a thing was possible—maybe for some women but not her. She had been happy with her last encounters—as infrequent as they were—but to get not just one real good one but two? Wow!

No, actually, Blade had given her four. She couldn't forget the night in the parked car and Monday night here on this same floor. A total of four orgasms and he hadn't fully penetrated her yet.

She opened her eyes and gazed up at him. He was looming over her and still had her pinned to the sofa. It was evident he wasn't planning on letting her go anywhere. He was probably thinking that she'd had four orgasms to his one and that he was due a few more. She hated to disappoint him, and she wouldn't. She was tired of fighting with him, tired of denying herself the very thing she wanted.

She had tried teaching him a lesson, humiliating him in a way most men would not have put up with. But he was still here. The man had staying power if nothing else. Did he want her as a notch on his bedpost *that* bad? Evidently. But still, she wouldn't be easy. Di Meglios never were.

"Well?"

She glanced up at him, ran her fingers through her hair and said, "Well, what?"

"Ready to go again?"

She would have laughed if she'd had the breath to do so. He really thought highly of himself. "Two is all I can do in a twenty-four hour period. Sorry."

"Says who?"

"Me. I know my body."

He moved his fingers and it was then she realized they were still inside of her. "I know your body, too. I'm getting six out of you today."

He had to be kidding. "Six?"

"Yes."

"And how did you come up with that number?" she asked.

A smile touched both corners of his lips. "That's the number you stopped at. The number when you gave in."

She didn't like the sound of gloating in his voice. "Doesn't matter. You still didn't make me beg."

"Yes, I did."

"No, you didn't." She would have remembered. Wouldn't she?

"You said please."

She frowned, vaguely remembering what she'd said. "So what if I did? That wasn't begging."

"Yes, it was."

She didn't intend to argue with him.

"Say it was, so I can get you out of these shorts," he said, not letting the matter drop.

He was working his fingers again and the feel of them was sending tremors through her body, and then she began feeling a wave of hunger building up inside her once more. How in the world was that even remotely possible?

"Blade?"

"Hmm?"

"Why are you doing this?"

"I'd rather show you why rather than try to explain," he whispered, his voice confident and arrogant, yet at the same time tender and warm.

She stared at him as he continued to work his fingers, while the hunger kept growing inside of her. And she knew as miraculous as it could be, if he kept it up that she would come again. But this time, she didn't want his mouth or fingers to deliver such pleasure. It was time to stop evading what she really wanted—total and complete penetration.

He was still holding her gaze and wouldn't let it go. And in a move that she figured surprised him, she leaned up and took her tongue and ran the wet tip along the edges of his lips, those same lips that could arouse her just from looking at them. She smiled when he released a quick rush of breath.

And then she used the tip of her tongue and wiggled it through the center of those lips, and when he all but sucked it inside his mouth to join with his, she flicked it all over the place.

Moments later, he pulled back and stared hard into her eyes. "Just what do you think *you're* doing?" he asked in a strained voice.

She knew this response would be easy. "I'm begging, Blade."

But not for long, Blade thought, when he shifted his body to remove her shorts. He was stripping her and stripping his control all at the same time, obsessed with anticipating the feel of her muscles clamping him and pulling him in as they had done before. But first he had to make certain of something. More for her benefit than for his.

"Are you on the pill?"

She blinked. "The pill?"

"Yes?"

She nodded. She was on them more so to regulate her period than anything else, but he didn't have to know that. "Yes, why?"

"If you want me to use a condom, I will, but I like the feel of being inside of you bare. I'm healthy," he said, twisting around to pull his wallet out of his back pocket and then taking something out of it to hand to her.

She took what looked like a laminated business card, but when she studied it, she saw that it was a health card. She glanced back up at him. "You carry around a health card?"

"Yes. Don't you?"

"No."

"It doesn't matter," he said, when she handed the card back to him. "I'm making love to you regardless."

"Why?"

He stared down at her. She was totally naked as he straddled her, and he would be removing his own clothes shortly. Now would be a good time to tell her how he felt, but he knew he couldn't. His woman was a "show me" woman and he intended to show her in both deeds and actions.

"Because of this." And then he leaned closer and captured her mouth in a way he'd gotten used to doing, yet still found exciting. When he eased off of the sofa to remove his shirt, she sat up with him.

"Let me, Blade," she said.

Sam's voice was filled with sexual desire, so much that she could hear it herself and knew he had to be aware of it, as well. He stood there as she pulled his T-shirt over his head and proceeded to toss it aside. Instead of going straight for his pants she used her hands to roam all over him, touching places on his chest she had often fantasized about. He was built. He was masculine. He was all man.

She felt him tremble at the touch of her hand. She liked the feel of the crisp hair beneath her fingers.

"Having fun?" he asked in a tense tone.

She smiled at him. "Not as much as I intend to have."

Surprise glinted in his eyes. "You're dangerous."

"You should have considered that before taking me on, Blade Madaris."

And then she leaned forward and captured one of the dark pebbles on his chest in her mouth, doing just what he'd done to her nipples earlier, licking and sucking.

She liked the guttural sound that he made and enjoyed the way his heart felt beating wildly in his chest pressed against her lips. Knowing she needed to take things to the next level, she pulled back and lowered her hand to undo his jeans, slowly easing down the zipper. It didn't take her long to work both his jeans and his briefs down his legs and toss them aside.

"I need you to sit on the sofa so I can remove your socks," she said, taking a look at him and enjoying the view. He was totally naked except for his socks.

He eased back on the sofa to sit down and she crouched down in front of him and slid the socks off his feet and tossed them aside. He then reached out for her, but she pushed him back against the cushion and, while still on her knees, leaned forward and licked his stomach, tracing wet rings around his navel with her tongue. She felt him clench his abdominal muscles as her mouth brushed against them.

She leaned back on her haunches and looked up at him. "You didn't ask, Blade, but I'm healthy, too. I get regular checkups. Now move your hips toward me."

He eased forward as she requested and the moment he did she dipped her head to his lap.

Mercy!

That was the only word Blade could think of when his head fell back against the sofa. What was this woman doing to him? She had taken his heart, so what else did she want? He knew at that moment Samari Di Meglio had his soul, as well.

This woman who was kneeling in front of him with his full erection in her mouth was doing things to him with her tongue that had him shuddering deep in his groin. He reached down and grabbed ahold of her head, tightened his fingers in her hair as he was devoured by what had to be the naughtiest mouth on earth.

"Samari."

Her name was a tortured moan from his lips and he quietly conceded that he wouldn't be able to handle what she was doing to him much longer. If she was retaliating for his earlier actions, she was getting retribution many times over. And when he felt his body nearly ready to explode, he slid his hands from her hair to her shoulders and, before she realized what he was doing, quickly eased her back, tumbling her to the carpeted floor and then swiftly joining her there.

The moment he straddled her body, he parted her legs and, gripping her thighs, eased into her warm, wet womanly charm. This time he didn't intend to stop until he thrust to the hilt.

Her body was tight and clenched him mercilessly as he stared down at her and pushed forward, only pausing when she needed to draw in a deep breath. "When was the last time you did this?" he asked. If he didn't know better he'd think she was a virgin. Her passageway was just that tight.

She looked up at him and for a moment he didn't think she was going to answer. "Over four years ago."

He blinked and decided that would be a discussion they would have later. But for now, he knew he intended to make this the best she'd ever had. Make it worth waiting four years for.

She dug into his shoulders as he moved deeper, stretching her body to accommodate his size. If there was any other way than this he would try it. However, he needed to feel her clenching him. He needed to give her all the pleasure she could handle.

When he had spread her to the hilt, he again gave her time to adjust. "You okay?" he said, wiping sweat off her brow.

She smiled up at him, "Yes, I'm fine now. I feel you."

He chuckled. "Good, because now I'm going to *fill* you."

By the time he figured that she'd gotten his meaning, he had begun moving, lifting her hips to receive his thrusts, easing in and out of her as if it was natural…and one day it would be.

Over and over he made love to her, stroking inside of her, slow and deep, imbedding himself to the hilt and then almost completely pulling out before going deep back inside again. Then he leaned forward and captured her mouth, making love to it with the same rhythm and pace of his thrusts.

When he felt her body buck underneath him, felt her detonate as her feminine juices began drenching him, he threw his head back and clamped down on her thighs and thrust as deep as he could go and then he exploded.

His semen shot straight to her womb. Hot, thick and potent. And he knew it had to be coating her insides, *filling* her. Once his sperm realized they were free, and no longer confined to a condom, he bet they would instinctively swim around like crazy to find an egg.

Not this time, fellas, he thought. He knew that had it happened this time, it would not have bothered him in the least. This was his woman. One day he wanted her to have his babies. He loved her and he wouldn't be satisfied until she loved him back.

Before he could pull in a deep breath, more shudders racked his body, and another release shot straight to her womb when yet another orgasm claimed him. And he knew at that moment that he would never, ever get enough of her.

"Why haven't you done this in four years, Sam?"

Sam refused to open her eyes, doubting she had strength to do even that. She pulled in a deep breath. That had been her sixth orgasm. Back to back. Once they'd christened the floor, he had taken her to the sauna, saying he'd never made love in a sauna before and wanted to try it. They had added to the steam and by the time he had stretched her out on the bench and entered her, thrusting in and out of her like he needed to mate with her as much as he needed to breathe, she could still feel the tremors that had rammed through her body.

Afterward, they had drunk plenty of water and then together had prepared lunch. After lunch he had taken her on the kitchen table, claiming he was getting his dessert again, and then they'd made love in the shower. The remaining times had been in her bed.

She glanced over at the clock on the nightstand. It was six o'clock and time for dinner, but she didn't think she would ever be able to move again.

"Sam?"

She forced her eyes open to look at him. "What?" she said in a near whisper.

"Why haven't you made love in four years?"

She closed her eyes. Moments later she reopened them, figuring he wouldn't let her be until she told him. "I've been too busy setting up players. Building them up and letting them down."

He lifted a brow. "At the risk of your own pleasure?"

She rolled her eyes. "What pleasure? At the risk of your ego getting inflated more than it probably already is," she said. "This is a sensual confession that you can take to the grave. What I've shared with you today is the first time I've done this and gotten any real pleasure out of it. I've only done it three other times and the men were selfish."

"But I wasn't?"

She chuckled and rolled her eyes. "You can ask me that after six times? Pleeeze."

He grinned as he shifted his body to lean over her. "Did I hear you say *please?* That's the magic word. I think you should get ready for number seven."

And before she could tell him he was crazy if he thought that, he lowered his mouth and proved that he wasn't.

Chapter 20

"If I wasn't seeing it with my own eyes, I wouldn't have believed it. Blade actually brought a woman to the party," several voices whispered.

A number of heads turned to stare at the couple who had just walked in.

"Who is she?"

"Don't know."

"Her face looks familiar."

"Hey, wait a minute. Isn't that one of the girls who was in Luke and Mac's wedding, one of Mac's attorney friends?"

Blade knew that he and Sam were being discussed the moment they entered the huge room at Whispering Pines, his uncle Jake's ranch, where most of the Madaris parties were held. He and Sam had arrived in Houston late yesterday evening, but had only notified Slade when they had gotten to town. Blade knew for his family to see him and Sam together would be a shocker.

He'd gone through the receiving line and had met Rasheed's wife, Johari. The rumors he'd heard were true. She was a beauty, but he thought that no woman was as beautiful as the one standing beside him.

Getting Sam to come with him to Houston hadn't been easy. She had grumbled all the way, claiming he was just trying to boss her around. He'd finally convinced her that due to Alex's hectic schedule it would be better if she came and talked to him here. The sooner Alex got a handle on things the better.

Blade still didn't like the fact that Sam's life could be in danger. That day when they had finally made love had turned into a lazy day filled with sex, sex and more sex. She would blush every time he teased her about the number of times she'd come. By the time they had closed their eyes that night it had been a whopping ten. And he had awakened the next morning ready to make love to her again. He had set a record not only for her but for himself, as well. He'd never wanted any woman that much and for that long. He had driven her into work at ten on Thursday, a time he considered a reasonable hour.

Her security team at the office had been apprised of the threat by Mac, and everyone was being cautious and alert. No packages were to be accepted that looked suspicious, and the only persons allowed in to meet with Sam were those appointments previously scheduled with current clients.

Blade had taken the initiative to speak with the security force himself and everyone was ready to do whatever had to be done to protect her. Even Rita had pulled her head out of her romance novel long enough to listen, and by the look in her eyes Blade had a feeling this was probably the most excitement she'd ever experienced as a security guard.

"Do you get the feeling that we're being watched, Blade?"

Sam's question reined in his thoughts and he could only smile. Being watched was just the tip of the iceberg. Wait until his great-grandmother saw them. That's when the interrogation would begin.

He glanced around, not surprised to see a number of curious eyes on them, mostly those of his relatives. They were trying to digest it all, making sure they weren't seeing things, or drawing the wrong conclusion. In this case the conclusions they reached would probably be right. The woman standing by his side would one day become Mrs. Blade Madaris.

He smiled at her and said, "We *are* being watched. I usually don't bring anyone to family functions."

"Why not?"

"I'm a player, remember. It's not good for my image," he teased, and couldn't help but laugh when he saw the frown on her face.

"Come on," he said, taking her hand. "I see my parents over there, as well as my grandparents. And I'm sure my great-grandmother is around here somewhere. I want to introduce you. The last thing I want is for them to get ideas about us. We're nothing more than friends and the sooner they know it the better."

Sam nodded. "I agree."

Blade figured she would. What he didn't tell her was that although he would tell his family she was nothing more than a friend, there was not a single one of them here tonight who would believe it.

An hour or so later Blade had made the rounds with Sam by his side, introducing her to everyone. After claiming he needed to go discuss a business matter with

Slade, he had left her in his great-grandmother's and Syneda's care, something that hadn't gone unnoticed. Mama Laverne and Syneda were two of the most opinionated and nosy women in the Madaris family.

Felicia Laverne Madaris, who was sitting on one of the sofas, glanced up at Sam and smiled before asking, "So, how long have you and my great-grandson been seeing each other?"

Syneda noticed the surprised look on Sam's face before she responded. "Blade and I aren't seeing each other. We're just friends. He's sort of helping me out of a jam."

Syneda and Mama Laverne exchanged knowing looks. First of all, Blade didn't have female friends, he had bed partners. And Blade wouldn't help any woman out of a jam unless there was something in it for him. But what was so crystal clear to both women, although the waters were evidently still rather murky to Samari Di Meglio, was that somehow, someway, Blade had singled her out. It was also rather obvious Ms. Di Meglio had no earthly idea just what that meant.

"I understand you're expecting," Sam said to Syneda, breaking into her thoughts. "Congratulations."

Syneda beamed. "Thanks. I'm happy about it, although it did come as a shock, since I was on birth control. But that's the thing about a Madaris man. If he wants to get you pregnant, a simple thing like a birth-control pill or a condom isn't going to stop him."

"Oh," Sam said, and quickly looked away. She had nothing to worry about, since the last thing Blade would want to do was to get her pregnant. She was sure of it.

After meeting them, Sam was convinced that she liked Blade's family. Some of them she'd met before, at Mac and Luke's wedding. They were friendly then and they were friendly now. Christy Madaris Maxwell had pulled out a bunch of photos of her little girl and Sam thought she looked like a doll, absolutely adorable. For a moment Sam could envisioned her own little girl, who would look like her father. And for some reason a little girl with Blade's features flashed across her mind.

She almost choked on the wine she'd been drinking. Lorren Madaris, who was married to Blade's cousin Justin, and Caitlin Madaris, who was married to his cousin Dex, glanced over at her with concern. "Are you okay?" Lorren asked.

She nodded after clearing her throat. "Yes, I'm fine." Deep down she knew she wasn't fine. For some reason she'd just thought about being the mother of Blade's baby.

Deciding that was the last thing she wanted to think about, she glanced around the room and smiled when she saw how attentive Sheikh Rasheed Valdemon was to his wife. She thought they made such a beautiful couple, and Johari Valdemon was practically glowing. Sam knew why. They had announced to everyone a few moments earlier that they would become parents this fall.

Sam knew that her own parents would jump for joy if either she or Angelo presented them with a grandchild. The thought of having a baby had never crossed her mind before, but now with so many pregnant women here tonight, she found herself thinking about it. And whenever she did, those thoughts would include Blade. She wasn't ready to think about why that was the case; for now she would just accept that it was.

She turned, knowing the object of her thoughts had returned to her side. He smiled at her. "Missed me?"

She chuckled. "Of course."

He glanced over at his family. "Excuse us for a minute." He took Sam's hand in his and led her over to a secluded spot near where the band had been playing earlier.

"I've made arrangements," he whispered. "Alex wants to talk to you before the party ends tonight. We'll use Jake's office. Will that be okay?"

"Yes, that will be fine. The sooner he finds out something the better. It's been crazy at the office with everyone looking over their shoulders."

He nodded in understanding.

"Sam! I didn't know you would be here."

Blade and Sam turned when Luke and Mac walked up. Sam gave her best friend a hug. "When I saw you in the office before you left town on Thursday, I didn't know, either," she said to Mac. "Blade had asked me the day before but I turned him down. And then he kept pestering me about coming, so I changed my mind Friday morning." She chuckled and added, "He finally asked me nicely instead of making it an order."

Mac nodded as she and Luke glanced over at Blade, who only shrugged his shoulders. "I thought it was best to bring her with me instead of leaving her in Oklahoma with that crazy person still on the loose."

Luke stared at Blade a moment. "I can see you thinking that way."

Luke knew it was a lie even as he said it. He couldn't see Blade thinking that way at all. For Blade to bring Sam to the party could only mean one thing. A woman had finally captured his cousin's heart.

Chapter 21

Sam glanced around at all the people gathered in Jake Madaris's office. She had assumed that only she, Blade and Alex would be there, and was surprised when she walked in and found others waiting.

When Alex Maxwell saw the obviously confused expression on her face, he explained, "I'm going to do everything I can to find out who sent you those flowers, Sam. But these other folks are sort of my backup just in case things get crazy, like they did with Mac last year. Besides, I'd like them to hear everything in case they latch onto something that I might miss."

Sam smiled. She'd heard all about Alex Maxwell and his ability to solve cases, so she doubted he would miss anything. And then, glancing around the room, she realized she knew about four of the others, as well. They were former members of the U. S. Marines recon forces. And two of them were former CIA agents.

"I'm sure you know everyone, but I'd like to reintroduce everybody anyway," Alex said.

"All right."

"First is Ashton Sinclair."

She smiled and then walked straight over into Ashton's outstretched arms. She knew Ashton very well, since he was Mac's cousin.

Ashton glanced down at her with a grin on his face. "Have you been behaving yourself?"

She smiled. "Trying to."

A serious expression then appeared on Ashton's face. "Alex will find the person responsible. In the meantime take every precaution."

She nodded. "I will." She smiled widely. "I understand congratulations are in order for you and Nettie."

He laughed. "Yes, we're having a girl. Nettie and I are ecstatic and the boys are excited," he said of his sons, six-year-old triplets—Hunter, Wolf and Brody.

She was introduced to Drake Warren and his wife, Tori. They were former CIA agents. She gave them hugs, as well. "And how is the newest member of the Warren family?" she couldn't help asking.

The couple beamed proudly. "Dior is doing marvelous and is giving her big brothers a lot of grief already," Tori said of their two other children, sons Deke and Devin, ages five and three respectively. "She'll be celebrating her first birthday soon."

Sam then met Trevor Grant, another former marine and close friend of the Madaris family. She knew from talking to Blade that Reese would be replacing Trevor as foreman of Madaris Explorations, a company owned by Blade's cousin Dex. Trevor wanted to pursue his dream of opening a tactical operations facility, and Drake and Ashton would be partners in the business venture.

"And how is your family, Trevor?" she asked. She remembered meeting Trevor's wife, Corinthians, and their two children, a seven-year-old son named Rio and a five-year-old daughter named Phoenix.

"Everyone is doing fine," Trevor said, smiling. "Thanks for asking."

Sam thought that all of them—Alex, Ashton, Drake and Trevor—were definitely handsome men, and Tori was certainly a beauty. And it was obvious that she was adored and loved by Drake.

"Now that we all know each other," Alex said, grinning, "we can get down to business. I want you to sit next to Blade, Sam, while I ask you some questions."

"Sure," she said, easing down beside Blade on the love seat. She smiled when he took her hand in his, tucking it into his lap.

"Now then," Alex started. "I understand you were questioned by Detective Adams, who I worked with to solve the Coroni case, so I got to know him pretty well. He's an intelligent man who's good at what he does, so I'm sure he's probably asked some of the same questions I'm about to ask. However, I might want you to elaborate some more in your answers. That will help me in my investigation."

"All right."

He paused for a second. "Now, I need the names of all the men you've been associated with. Since your secret admirer claims to be an old friend, you need to go back as far as you can, even during your college days. So let's start there."

Sam shifted to a more comfortable position in the love seat, but Blade held tight to her hand. "I didn't date a lot in college, especially after what happened my first year at Yale."

"What happened?" Tori asked.

Sam glanced across the room and met Tori's gaze. "My roommate, Vivian Randall, committed suicide in our dorm room. I was away in class at the time."

"And why did she kill herself?" Ashton asked.

She noticed that, like Detective Adams, Alex was jotting down information on a notepad. "She had met this guy at school, Tyrell Graham, and he convinced her that he was madly in love with her. She found out differently when a video of them making love showed up on the Internet. She questioned him about it and he brushed her off, admitted to putting it out there and laughed in her face about it. She came back to our dorm room and overdosed on some of my pills."

"Your pills?" Trevor asked, lifting a brow.

"Yes. The doctor had prescribed them for my migraine headaches and she took them." Sam lowered her head as if the memory was almost too much for her.

Blade tightened his grip on her hand. He'd known about her roommate committing suicide, but hadn't known the woman had used Sam's prescription to do so. No wonder she still felt guilty after all these years.

The room was silent for a moment. "Evidently you were upset about the entire incident. Did you ever confront Tyrell Graham about his part in your roommate's death?" Sir Drake said.

Sam's eyes blazed with fire. "Yes, of course. He didn't have any remorse."

"And what did you do?" Ashton asked, figuring she would have retaliated.

"Nothing at the time. I was too upset about it. Before the semester was over I had changed universities and returned home to New York and attended NYU. But I did run into Tyrell a few years later."

"How long ago was that?" Tori asked.

"Three years ago. I was invited to be one of the judges in a bodybuilding contest he was entered in. There were five judges, but of course he thought it was my fault that he didn't win."

"And *was* it your fault that he didn't win, Sam?" Blade asked, looking at her as if he knew she'd had something to do with the outcome.

She smiled at him. "Well, I did mention what he'd done to my godfather, who happened to be one of the major sponsors of the event."

Alex chuckled, reading between the lines. "Did Graham threaten you?"

"No, but I could tell he was mad. Not only did he lose the competition, but he was banned from every contest my godfather sponsored."

"You do know that if he was a career bodybuilder, one who spent hours and hours working out to compete, what you did could have ruined him for life," Trevor pointed out.

She pressed her lips together a second before saying, "Then I guess that was unfortunate for him. I had no pity for him, like he had no pity for Vivian."

Alex cleared his throat. "Okay, moving on. You said you didn't date seriously during college. What about later, in law school?"

She shook her head. "No, I didn't date seriously then, either. I met the man I thought I would marry a few years ago, not long after I finished law school and went to work at my family law firm. Guy Carrington was an associate attorney there. We became engaged and planned to marry."

"What happened?" Drake asked.

Sam didn't say anything for a moment. "On the day of

the wedding, in the middle of the ceremony, two women showed up claiming Guy was the father of their children and that he was still seeing them both. One of the women was pregnant again."

"Have you heard from Carrington?" Alex asked.

"Not since he contacted my family's firm for a reference and I found out about it."

"And what did you do?" Ashton asked.

She smiled. "My parents were out of the office and the paperwork came across one of my uncle's desks. He passed it on to me. Of course I gave Guy a glowing recommendation."

The look in her eyes said it all. They could just imagine just how glowing the recommendation was. Hell knows no fury like a woman scorned.

"So there's a chance you're not one of Carrington's favorite people," Trevor said, trying to hide his smile.

"No, but then he's not one of mine."

"When was the last time you saw him?" Tori asked.

"The day of the wedding."

The room got quiet again. "How about telling what happened after your broken engagement, about the men you dated and why you dated them," said Blade.

Sam shifted her gaze from him to the other five pairs of eyes focused on her. "After Guy, I was on a mission to make men pay. So I decided to get even and became a bona fide player hater."

Alex lifted a brow. "A player hater?"

"Yes."

Five pairs of eyes shifted from Sam to Blade. He returned their stares with a shrug.

Alex cleared his throat and returned his gaze to Sam. "So as a player hater, what exactly did you do?"

"The usual."

Sir Drake, who had been leaning against the edge of Jake's desk, asked, "What's the usual?"

Sam smiled. "I would lead them on, convince them I was interested in them and that I was easy. I would build up their sexual expectations and when the time came for me to deliver, I didn't."

"You deliberately set them up? Strung them along? Teased them?" Trevor asked incredulously.

"Yes," she responded proudly. "I played them."

Trevor shook his head. "I'm sure a number of them must have been angry, even have threatened your life," he said.

"Yes, they did."

"Didn't you take any of them seriously?" Alex asked.

"No. I figured they would eventually get over it. I just wanted to show them that two could play their games."

"What about that guy a few years ago, Sam?" Ashton asked. "Mac mentioned that some guy was arrested and served time for trying to exact revenge on you."

"Someone tried to get even?" Blade asked.

She rolled her eyes. "Yes, Belton LaSalle. I met him the first year I moved to Oklahoma. He believed that he was God's gift to women."

Five pairs of eyes sought Blade out again. This time he smiled.

"Anyway," Sam said, "I thought he needed to be taught a lesson. I must have seriously pissed him off. About a week or two later, he called and invited me out, claiming he just wanted to apologize and show me that there were no hard feelings."

She shifted in her seat and noticed the she had everyone's attention. "Mac and Peyton didn't trust him and suggested that I meet him in a public place. I picked a well-known restaurant downtown, but I didn't know that Mac still had misgivings about him. She and Peyton had made reservations at the same restaurant and got a table not far from ours."

She drew in a deep breath. "To make a long story short, when my back was turned, Belton slipped a date-rape drug into my drink."

"The bastard!" said Alex, to everyone's surprise.

Blade and the others understood Alex's outburst had to do with a situation involving Christy a few years ago.

"Lucky for me, Mac and Peyton saw the whole thing before I drank anything. They called the police, and Belton was arrested and sent to prison. He was given four years, but only served two."

"So you know for a fact that he's out of prison now?" Ashton said.

"He's supposed to be. I got a letter from the parole board a few years ago saying he was being released two years early for good behavior."

"Have you seen him or has he tried contacting you in any way?" Drake asked.

"No, the last time I saw him was in court—the day he was sentenced."

"Okay, what about male friends?" said Alex.

"There's only Frederick."

"Frederick?" Ashton asked.

"Yes, Frederick Damon Rowe. We call him FDR. We started working at my family's law firm on the same day and became best friends."

"When was the last time you saw him?" Alex asked.

"I saw him when I was home visiting my family about three weeks ago. He calls periodically to check up on me, and even comes to visit me. However, he's been busy lately and hasn't had a chance to get away," Sam said.

"Are there any other names that come to mind—male or female—that you feel I should check out?" Alex asked.

Sam shook her head. "No, I can't think of anyone."

"What about cases you've handled? Anyone that you've really pissed off?"

She shrugged. "There's always one or two, but none that I think would want to retaliate."

Alex smiled. "Share the names with me and let me be the judge of that. And I would like a list of the names of all your employees." He closed his notepad. "How soon can I get it?"

"I can fax that information to you when I return to the office Monday," Sam said.

"Good. I have some free time between assignments. I should have some information for you in a couple of weeks."

"That soon?" she asked.

Alex smiled. "Yes. I have contacts, and usually they're not only efficient, they're fast."

"When will you be returning to Oklahoma, Sam?" Ashton asked.

"Tomorrow."

"What about protection for her until I find out something?" Alex asked, turning to Blade.

Blade smiled. "She's with me, and I don't plan on letting anything happen to her. Trust me."

Blade opened the door to his condo and stood back and let Sam enter first. She glanced at him when he followed her inside and shut the door behind them. "I'm glad that's over," she said, tossing her purse on a table.

"It wouldn't surprise me if he contacts us sooner," Blade said, removing his tie. "Alex is good at what he does. And like he said, he has good contacts."

Sam sat down on the sofa, kicked off her shoes and crossed her legs. Blade watched her every move as he went behind the bar. "Would you like something to drink?"

"Yes, please. A glass of wine would be nice."

"A glass of wine coming up. It's a beautiful night. Would you like to sit outside on the balcony?"

"Yes."

"Why don't you go ahead and I'll follow shortly with the wine."

"Thanks."

He tracked her with his eyes as she walked barefoot toward the French doors. The dress she was wearing, a yellow, tiered silk number, looked good on her. It wasn't too short, but showed off her beautiful legs. He had noticed a number of men at the party admiring them. He had told her before leaving for the party and again on the drive back home just how good she looked in that dress.

He finished pouring their drinks and moved to join her outside. When he opened the French door she was standing at the rail looking out. She turned to him and smiled. "You're right. It is a beautiful night," she said, accepting the glass of wine he offered. "Thanks."

"You're welcome."

She swung back around and looked at the view. "Your company did a wonderful job on the Madaris Building. I love the way it's all lit up at night—all fifteen stories."

He stood next to her and followed her gaze. "That was Slade's idea. He figured the lights would reflect on Laverne Park."

She turned back to him. "Which is named after your great-grandmother," she said.

He took a sip of his wine. "Yes. Although we all might joke about her trying to keep up with all of us, there's no doubt in our minds how we feel about her. We wouldn't trade her for the world. She raised seven sons after my great-grandfather died. They all got a good education and they're out on their own. She was also there for her grands."

He chuckled. "My dad, Justin, Dex, Clayton and Felicia had some stories to tell about her. Like the time she caught my dad and Cousin Nolan skipping school. I heard she drove them back to school and sat in the back of their class that day to make sure they stayed there."

Sam laughed. "After talking to her tonight I can tell she's made of sturdy stuff. I was close to my grandmother and felt a great loss when she died while I was in high school. I never knew my great-grandmother, but I'm told she was a strong woman just like your great-grandmother."

She took a sip of her wine, looked over at him. "You know your family thinks something is going on between us, don't you."

He grinned. "Something *is* going on between us."

"No, I think they believe we're more than bed partners."

We are more than bed partners, sweetheart. Instead he said, "You do understand why they would think that."

"Yes. You've never brought a woman to a family function before. But they don't know why you brought me."

Oh, they know, trust me. "It doesn't matter," he said.

"In a way it does, because I like them, Blade."

And they like you.

"I don't want them getting the wrong idea," she said.

Too late. It's a done deal.

Sam turned back to look at the view of the impressive building. "So, what floor is your office on in the Madaris Building?"

"The Madaris Construction Company is on the fifteenth floor."

"Wow, all the way at the top."

"Yes."

"And will I get to tour the Madaris Building tomorrow?" she asked.

He smiled. "Of course, I'll give you a personal tour before we return to Oklahoma."

She turned back to him, surprised to see he had moved closer, and looked up at him. "Promise?"

His smile widened. "I promise."

Blade couldn't remember the last time he'd enjoyed talking to a woman this much. Usually when he was with a woman they didn't talk at all. Their only communication was in the bedroom. But Sam was different. He wanted her. He loved her and could actually feel that love all the way to the bone.

Besides loving her, he desired her. His gaze roamed up and down her body, remembering the times he'd been inside of her and wanting to get back inside her again. "Did I tell you how good you look tonight?"

"Yes, about three times, I think," she said, grinning.

"Now I've made it four." He reached out and traced his fingers along the spaghetti straps of her dress.

The strong, lean fingers that were lightly touching Sam, caressing her shoulders, were sending delicious shudders through her body.

"Do you know what I want to do? What I've fantasized about doing?" he said, in a deep, husky tone.

"No, what have you fantasized about, Blade?"

He eased closer to her, so close that his chest was pressed against her, and he subtly pried her thighs apart with his knee to get closer to the opening between her legs. Not surprisingly, she felt his arousal.

He leaned in closer and whispered in her ear. "Bending you over this railing and taking you right here…from behind."

Sam's heart began beating wildly when the image of Blade's fantasy flashed in her mind. She imagined herself with her dress hiked up and her backside tilted to him and Blade standing behind her with his pants down past his knees, his erection hard and ready to go deep inside of her.

She swallowed and glanced around. "What would your neighbors think?"

"They won't be able to see a thing," he assured her, using his tongue to lick her earlobe. "This balcony is private, secluded, flanked by solid brick walls. It's dark, and as you can see, no one is in the Madaris Building tonight."

She looked across the park at the building.

"I want you," he said, as he began tracing kisses around the side of her neck. "I want to get inside your body and ride you hard, Sam."

He lifted his head and her eyes stared into his. She felt the heat coming from his lips and saw the way his nostrils flared. As if they had a mind of their own, her arms reached out and encircled his neck and she pulled his mouth to hers.

The kiss was long, deep and intoxicating, and had her groaning in the deepest part of her throat. She knew he was lifting the hem of her skirt when she felt the cool night air caressing her thighs. And her heart began thumping harder against her chest as his hands slid off her panties.

"Oh."

His fingers trailed over her Brazilian wax job, caressed the clean smoothness of the skin before easing a finger into her wetness. She groaned again from the probing, and when his finger began making circular motions inside of her, she pulled her mouth from his and threw her head back.

In an effortless move, he turned her to face the railing and stepped up behind her, letting his erection press hard against her buttocks. "Feel me?" He leaned forward, licking the side of her face with his tongue.

"I feel you," she responded, barely able to get the words out. "You're hungry?"

A smile touched his lips. "Starving, sweetheart. Can I make a sensual confession?"

She moaned deep in her throat. His finger was still inside of her, making her clutch him fiercely with every stroke. "Yes." Her response was followed by another moan.

"I like shooting off inside of you, combining our juices while I thrust in and out."

His words were killing her softly, arousing her even more. "I heard you have cases of condoms," she panted.

He smiled again. "I do. Make sure I show them to you sometime. But I like being skin to skin with you without anything between us. I like giving you a part of me that no other woman can ever claim. I hope you don't mind."

"If I did mind, it wouldn't have happened the first time or all those other times after that. Now stop talking and take me, Blade, like in your fantasy."

"Hmm, not yet. I need to cop a taste first. Hold this position and don't move until I tell you to do so."

She was tempted to turn around when she heard him pulling a couple of pillows off the patio furniture, and then she glanced down and saw that he had nestled his body flat on his back between her open legs. His hands grabbed a hold of her knees. "Come on, baby. Lower yourself, down to my mouth." He licked his lips. "I'm waiting. I'm starving."

"Blade." His name came out as a sensuous sigh as she lowered her body. When her womanly center was directly over his face, he raised up to settle his mouth between her legs.

She swallowed a scream when his tongue entered her, and her hands tightened on the railing. With intense thrusts of his tongue inside of her, her body began to quiver—shuddering as it had never done before. She took in deep breaths and when she thought there was no way she could handle any more, her body exploded.

"Blade!"

How could he do such things to her? And why did she let him? She knew the answer before the last shudder left her body. She loved him. The man who'd told her that he would never love a woman, would never marry—against all odds—had captured her heart.

Sam held tight to the railing as all her strength left her, making her weak in the knees, even as he held them. Moments later he released her and slid from under her. And then he was there, behind her. She heard his zipper open and his pants drop. The erection pressing against her was large, hot and ready—just like she'd imagined.

Before she could utter a sigh, he had tilted her up and entered her from the back. He began moving into her wetness in firm, easy strokes, holding tight. She could hear his thighs beating against her buttocks in repetitive thrusts.

And then he leaned over her, lowered the zipper on her dress and placed a wet kiss at the center of her neck, followed by a nip to her skin. "Now I've branded you," he whispered, just seconds before he exploded inside of her.

Sam could feel his hot release shoot all the way to her womb. She shivered at the very essence of his virile semen as it mixed with her own juices, and her body shuddered in intense pleasure again.

She heard him let out another guttural groan and gasped when another release shot from him, heading straight for her womb a second time.

"You are mine," he breathed against her ear, at the same time she felt his hot tongue trailing a path from her neck to the side of her face. Moments later, while their bodies were still intimately connected, he eased them down to the cushions he had placed on the balcony floor. And there he continued to hold her in his arms, with his erection still locked deep inside of her.

As she closed her eyes, drained and sated, she knew it wouldn't matter to her if he never took it out.

The woman opened the door and smiled brightly when she saw the man she had been thinking about. "You should have called. I would have come to the airport to get you."

He smiled down at her. "I know, but it was no bother. Got any news to tell me?"

"Yes," she said, leading him over to her sofa. "Ms. Di Meglio is out of town. She went to Houston with that man, Blade Madaris. I think he's appointed himself her bodyguard."

The man laughed as he pulled her down to the sofa with him. "That doesn't matter. When I'm ready to make my presence known and remind her of the reason I hate her, neither Madaris nor anyone else will be able to stop me from doing what I want to do."

Chapter 22

Sam stood at the window in her office and looked out. Blade was pulling up in the parking lot, and in no time at all Rita was racing over to the car, no doubt to squeal on her.

Rita was probably telling Blade that earlier that day Sam had tried defying security to go out and grab lunch at the restaurant on the corner. Mac had come back to the office just in time to talk her out of leaving.

She ran her fingers through her hair, feeling a moment of frustration. She had been back from Houston for over a week and her secret admirer had not once tried contacting her. She was beginning to think it had all been a sick joke played by one of her former clients, or someone she had opposed in a court case. Some people took a loss in the courtroom personally.

She moved away from the window when she saw Blade heading toward the building with an unhappy look on his face. A fierce frown tightened his features. Evidently Rita had told him—the traitor. The woman needed to stick to reading her romance novels.

Sam rolled her eyes. Maybe it was time to make Blade see reason and let up a little. She had no complaints about the amount of time they spent together, especially since he stayed at her place every night. But she thought he was overdoing it a little with this protection thing.

She couldn't go to her front door unless he was dead on her heels. And when he took her home in the afternoons, they stayed there. They either stopped for takeout on the way home or had food delivered to them once they got there. More than once she'd suggested they go out someplace, and he wouldn't hear of it. Well, she was determined that he would listen to her today. Somehow and someway she was determined to get his attention.

She looked up when he flung open her office door. She swallowed the knot caught in her throat and smiled sweetly at him. "Is something wrong, Blade?"

He closed the door with just about as much force as he'd opened it, and crossed his arms over his chest. They were about to have an argument and it was bound to be a doozy. It was a good thing that Priscilla and most of the staff had already left. Peyton had been in court all day and Mac's office was at the other end of the long hallway. Even if Mac heard Blade scolding Sam, she wouldn't have lifted a finger to help, since she believed the tongue-lashing was much deserved.

"Are you out of your mind? I can't believe you planned to go out for lunch by yourself."

"It was to the restaurant on the corner to grab a burger," she said defensively.

"I don't care if it was to go outside on the sidewalk to buy a bag of peanuts. I bring you here every morning and you are to stay put until I come back and pick you up," he said, raising his voice.

That got her dander up. "I've told you before, Blade. You are not my daddy."

He crossed his arms over his chest. "Then maybe I should call Mr. Di Meglio and let him know just how difficult his daughter is being about staying alive."

She glared at him. She still hadn't told her parents anything. "You wouldn't dare."

His smile formed slowly and didn't quite reach his eyes. "Try me, sweetheart."

She continued to glare at him. He *would* call her parents—she had no doubt of that. Already she knew they were getting suspicious, but she wasn't sure of what. When she had talked to them last week they had mentioned possibly coming to see her. Fortunately, she had managed to talk them out of it, telling them she was working on a very important court case. Since they were both attorneys, they understood and had relented. However, they'd informed her that they would be calling her again this week. She dreaded their calls because it meant she would have to lie to them again.

"I want your word, Sam, that you won't be trying something like that again."

She lifted her chin. "You might want my word, but you won't get it. I feel like I'm a prisoner at work and in my home. I want to go out and eat at a restaurant without having to look over my shoulder. I need to get my nails done this week and go to the spa."

"And I told you that I would take you wherever you needed to go."

"But I don't want you to feel obligated to take me places and be my bodyguard. You have your own work to do."

"And I'm doing it. I met with my surveyors today. Everything with the Mosley project is on schedule and we'll hand Luke the keys to the rodeo school on Friday."

She let out a long, frustrated sigh. She had to get him to understand. "Blade, I want to take my car and just drive. I want to feel my hair blowing in the wind without fear that someone's trying to kill me."

"And that time will come, Sam. In fact, I got a call from Alex earlier today, and he's flying into town tomorrow. He has information he wants to share with you."

Blade could tell by the expression on her face that she needed to hear that.

"Really? Do you think that he—"

"Let's not jump to conclusions. Let's just wait to see what he has to say." He dropped his hands to his side. "Are you ready to leave?"

"No."

"No?"

"That's what I said," she told him as she moved from behind her desk, walked over to the window and closed the blinds. Then she glanced over her shoulder. "Lock the door, Blade."

Blade wasn't sure how long he stood there staring at her before he finally reached behind him to lock the door. It was probably when she began stripping off her clothes. He took a deep breath as he watched her, and in no time at all, she had stripped down to nothing more than a pair of black lace panties.

"Is there a reason you're taking off your clothes in here?" he asked, although he was now following her lead and removing his.

"Yes, there is one fantasy I have that we haven't played out yet."

He glanced over at her as he unzipped his pants. "And what fantasy is that?"

"Being taken on my desk. Think you can handle it?"

Blade couldn't help but smile. Hell, at times he wondered if he *could* handle her. When they arrived in Houston, she had declared that it was fantasy week, and each night one of them would act out their wildest sexual fantasies. Some had been real doozies. They had even made out again in a car—the backseat this time—although it was parked in Blade's garage. It hadn't mattered. He had taken her in the car, against the door, as well as on the hood and the fender. The fantasies had been worthwhile.

Sam was everything he could possibly want in a woman—sexually daring, provocative. He loved her and he respected her. There were times when he would find her staring at him as if he was a puzzle she needed to solve that was missing one piece. It was during those times that he wanted to reach out and pull her into his arms and tell her just how much he loved her and that everything would be okay.

Sam slowly walked toward him, swaying her hips, and he moved away from the door to meet her halfway. They were two naked bodies about to intimately become one. She wrapped her arms around his waist and began rubbing her body against him, flesh against flesh and skin against skin.

He picked her up in his arms and carried her to her desk and plopped her naked rear end on top. He then leaned forward and captured her mouth, mating their tongues in one ravenous exchange.

He reached down and used his finger to test her, to see if she was ready for him, and wasn't surprised to find that she was. He pulled his mouth back and whispered against her lips, "You're hot and wet."

"Then make me hotter and wetter."

He tilted her back on the desk and spread her legs in the process. And then his erect and protruding shaft homed in on just where it wanted to go. He teased the well-lubricated opening of her legs before slowly easing inside of her.

His breath caught the moment he sensed the pleasure he always felt when he entered her like this. He'd never thought he would find a woman like her, a woman whose sexual fantasies mirrored his, and who met his every need, not just in the bedroom.

She wrapped her legs around him as he moved inside her, while her inner muscles clenched tight around his engorged erection. Her muscles were working him and he was determined to work her just as hard. Each thrust into her body mirrored just how much he loved her, how much she meant to him, and just how determined he was to never let her go.

When he felt her shudder around him he rolled his hips and rocked into her one final time before exploding, releasing the orgasm he could no longer hold back, and joining her as the two of them climaxed together.

An hour or so later, in a better frame of mind than she had been earlier, Sam got out of the car when Blade parked it in her driveway. He had fulfilled another one of her fantasies and she was happy about it. Sex had to be one of the best stress relievers.

And to top things off, after leaving the office he'd taken her to the restaurant on the corner. Instead of getting takeout, as she assumed they would, he had parked the car, come around and opened her door, took her hand and led her inside the restaurant, requesting a table at the window.

During dinner, it had been quite obvious that he was

watchful and alert. Every so often she would see him looking around, checking out anyone who'd entered the restaurant. But sitting across from him, sharing a meal and telling him how her day had gone had been nice.

"Other than the nail salon and spa, do you have any other appointments this week?" he asked as he waited for her to walk around the car.

She didn't look at him as she pulled her key out of her purse. "Yes, I have a doctor's appointment on Friday."

"A doctor's appointment?"

"Yes," she said, still not looking at him. "My regular checkup."

It wasn't completely true. There was nothing regular about the appointment she had made with her doctor. She was late, and for someone whose cycle was always regular, that concerned her. But then, she knew all the stress of what she was going through might have had something to do with it.

But something Syneda Madaris had said that night at the party in Houston still stuck in her mind.

…the thing about a Madaris man. If he wants to get you pregnant, a simple thing like a birth-control pill or a condom isn't going to stop him….

She glanced over at Blade when he took the key from her hand. Although the two of them had spent the last three weeks making love practically each and every day, there was no reason for her to assume he wanted more out of the relationship. And he was definitely not a man who'd want a baby.

He enjoyed her. She was a novelty. She was a first for him in many ways. A woman he had shared sensual confessions with. But she knew that once he got tired of her, he would walk away without looking back. She knew it and she accepted it because she loved him. She appreciated him caring enough to protect her. But he'd explained in the beginning that the reason he was doing it was to keep Mac, Peyton and Luke from worrying.

"You're expecting a delivery?"

She glanced up at Blade and then at the box that was sitting on her doorstep. "No." She glanced at the label. "It looks like a box from Mom. She's always sending me stuff if she sees something she thinks I'd like. Unfortunately, I inherited her shoe fetish. I'm sure you've noticed I have quite a few."

Blade nodded. He had noticed. But still…

"When you get inside I want you to call your mother to verify she sent you this package."

Sam rolled her eyes. "Is that really necessary?" she asked, opening the door.

"Yes," Blade said. "It's necessary."

"Fine, I'll do it," she said, tossing her purse on the table. "Will you at least bring the box inside the house?"

Blade looked over at her. "I'm not touching that box and neither are you. Just get your mother on the phone, Sam."

Sam glared. "I hope you know if I call her she's going to wonder why I'm even asking, when I know she's sent me stuff before."

"Doesn't matter, Sam. Call her."

When she narrowed her eyes, he said, "Please."

She smiled sweetly as she went back to the sofa and grabbed her cell phone out of her purse. "Sure, Blade, now that you've *begged*."

He ignored her comment as he thought about the box sitting on her doorstep. He wasn't a paranoid person, but for some reason he felt the hair on the back of his neck stand up. He heard the conversation between Sam and her mother and knew what she was going to say before she'd hung up the phone.

Blade was already pulling out his cell phone and dialing 9-1-1.

Chapter 23

The man meant to kill her.

That was a fair enough assessment to make, Detective Adams thought, as he glanced over at Sam and Blade. Blade was holding her in his arms while her face was pressed against his chest.

The bomb squad was leaving after detonating what had been a bomb. Had she opened the box, it would have blown her and anyone standing within twenty feet of her to smithereens. He could tell that Sam was upset and afraid, and rightly so. To finally realize someone meant to kill you was enough to cause anyone distress. And it hadn't been one of those amateur, homemade bombs. Whoever had put it together knew exactly what he or she was doing. It was someone who knew enough about chemistry and physics to make a fairly sophisticated explosive device.

"I suggest the two of you find somewhere else to go

tonight," Detective Adams said. "And the fewer people who know where you are the better until we can find out who's behind this. The only thing the guard at the security gate knows is that the package was delivered by the regular FedEx deliveryman for this route."

Detective Adams took in a deep breath. "Chances are the deliveryman didn't have a clue what he was delivering. In fact, if someone had broadsided his truck, he and everything within twenty feet would have been blown up."

Blade's lips tightened. Although he had called the police he had hoped it was a false alarm. The bomb squad had closed off the area while they investigated the package, and once they discovered it contained live explosives set to go off when the package was opened, they went to work.

"Mr. Madaris?"

"I heard you," Blade said, trying not to show his anger, especially toward anyone associated with the police. They had been more than helpful, considerate and very efficient. He just didn't want to think about what could have happened to Sam if she'd opened that box. His arms tightened around her just thinking about how he could have lost her.

"I understand you've called Alex Maxwell into this," Detective Adams said.

Blade nodded.

"Then I'm confident we'll have the person responsible sooner rather than later. We don't have the manpower or resources that he seems to have. With Maxwell's help, we'll have this lunatic behind bars before he can try anything else."

Blade hoped so, too. He wouldn't rest until the person who had tried to hurt his woman was captured.

He leaned back and looked down at Sam, and could tell she was still in a state of shock. "We're leaving here tonight, Sam. I want you to go upstairs and grab some things. We'll be gone for a few days, at least three to four."

The police and bomb squad had already done a thorough sweep of her house to make sure that nothing had been tampered with and there had been no forced entry. But until the authorities talked to the FedEx driver, no one was taking any chances.

She glanced up at him, and the look Blade saw in her eyes nearly ripped his heart out. The fire was gone from her eyes. But he knew that eventually it would return and when it did it she would be mad as hell at the person responsible. Her temper would be out of control, and it would be the one time he wouldn't mind seeing it.

"Do you need me to help you pack, sweetheart?" he asked softly.

She shook her head as she stepped out of his arms. "No, I can do it. I'll be back in a few."

He watched as she walked up the stairs.

Ignoring how badly her hands were shaking, Sam hurriedly went through several drawers in her bedroom, pulling out items and throwing them in the suitcase on her bed. Enough for three or four days, as Blade had said.

She paused for a moment to take a deep breath when reality hit hard once again. Someone had tried to blow her up. Someone truly wanted her dead. She actually felt weak in the knees knowing there was a person who hated her enough to want to end her life.

"Samari?"

She quickly wiped the tears from her eyes, then turned around. Blade rarely called her Samari except when they were making love. "Yes?"

"Come here, baby."

She quickly crossed the room and walked right into his open arms. "I promise you that we will get this guy," he whispered.

She heard the conviction and the determination in his voice. "I know. But all this time I thought… I was really hoping that it was a bad joke. I never really thought that someone actually wanted to hurt me."

She drew in a deep breath. Now she knew and she would never be caught off guard again.

"Luke, this is Blade."

It took Blade a good fifteen minutes to tell his cousin what had happened. It would have taken less time if Mac, who'd been standing next to Luke, hadn't kept interrupting by asking questions.

"Assure Mac that Sam's okay, just shaken up a bit. We're at one of those resort hotels in the mountains that have a cluster of chateau-style villas, and we're staying put for a while. Alex is supposed to arrive in the morning and he'll head straight to your place. I want you to bring him here, Luke. And you might want to check your rearview mirror periodically to make sure you aren't being followed."

Blade gave Luke the name of the resort and their villa number. "I don't know what information Alex has for us, and other than contacting you, I haven't made any other calls. The fewer people who know where we are the better. And have Mac clear Sam's calendar, because she won't be back in the office this week."

Moments later he ended the call and placed the phone on the dresser. The resort was a pretty nice place if you needed somewhere to hide out, and until that lunatic was caught he intended to keep Sam right here. What nearly happened today had taken a good twenty years off his life.

He glanced up when he heard the bathroom door open. She had showered. They usually took showers together, but he'd needed to call Luke to apprise him of what had happened. Of course, both Luke and Mac were furious, but grateful Sam was okay.

Blade saw that she was wearing the bathrobe supplied by the hotel, and knew that she was naked underneath. Sex should have been the last thing on his mind but it wasn't. He would always want her, anytime and anyplace. But now, what she needed was for him to hold her, assure her that she was safe.

"Are you okay?" he asked softly.

She nodded as she tried drying her hair with a towel. "Yes."

He crossed the room and took the towel out of her hand. "Sit," he said, pulling out the chair at the desk for her.

She glared up at him and he saw some fire returning to her eyes, but not enough to suit him. When she sat in the chair he went about drying her hair. This was the first time he'd dried a woman's hair, but then there had been so many firsts with Sam.

"I called Luke and Mac and told them what happened," he said.

She didn't say anything. She simply nodded.

"Mac is going to clear your calendar for the rest of the week."

She nodded at that, too.

"We're staying here for a while. At least till Sunday, and then we'll decide where we'll go. If I have to, I'll take you back to Houston, to Whispering Pines. Nobody can get on that ranch unless Jake wants them there."

When she still didn't say anything to that, he said, "And I want you naked for the entire time we're here."

She turned around, glared at him, stood up and snatched the towel out of his hand. "You horny bastard, don't hold your breath!"

He laughed. "Hey, the fire's back and I love it. I was beginning to miss your smart mouth."

When Sam realized what Blade was trying to do, she threw herself into his arms and pressed her face against his chest and wrapped her arms around his waist. She needed his strength. And she would give just about anything for his love.

Blade held Sam tight for a long moment and then picked her up in his arms and carried her over to the bed. "I just want to hold you, sweetheart. Nothing more, I promise," he said, tucking her close to his side as he stretched out in the bed. "I really need to hold you."

There was no conversation between them as he held her, needing to have her close to him as much as it seemed she needed to have him close to her. A few moments later, he said in a strained yet husky voice, "I could have lost you, Sam. Damn, I could have lost you. And what scared me most is the thought of losing you without letting you know how much I love you."

Her body went still and for a moment he wasn't sure she was breathing. "Sam?"

She shifted slightly and turned in his arms to meet his gaze. "You love me?"

He reached out and traced the tip of his finger down the side of her face. "Yes. And I'm not saying that to try and put pressure on you or anything. I know you don't love me yet, but I might as well warn you that if I have anything to say about it, you will eventually."

Sam had to fight the tears from falling from her eyes when she whispered, "I do."

Blade lifted a brow. "You do what?"

She reached out and placed the palm of her hand against his cheek. "I do love you."

He pulled back slightly and stared at her. "You do not."

She couldn't help but grin. "I do, too."

She moved up in the bed and leaned over him. "I love you, Blade Madaris, and that's what scared me the most, too. The thought that I could have died and you would not have known how I felt. You would have had no idea how much I love you."

"Oh, baby." Blade pulled the woman he loved into his arms and covered her mouth with his. This was his woman. He loved her more than life itself and was determined more than ever to protect her. Nothing in this world was more important to him than her.

Chapter 24

When Sam awoke the next morning it was to find her body curled up close to Blade with his large arm slung over her hip, as if he needed to make sure she was there, plastered to him and safe from harm. She shifted her body and smiled, knowing she truly had something to smile about.

Blade loved her.

She never considered herself a crybaby, but she felt tears welling up in the back of her eyes. The two of them were an unlikely couple. He had been the player and she, the player hater. And she had done all the things to him that had been her trademark. And he still had come back. He had been there when she needed him. If she would have defied him and opened that box, she would not only have taken her life but taken his, as well.

She closed her eyes when she realized just how close she'd come to doing that. That damn lunatic. That crazy person had a lot of friggin' nerve to want her dead. She couldn't wait until he was caught and when he was, she would—

"The fire is boiling over in your eyes now. You're pretty hot in more ways than one," Blade said, lifting her up and placing her on top of him. She'd known he'd only wanted to hold her, but after his sensual confession that he loved her, she had wanted him to make love to her, and he had, several times. And she had drifted off to sleep with him still embedded deep inside of her. It hadn't been the first time they'd gone to sleep that way, and she was going to make sure it wasn't the last.

"What time is Alex arriving?" she asked. She was ready to hear what he had to say.

"His flight got in a couple of hours ago."

Her eyes widened. "That means he could be on his way here," she said, trying to pull out of Blade's arms.

"Doesn't matter. I'm getting this."

And then he kissed her in the way she was getting used to being kissed by him. It was a long, drawn-out, make-your-panties-wet kiss. The only problem was she wasn't wearing any panties.

She pulled back and broke off the kiss. "Come on, Blade, we have plenty of time for that later. We need to get dressed."

He released her and she eased out of bed. "I want to be dressed with the coffee brewing when he gets here, and I need to shower first."

Blade watched her walk into the bathroom in all her naked splendor, and when he heard the sound of the water running, he decided he wanted to take a shower, as well. He eased out of bed and followed the woman he loved.

"Thanks, Sam," Alex said, accepting the cup of coffee. He glanced over at Sam and Blade and thought something was different. Oh, he'd known since the other night in Houston that they were having an affair, but Christy thought it was more than that. Seeing them together now, he was beginning to think so, too.

He watched how Blade was keeping her within easy reach, and when she moved, so did Blade's eyes. She was rarely out of his sight. If Blade hadn't already fallen in love with her, then he was more than halfway there.

Alex bit into his bagel. Luke had stopped by a deli and bought a dozen of them. Sam had eaten only one. He, Luke and Blade had practically finished off the others.

"So, you think you know who sent the bomb, Alex?"

That question came from Blade. He, Alex and Luke were in chairs in the sitting-room area of the hotel room. Sam was perched on the arm of Blade's chair and his arm was wrapped around her waist.

Alex took a sip of his coffee. "I think so, but first let me tell you who I don't suspect any longer."

Blade nodded. "All right."

Alex opened his notepad. "First, Tyrell Graham."

Sam's gaze sharpened. "And just what is good old Tyrell doing these days?" she asked.

Alex met her eyes. "Nothing. The man is dead. He was shot by his girlfriend last year and she's presently serving time for it. She caught him cheating and blew him away."

Sam flinched upon hearing about Graham's death. Although she thought he was scum, she felt bad about it.

"And I think we can scratch LaSalle off the list, as well. In fact I'm pretty sure of it," Alex said.

Luke, who had heard the story about Belton LaSalle from Mac, asked, "Why is he off the list?"

"Because he hasn't lived in the United States since his probation ended. He found religion and moved to Africa to work as a missionary," Alex responded.

Sam leaned forward, clearly astonished. "You've *got* to be kidding me."

Alex shook his head and tried hiding his smile. "Trust me, I'm not."

"Wow."

"And as far as Guy Carrington is concerned, he is practicing law at a firm in Miami and has a nice place on the beach. He's a happy-go-lucky bachelor, although he's paying out the yin yang in child support."

Blade had been quiet, listening to what Alex was saying. "If all those people have pretty much been eliminated, then who's remaining?" he asked.

Alex met Sam's gaze, and hesitated. "I've narrowed it down to one person who is our prime suspect right now."

Sam swallowed and pulled in a deep breath. She felt Blade's arms tighten around her. "And who is he, Alex?"

The room got quiet as Alex leaned forward in his chair and held Sam's gaze. "I know you're going to find this hard to believe, Sam, but all my evidence points to Frederick Rowe."

For a moment Sam just stared back at Alex and then she stood. "That's impossible. There has to be a mistake. I don't believe it. I refuse to believe it. And I hope you have a good reason for saying something like that!"

Everyone could tell how upset Sam was. Anyone who knew her for any length of time knew she didn't do anything halfway, whether it was seeking revenge, settling a score, defending a client or choosing her friends. Rowe was a friend she trusted, and she refused to believe the worst about him.

Alex flipped a page in the notepad, then glanced over at Sam. "These are my reasons for making him the prime suspect. Maybe there is an explanation, but until we know what that is, he heads the list."

Drawing in a deep breath, she went back to sit on the arm of the chair beside Blade. Instinctively, he wrapped his arms around her waist.

"First of all," Alex said, "were you aware that over the past three months Rowe has come to Oklahoma City at least a dozen times?"

Sam blinked. No, she hadn't known that. Why would FDR come to town without contacting her, or not even stay at her place? "No, I didn't know," she said honestly. "But maybe he has business interests here that he's keeping private," she added in his defense.

Alex shrugged. "Possibly. And did you know he's in town now and has been since the beginning of the week?"

Sam pulled away from Blade to stand up again. Surprise was etched all over her face. "FDR is here? In Oklahoma City?"

Alex nodded. "Yes. I had someone track him to a hotel last night, where he is staying."

Sam didn't say anything. She couldn't help wondering what FDR was up to. When she had talked to Angelo earlier in the week, he'd said Frederick had taken a few days off to visit the aunt who'd raised him. She lived in Florida.

Knowing everyone in the room was waiting for her to respond, she said, "No, I didn't know that, either. My brother mentioned he'd taken some time off to visit a relative in Florida."

She rubbed her hands down her slacks. She knew those two things alone raised suspicions about FDR, but she still wasn't convinced. "Still," she said, "that doesn't mean anything other than he's keeping his comings and goings a secret for some reason and—"

"And we've discovered the secret," Alex interrupted. "It baffled me how your 'secret admirer' knew when you were out of the office, which is the reason flowers weren't delivered that week you went home to New York to visit your parents. Now I believe I know why."

Needing the comfort of Blade's touch, Sam sat back down on the arm of the chair and he automatically reached out and again wrapped his arms around her waist. "Why?" she asked.

Alex hesitated for a moment. "He's having an affair with someone in your office, Sam. And from what I gather, the affair has been going on for about six months now."

Sam threw her head back and closed her eyes. This was crazy, simply crazy. FDR was having an affair with someone in her office and she didn't know about it? She lowered her head, opened her eyes and looked back at Alex. "Who is it?"

Alex's gaze was unwavering. "Your secretary, Priscilla Gaines."

If Blade's arms hadn't been around Sam's waist, she would have toppled over and literally fallen and hit the floor. Priscilla had been the law firm's secretary since day one, and Sam knew she rarely dated anyone. Not that it mattered, but Priscilla was twelve years older than FDR and she was a single mother raising her twin boys.

Sam glanced around the room and saw the way the men were all looking at her. Alex was right—all of FDR's secrets were incriminating. However, she still refused to believe the worst about him.

"Fine, those things make him a suspect. But there is the one thing that as an attorney I know you haven't presented, and that's a motive."

Alex leaned back in his chair as he flipped to another page in his notepad. "I think this would be sufficient motive," he said, tearing out the sheet and handing it to her.

Sam hesitated, refusing to even look at it as she passed it on to Blade. "What does the paper say? What would have been his motive, Alex?" she asked softly.

Alex took a deep breath. "Revenge. Does the name Alvin Quincy ring a bell?"

Sam scrunched up her face for a moment and quickly said yes. "Years ago, when my father was a prosecutor, he sent him to prison. Quincy escaped around six years ago, a little after I moved here. He'd always made threats about getting back at my father, and when he was freed, he went after my brother, Angelo, running him off the road, nearly killing him. Everyone figured he'd come after me or my parents next, which is the reason my family talked me into moving to Windsor Park, for security reasons."

"Was the man ever captured?" Luke asked.

Sam shook her head. "Yes, but he swore he would never be taken alive and was killed in a shoot-out when the police tried to apprehend him."

She glanced over at Alex. "But what does any of that have to do with FDR?"

Alex closed his notepad. He met her gaze. "It seems that Frederick Damon Rowe is Alvin Quincy's son."

Those were the last words Sam heard before everything around her suddenly turned black and she passed out.

Chapter 25

Luke glanced up at Blade when he reentered the room. "How is she?"

"I think she's in shock. I know for a fact she's still in denial." He glanced over at Alex. "Even after all you've told her, she still wants to believe FDR isn't a suspect."

Alex nodded in understanding. "It's hard to comprehend that someone you trust has betrayed you."

"Betrayed, hell!" Blade stormed, his anger escalating. "The man tried to kill her. Blow her up. What kind of damn friend is that?"

"Calm down, Blade," Luke said.

"I won't calm down until Rowe is put in jail and the keys are thrown away. But not before I kick his—"

The sound of Luke's cell phone ringing drowned out Blade's words, and Luke was glad. He'd never seen Blade this angry before about anything, and definitely not over a woman. He saw the caller was Mac. "Hello, sweetheart."

"We have trouble," Mac said, almost whispering into the phone.

Luke stood. "Why? What's up?"

"Sam's parents are here. They arrived this morning and want to know where she is, and have threatened to turn this city upside down until they find her. When they first got to town they went straight to her town house, and someone at the security gate told them about the bomb."

Luke ran his hands down his face. He had met Sam's parents before. They could be a force to deal with when it came to their children. "Hold on a minute, Mac." He then relayed to Blade and Alex what Mac had told him.

Blade released a curse. "Great! That's all we need."

"Yes, but at least we got our prime suspect under surveillance, and I'm going to contact Detective Adams to pick him up from the hotel and bring him in for questioning."

"And I want to be there when you do," Blade almost growled.

Alex rolled his eyes. "I don't think that's a good idea."

Blade met his friend's gaze. "My woman was almost killed, Alex. There's no way I'm not going to be there when Rowe is brought in."

Alex pulled in a deep breath of air, then pushed it out. "Fine, but I wouldn't suggest that Sam be there. Are you going to leave her here alone?"

"Damn," Blade uttered. He'd forgotten about that.

"Two of Jake's men are parked outside," Luke said. "I had them follow us to make sure we weren't followed by anyone. I can leave them here to keep an eye on things until we get back."

Blade nodded. He knew all of Jake's men, since most of them had worked for his uncle for years. Since Jake and Mac were partners in a land-grazing deal, Jake's men rotated periodically to stay with the herd. They were men who could be trusted.

"That's a good idea," Blade said. "I'd feel better about leaving her, knowing they're here. Let me go check on Sam again. I want to tell her our plans and also tell her that her parents are in town."

"Handling my parents won't be easy, Blade. Maybe I should go," Sam said, easing off the bed.

"No, you should lie down awhile longer. I wish you'd let me call the doctor. Are you sure you're okay?"

Sam took a deep breath. She had no recollection of ever fainting before, even when she'd been told about Vivian. "I'm fine, really. But maybe you're right. I should rest up to deal with my parents later. And Blade, I know everything that Alex said about FDR makes it look bad, and I know this might sound crazy, but I still refuse to believe he did it."

Blade pulled her into his arms. "There's nothing wrong with not wanting to believe the worst about someone you care deeply about, sweetheart."

"But that's just it, Blade. I don't believe the worst in FDR. No matter what evidence there is stacked against him. He would not want me dead. I just won't believe it."

As he drove to the law offices of Madaris, Di Meglio and Mahoney, Luke glanced toward the backseat of his truck. "You're quiet, Alex."

Alex looked up from his mini laptop. "I'm just checking out a few things. I've learned from prior cases that it's not over till the fat lady sings, and for some reason she hasn't taken center stage with this one yet."

Blade, who was sitting up front in the passenger seat, turned around. "Are you beginning to think that it's not Rowe?" he asked.

Alex shrugged. "I'm beginning to think we need to get him in and question him as soon as possible. I called Detective Adams and asked that he bring him to the law firm instead of picking him up and taking him down to headquarters. That way we'll have him and Priscilla Gaines there together. I met Ms. Gaines last year while handling that case for Mac, and she genuinely seemed to care for Mac, Sam and Peyton. She was almost overprotective of them. I can't see her wanting to hurt one of them."

"Not even for love?" Blade asked. "If she thinks she's fallen in love with Rowe and he's convinced her that he has a legitimate gripe with Sam, then she would possibly go along with anything he has planned—including murder."

"Yes, but…" Alex shook his head. "Even with a motive of revenge on Rowe's part, why lash out at Sam when he was there working at the firm every day with the very man who had put his father behind bars? Why not lash out at Antonio Di Meglio, Sam's mother or her brother?"

Alex didn't say anything for a moment. "There is something I need to check out. I can feel it," he said, looking back at his laptop.

Luke and Blade didn't say anything. They'd known Alex long enough to know that he wouldn't leave any stone unturned in this investigation, and that if someone other than Rowe was involved, Alex would uncover it.

Blade didn't know what to expect upon meeting Sam's parents, but it hadn't been a slightly older version of Clayton and Syneda. In their early fifties, the two were dynamic together.

Sam's mother, who looked like an older version of Sam, was simply beautiful, gorgeous in her own right. And her father was tall, dark and dashingly handsome.

Blade would bet any money that the man had been a rogue in his day. And with his striking looks, Blade would also bet he had been a heartbreaker. Like his daughter, he had sharp eyes, and also like his daughter, an even sharper tongue.

Antonio and Kayla Di Meglio lit into him the moment he walked into Mac's office, and began questioning him as if he was on the witness stand. Who was he to their daughter? Where was she? Who would want to hurt her? And what steps were being taken to assure her safety?

He was grateful that, like Sam, Mac had a large office, big enough to accommodate the eight people crowded into it. He decided not to beat around the bush, and to let Sam's parents know his role in their daughter's life.

"I'm Blade Madaris, the man who's going to marry Samari," he said, shocking everyone in the room.

"Marry her?" Sam's father said, with an expression indicating he was stunned, as well. "I just saw my daughter a few weeks ago and she never said anything about being serious about anyone."

"We became involved after she returned," Blade said. "Just believe me when I say that I love Sam, she loves me, and when all this is over, I am marrying her."

"And what about babies?" Kayla Di Meglio quickly asked. "You do want children one day, right?"

"Yes," Blade said with a serious expression on his face. "We will have lots of children." He thought about the text message he'd received from Slade that morning, saying their great-grandmother had dreamed about fish yet again. What was this for her, a bonus year? That made him wonder.

"And as far as where Sam is," he continued, "she's in a safe location for now, until we discover who sent that bomb yesterday. I hired a family friend, Alex Maxwell, to investigate and—"

"Alex Maxwell?" Sam's father interrupted, glancing across the room at Alex, who was sitting alone in a corner, working on his laptop.

Alex glanced up. "Yes?"

"I've heard of you," Sam's father said. "Your name and reputation precede you—admirably, I might add."

Alex nodded. "Thank you." He then turned his attention to whatever was on his computer screen.

Antonio turned his attention back to Blade. "Do you have any idea who would want to hurt my daughter?"

"Yes. Our prime suspect right now is a man who works for you, and we believe his accomplice is someone who works here for this firm."

Shock showed on Sam's parents' faces. "Who?"

"Frederick Rowe."

"Frederick?" Sam's father said in disbelief. "That's absurd. My wife and I wouldn't believe Frederick any more capable of hurting Sam than her own brother would."

"Thanks for the vote of confidence, Mr. Di Meglio," a deep voice said from the doorway. "Especially since it seems I might be in need of an attorney, if I don't decide to represent myself."

Everyone turned toward the door, where a man Blade figured to be Frederick Rowe stood flanked by Detective Adams on one side and a police officer on the other.

Sam was sitting at a table drinking a cup of coffee and awaiting word from Blade. She hoped that he believed her when she said that there was no way that FDR was involved.

She nearly jumped when there was a knock at the door and wondered if it was the cleaning lady, come to straighten up the villa. As Sam walked to the door to look out the peephole, she tried to stop her heart from racing upon remembering that two of Jake's men were stationed outside in the parking lot.

She was surprised to see the person standing on the other side. She took the chain off the door and opened it. "Frank? What are you doing here?"

The man who'd worked as a security guard at their law firm for the past year flashed a friendly smile. "Mr. Madaris asked me to come and get you. Something has come up and they need you at the office."

Sam nodded. Evidently her parents were out of control and giving everybody grief. "Okay, let me grab my purse. I thought you were still out of town, skiing in Colorado," she said, rushing over to the table to get her purse and slip into her shoes.

"I returned to town early and they called me to come in when Rita phoned in sick this morning."

"Oh."

Sam picked up her purse, turned around and smiled at him. "Okay, I'm ready to go."

Antonio Di Meglio glanced over at Blade. "Why did you think Frederick had anything to do with this threat against Sam?"

"Motive."

"And what motive is that?" Kayla Di Meglio asked, pushing her hair away from her face, a habit her daughter had evidently inherited.

"Revenge. Do you know who his father is?" Blade asked.

Antonio Di Meglio nodded. "Yes. A man I sent to prison when Frederick was no more than ten years old. My wife and I kept up with Frederick, who was sent to live with his grandmother when his father was put away.

His mother was killed driving the getaway car. It was a bank robbery, planned by Alvin Quincy and his girlfriend, in which three innocent people were killed."

Frederick continued the story. "The Di Meglios were there for me when I was growing up. Not that they had to be, but because they are good people. And when I got older and expressed an interest in law, they provided me with money for law school and made sure I had a job afterward."

Blade nodded. "Sam didn't know." It was a statement more than a question.

"We never told Sam," Kayla Di Meglio said. "We felt that if and when Frederick wanted her to know, he would tell her."

"Eventually, I would have told her," Frederick said. "In the beginning it was important that she accepted me and got to know the man I am. Then, after a while, when she did accept me for who I was, it didn't matter. So, no, she didn't know."

"Even when she found out about your relationship to Quincy and about all your trips to Oklahoma that she didn't know about, she still believed you were innocent," Blade said.

"And the reason he didn't tell anyone about those visits was mainly because of me," Priscilla said, as she nervously entered the office.

She moved over to Frederick's side. "We fell in love, but I wasn't ready for anyone to know I was involved with a younger man. And I made him promise not to tell anyone."

Mac leaned back in her chair. "So, we still don't know who sent that bomb."

"Yes, we do." Alex, who'd been quietly working at his laptop, suddenly jumped up. "Damn. The bastard covered his tracks well."

He looked up, saw everyone staring at him and decided to explain. "According to the statement received from the FedEx driver, he'd made deliveries in Sam's complex that day, but he didn't leave one for Sam, which meant it had to be personally delivered. I asked the security company for Sam's complex to provide me with the names of all their employees, regardless of whether they were working that day or not. I just compared that list to the list of employees Sam sent me, of who works here, including your security staff. I saw a number of them work at both places."

Mac nodded. "That can be explained. When Sam, Peyton and I decided to hire security service here, Sam recommended that we use the same company that was being used in her gated community. They had a good reputation."

"Yes, but one of their employees is someone we need to question immediately," Alex said.

"Who?" Blade asked, moving toward Alex.

"Frank Denson."

"Frank?" Peyton asked, surprised. "Why would Frank want to hurt Sam?"

Alex sighed deeply. "I just finished doing an extensive background check on Denson, who changed his last name, by the way. The man has a degree in chemical engineering from MIT."

"Why would someone with that kind of degree and from such a prestigious school work as a security guard?" Detective Adams asked.

"According to the report I received just now," Alex said, "he had a mental breakdown after his last year of college. It seems he never got over his sister's suicide almost ten years ago. The two were extremely close growing up. Their parents had been abusive, so the two had always been there for each other."

"And who was his sister?" Mac asked.

Alex pulled in a deep breath, then said, "Vivian Randall."

"Vivian Randall!" Sam's father exclaimed. "She was Sam's roommate her first year at college. Randall committed suicide over some guy on campus. Why would Denson want to get back at Sam for that?"

"He probably blames her," Blade said, thinking out loud. "Damn. I bet in his mental state that he blames Sam for what happened to his sister."

"But why?" Kayla Di Meglio was asking. "Sam had nothing to do with that. Vivian Randall committed suicide. Sam wasn't even in their dorm room when she did it."

"Yes," Blade said, nodding. "But Vivian Randall used Sam's prescription drugs when she overdosed. I know that shouldn't matter, but I bet in Denson's sick mind, she's just as guilty as Tyrell Graham, the man who drove Randall to commit suicide."

"Then why not go after Graham and leave my daughter alone?" Antonio Di Meglio angrily asked.

"He might have," Alex replied. "Tyrell Graham was killed last year and his girlfriend was arrested for the crime. But she has always maintained her innocence. Now I'm wondering if perhaps she was set up."

At that moment Luke's phone rang, and when he saw the call was from one of the men posted to watch Sam, he quickly picked up. "Yes, Marvin, what's up?"

"Did you forget to call to let us know you were sending someone from Security to pick up Ms. Di Meglio? That security guard from her office showed up and they just drove off."

"What!" Luke exclaimed getting to his feet. "Follow them. Stay a safe distance behind and let us know where he's headed."

Luke clicked off the phone and look at everyone. "That was one of the men we left guarding Sam. It seems Denson showed up, probably convinced her we sent for her, and she left with him. The bastard has Sam."

Detective Adams pulled his cell phone out of his jacket pocket and, ignoring Blade's roar of anger, called in to headquarters. "I need police backup."

Chapter 26

They had been riding for a good ten minutes when Sam glanced over at Frank. "Why are we going this way? This is not the way to the office."

Frank chuckled. "I was wondering how long it would take you to notice. We aren't going to the office, Ms. Di Meglio."

Sam was confused. "Why? I thought you said Blade asked that you bring me to him and that—"

"I lied."

For the first time since being in Frank's presence, she felt the hair on the back of her neck stand up. "What's going on, Frank? I think you need to take me back to the resort."

The laugh that came out of his mouth chilled Sam to the bone. "And I think you need to shut up. You would be dead now if you had opened that box like I planned."

His words sent Sam's mind reeling. "You're the one who sent that bomb?"

"Guilty as charged, Counselor," he said, bringing the car to a stop. "And I found out where you were from eavesdropping on a conversation between Ms. Madaris and Ms. Mahoney this morning. It gave me another chance to take care of you once and for all."

"But why? What have I ever done to you?" She glanced around and saw Frank had brought her to a secluded area near an abandoned warehouse.

"You helped take away the only person who loved me. Because of you, I lost my sister."

Sam began racking her brain, trying to remember what case she'd handled that had involved anyone that could have been in Frank's family. "Your sister? There must be a mistake."

Frank grinned. "No mistake. Those were *your* pills."

Sam frowned. "My pills?"

"Yes. My sister took your pills and killed herself."

"Vivian?" Sam exclaimed.

Saying her roommate's name made Frank's face become more contorted with rage. "Yes, Vivian!" he screamed. "They were *your* pills, so you helped kill her. I've already killed Tyrell Graham for his part, and I was glad to let him know who I was before putting a bullet in his head."

Frank smiled, and the way his lips curled sent chills through Sam's entire body. "Then I set it up to make it seem that it was his girlfriend's doing," he said proudly. "That wasn't hard to do, since I heard them arguing that same day. A lot of the neighbors heard them, too. And since I worked security at that condo complex, I followed her back to her place so I'd know where she lived. When I killed Graham, it was easy for me to return to her place and hide the murder weapon inside her house."

He paused as if gathering his thoughts. "And now, Samari Di Meglio, I am going to kill you. Now get out of my car."

"They've turned off a road that leads to an abandoned warehouse," one of Jake's men said to Luke on his cell phone.

"We're there," Luke said, turning off the main highway and onto a dirt road. He heard Blade curse and knew exactly how his cousin felt. Luke had gone through the same thing when Mac's life had been in danger.

Detective Adams had reviewed a map of the area and figured out where Sam was being taken, so his men were already in place. But Luke knew that was not enough to satisfy Blade, since anything could go wrong.

Before they'd left the law firm, Patsy Ackerman had admitted to the police that she was the one who'd kept Frank informed about Sam's whereabouts, and knew that he had been sending her the flowers. Frank had convinced Patsy that he wasn't planning to harm Sam, but just wanted to shake her up a bit. Patsy hadn't realized how obsessed he was until he had come over to her place and told her about the bomb. He had tied Patsy up and said he would take care of Ms. Di Meglio and then come back and deal with her.

Luckily, Patsy was able to untie herself. The police officer who'd accompanied Detective Adams to the office with Rowe had transported Patsy down to police headquarters for further questioning.

It hadn't been easy, but they had convinced Sam's parents to remain at the law office with Mac and Peyton, who seemed capable of handling the couple better than anyone.

Luke glanced over at Blade and saw the intense look on his face. "You love Sam, don't you? I mean really love her."

Blade, who'd been staring straight ahead, glanced back. "Yes, I really love her, and I'm not going to try and figure out how it happened. It happened. And like I told her parents, I'm going to marry her." Blade took a deep breath and shook his head. "I remember Justin saying that Lorren was his fate. In my case, Sam is my destiny."

Luke was about to ask another question when his phone rang. He listened for a short while and then ended the call. "Frank's at the abandoned warehouse and he's made Sam get out of the car," he told Blade.

Sam knew that Frank was unstable, and she didn't intend to become another one of his victims. She had every intention of getting way from him as soon as she could.

"Move," Frank ordered, breaking into her thoughts.

"Frank, please listen and—"

"Shut up or I'll shoot you now."

She'd seen the gun and, considering his mental state, knew she had to tread lightly. She began walking. "Shooting you now and getting it over with isn't such a bad idea," Frank said. "Stop and turn around."

She slowly turned as he'd ordered her to. At that moment she knew she didn't have a chance to escape, and talking to Frank was no use.

"Vivian died because of you. If you hadn't had those pills, she wouldn't have died," he snarled.

Sam pulled in a deep breath. There was no way she could reason with him to make him see that even if she hadn't had the pills, Vivian would have found some other way to end her life.

"And now you will die," he said.

She stared at him and saw the demented look in his

eyes and felt her knees weaken. At least she had told Blade she loved him.

Frank raised the gun and aimed it straight at her head. She closed her eyes, and the moment she did, a shot rang out, then a second. She opened her eyes and saw Frank crumple to the ground. Someone had shot him.

She looked around as police officers came swarming from everywhere. She heard Blade call her name, and then she saw him racing toward her. Somehow she found the strength to move, once she realized what had happened.

She threw herself into Blade's arms as he pulled her close and whispered that he loved her. She buried her face in his shirt, trembling with relief that he was there. Sam knew at that moment that she was safe and in the arms of the man she loved.

Sam opened her eyes, once again shivering while reliving the nightmare of Frank Denton aiming a gun at her head.

"It's okay, sweetheart. You're here with me."

She took a deep breath at the sound of the deep, husky voice so close to her ear. Instinctively, she leaned back against Blade's hard body, and the arm already around her middle tightened.

They were naked, in her bed, after having made love earlier. Now he was whispering in her ear, telling her how he wanted to make love to her so that she would forget the near tragic incident earlier that day.

After providing Detective Adams and the police with all the information they needed, Blade had taken Sam home and run warm, sudsy water in the Jacuzzi tub, then had gotten in with her. With strong gentle hands he had tried soothing away all her hurts and fears.

He had dried her off, wrapped her securely in a towel and taken her to the living room, where he had held her in his arms until she had gone to sleep. She had awakened hours later in bed and wearing the nightgown he had put on her.

She had gotten dressed and had gone downstairs to find Blade in the kitchen, preparing dinner. The moment he looked up and saw her, he'd stopped what he was doing, moved toward her and pulled her into his arms. He had swept her off her feet, taken her upstairs and had made love to her until they were both satisfied and completely drained. Then they had drifted off to sleep until she awoke from the nightmare of her recent ordeal at the hands of Frank Denton.

She shifted in bed and turned toward Blade and pulled his mouth to hers, eased her tongue between the lips she adored and kissed him in a way she needed to. He responded the way she wanted, taking over the kiss, and had her moaning moments later.

He pulled his mouth away and trailed kisses down her throat before returning to her mouth again. Later, he gathered her into his arms. "Hungry?" he asked in a deep voice.

She gave him an affirmative nod. Other than the bagel and coffee she'd had for breakfast, she hadn't eaten anything. "What were you cooking?"

"Baked chicken, rice pilaf, green beans and corn bread," he said proudly.

She smiled and licked her lips. "I can't wait."

He laughed. "I prepared enough, since I invited your parents over."

She blinked in surprise. "My parents?"

"Yes. I can expect Luke and Mac to entertain them for

just so long. The only reason they haven't shown up is because I convinced them you needed your rest."

Sam appreciated that.

"They were worried about you, which is why they flew into town in the first place. They suspected something was up. I talked to them earlier today and assured them I would take care of you."

"You did?"

"Yes, and I might as well confess right now that I told them I was going to marry you."

She studied him for a moment, trying to gauge if he was serious or not. "Are you?" she asked.

"Am I what?"

"Going to marry me?"

"I hope that I am. Will you marry me?"

She smiled. "Is this an official proposal?"

"Yes," he said with a serious expression on his face. "I thought I'd never ask a woman to marry me, but I need you in my life, Sam. And if you prefer to live here because of your law practice, then I can move to Oklahoma City."

"But what about your company?"

"I can set up a satellite office here. Houston is only eighty minutes away by air, and Slade and I have been thinking about purchasing a Cessna for the company, anyway."

"You can fly a plane?"

He laughed. "After the incident with Christy a couple of years ago, we decided to all get our pilot's licenses." He didn't say anything for a moment and then asked, "So, will you marry me?"

She reached up and placed her arms around his neck. "Yes, I will marry you."

Blade's smile spread from ear to ear. "I might as well do another one of those sensual confession things," he said.

"About what?"

He reached out and gently rubbed her stomach. "I told your parents that we would make lots of babies."

She held his gaze. "And you want babies, Blade? Lots of them?"

"Yes, I want babies, lots of them. And for a man who'd never given a thought to being a father, that's saying a lot."

Sam nodded. Yes, it certainly was. She swallowed, thinking she might as well tell him her suspicions. "What if I told you there's a possibility that—"

"You're already pregnant." He finished her sentence for her.

Her eyes widened. "Yes. How did you know?"

He told her about his great-grandmother's fish dreams.

"And your family believes there's a connection?" she asked in amazement.

He smiled. "Yes. So far she's been right most of the time. All the dream does is confirm that someone is pregnant. She doesn't always know who. But once she says she's had a dream about fish, then everyone starts looking at each other suspiciously."

"And how will you feel if they began looking at you?"

His smile widened. "It wouldn't bother me a bit. So when will you know for sure?"

"I can always take one of those pregnancy tests. But I'm an old-fashioned girl and I prefer hearing it from a doctor. I have an appointment on Friday."

"*We* have an appointment on Friday. We're in this together, and no matter the outcome, we'll leave there and go shopping for an engagement ring."

He leaned down and placed a kiss on her lips. "How does a June wedding sound?" he said.

"That's only two months away," she said, looking up at him.

He laughed. "Hey, I met your mom. She can handle it, and if she needs help, the women in my family will be glad to pitch in."

Sam's lips softened. "In that case, I guess a June wedding it is."

Satisfied, he pulled her closer and captured her lips in a kiss that was meant to seal what he knew was his destiny. She was the only woman for him, smart mouth and all. He would love her, adore her and cherish her forever.

Epilogue

Slade Madaris raised his champagne glass in a toast to the newlyweds. "Today, Blade and Sam, the two of you have made the oldest member of the Madaris family truly happy."

He glanced over at his great-grandmother and grinned before returning his attention back to the smiling couple. "May today be the first of many days the two of you will share in wedded bliss."

Blade took a sip of champagne and smiled at Sam. She'd had to settle for sparkling cider. Her doctor had confirmed what she'd suspected, that she was having his baby. He hadn't had to make an announcement to his family, since Mama Laverne's dream about fish had pretty much narrowed it down when Alex and Christy said they weren't expecting.

Blade proudly announced that he was going to be a father and was very happy about it, and that their wedding was going take place in June—not because he had to marry Sam, but because he wanted to.

Knowing that they would finally become grandparents in about seven months, Sam's parents were excited beyond measure. The news wasn't something they could tell them over the phone, so he and Sam had made a surprise visit to New York.

After Sam's parents learned that Frank Denson had confessed to killing Tyrell Graham, they fought to get the case reopened and get Tyrell's girlfriend, who'd been falsely convicted, exonerated and released from prison.

"I believe it's time for another dance, Mrs. Madaris," said Blade as he leaned over and whispered in Sam's ear, before taking the glass from her hand. He swept her onto the dance floor as the music began to play. The elaborate and elegant wedding had taken place in New York, and all the Madarises had traveled to the Big Apple for the event. Blade and Sam would be catching a plane out of JFK for London for a fifteen-day cruise to the Mediterranean.

With the help of the Madaris women, Sam's mother had done the impossible in less than sixty days, putting together an elaborate wedding the likes of which New York society hadn't seen in a long time. The guest list had included friends and family members from both sides. Not surprisingly, the Madarises and Di Meglios knew some of the same people.

"Did I tell you how beautiful you look today?" Blade asked, leaning closer and whispering in her ear.

Sam smiled up at her husband. He had told her several times, but she had also seen it in his eyes. His love had been so plain it almost brought tears to her eyes. "Yes, but you can always tell me again," she said.

"Samari Madaris, you are the most beautiful woman

I've ever seen, not only today but always. And I love you."

The smile that touched her lips also touched her heart. "And I love you, too, so very much."

He pulled her back into his arms and held her tight as their bodies swayed gently to the sound of the orchestra music. Sam glanced over at a couple standing on the sidelines, talking, before turning her gaze back to her husband. "Are you sure Reese and Kenna are just friends?"

Blade grinned. "That's what they say and no one has a reason to doubt them. But who knows? Friends can become lovers. Clayton and Syneda proved that."

Sam saw FDR and Priscilla. They made a great couple, and in fact, wedding plans were in the works.

Sam had decided to relocate to Houston when Clayton and Syneda decided to expand their law firm and wanted to add another Madaris to their practice. And what used to be Madaris, Di Meglio and Mahoney would soon become Madaris, Mahoney and Rowe, since Frederick would be moving to Oklahoma City for good.

Sam couldn't help noticing her brother dancing with Peyton, and wondered if Angelo had finally decided to make a move. If so, it was about time.

Sam wrapped her arms around her husband and placed her head on his chest. She was happy. She was having his baby and life was good. She had a Madaris man and she would love him for the rest of her life.

* * * * *

REQUEST YOUR
FREE BOOKS!

2 FREE NOVELS
PLUS 2 FREE GIFTS!

KIMANI™
ROMANCE

Love's ultimate destination!

YES! Please send me 2 FREE Kimani™ Romance novels and my 2 FREE gifts (gifts are worth about $10). After receiving them, if I don't wish to receive any more books, I can return the shipping statement marked "cancel." If I don't cancel, I will receive 4 brand-new novels every month and be billed just $4.69 per book in the U.S. or $5.24 per book in Canada. That's a saving of over 20% off the cover price. It's quite a bargain! Shipping and handling is just 50¢ per book in the U.S. and 75¢ per book in Canada.* I understand that accepting the 2 free books and gifts places me under no obligation to buy anything. I can always return a shipment and cancel at any time. Even if I never buy another book from Kimani Press, the two free books and gifts are mine to keep forever.

168 XDN E4CA   368 XDN E4CM

Name	(PLEASE PRINT)	
Address		Apt. #
City	State/Prov.	Zip/Postal Code

Signature (if under 18, a parent or guardian must sign)

Mail to **The Reader Service:**

IN U.S.A.: P.O. Box 1867, Buffalo, NY 14240-1867
IN CANADA: P.O. Box 609, Fort Erie, Ontario L2A 5X3

Not valid for current subscribers to Kimani Romance books.

Want to try two free books from another line?
Call 1-800-873-8635 or visit www.morefreebooks.com.

* Terms and prices subject to change without notice. Prices do not include applicable taxes. N.Y. residents add applicable sales tax. Canadian residents will be charged applicable provincial taxes and GST. Offer not valid in Quebec. This offer is limited to one order per household. All orders subject to approval. Credit or debit balances in a customer's account(s) may be offset by any other outstanding balance owed by or to the customer. Please allow 4 to 6 weeks for delivery. Offer available while quantities last.

Your Privacy: Kimani Press is committed to protecting your privacy. Our Privacy Policy is available online at www.eHarlequin.com or upon request from the Reader Service. From time to time we make our lists of customers available to reputable third parties who may have a product or service of interest to you. If you would prefer we not share your name and address, please check here. ☐

Help us get it right—We strive for accurate, respectful and relevant communications. To clarify or modify your communication preferences, visit us at www.ReaderService.com/consumerschoice.

KROM10